Disobedience

Naomi Alderman

TOUCHSTONE

New York   London   Toronto   Sydney   New Delhi

TOUCHSTONE

An Imprint of Simon & Schuster, Inc.
1230 Avenue of the Americas
New York, NY 10020

This Touchstone paperback edition March 2018

For information regarding special discounts for bulk purchases,
please contact Simon & Schuster Special Sales at 1-866-506-1949 or
business@simonandschuster.com.

The Simon & Schuster Speakers Bureau can bring authors
to your live event. For more information or to book an event,
contact the Simon & Schuster Speakers Bureau at 1-866-248-3049
or visit our website at www.simonspeakers.com.

Interior design by Lauren Simonetti

Manufactured in the United States of America

1   3   5   7   9   10   8   6   4   2

The Library of Congress has cataloged the hardcover edition as follows:
Alderman, Naomi.
Disobedience / Naomi Alderman.
p. cm.
"A Touchstone book."
1. Jewish families—England—London—Fiction. I. Title.
PR6101.L43D56 2006b 823'.92—dc22 2006045028

ISBN 978-1-5011-9966-0
ISBN 978-1-4165-4097-7 (ebook)

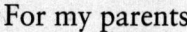

For my parents

Chapter One

And on the Shabbat, the priests would sing a song for the future that is to come, for that day which will be entirely Shabbat and for the repose of eternal life.

Mishnah Tamid 7:4, recited during
the Saturday morning service

By the first Sabbath after the festival of Simchat Torah, Rav Krushka had grown so thin and pale that, the congregation muttered, the next world could be seen in the hollows of his eyes.

The Rav had brought them through the High Holy Days, had remained standing during the two-hour service at the end of the Yom Kippur fast, though more than once his eyes had rolled back as though he would faint. He had even danced joyfully with the scrolls at Simchat Torah, if only for a few minutes. But, now that those holy days were over, the vital energy had departed from him. On this sultry, overripe September day, with the windows closed and sweat beading on the brow of every member of the congregation, the Rav, leaning on the arm of his nephew Dovid, was wrapped in a woollen overcoat. His voice was faint. His hands shook.

The matter was clear. It had been clear for some time. For months his voice, once as rich as red kiddush wine, had been hoarse, sometimes cracking altogether into a harsh little cough or a deep fit of retching and choking. Still, it was hard to believe in a faint shadow on the lung. Who could see a shadow? What was a shadow? The congregation could not believe that Rav Krushka could succumb to a shadow—he from whom the light of Torah seemed to shine so brightly that they felt themselves illuminated by his presence.

Rumors had spread across the community, were passed at chance meetings in the street. A Harley Street specialist had told him all would be well if he took a month's rest. A famous Rebbe had sent word that he and five hundred young Torah students recited the entire book of Psalms every day for Rav Krushka's safe recovery. The Rav, it was said, had received a prophetic dream declaring that he would live to see laid the first stone of the Bais HaMikdash, the Holy Temple in Jerusalem.

And yet he grew more frail every day. His failing health became known across Hendon and farther afield. As is the way of things, congregants who once might have skipped a week in synagogue, or attended a different service, had become fervent in their devotions. Each week, more worshipers attended than the week before. The clumsy synagogue—originally merely two semidetached houses knocked together and hollowed out—was not designed for this quantity of people. The air became stale during services, the temperature even warmer, the scent almost fetid.

One or two members of the synagogue board suggested that perhaps they might arrange an alternative service to cater to the unusual numbers. Dr. Yitzchak Hartog, the president of the board, overruled them. These people had come to see the Rav, he declared, and see him they would.

So it was that on the first Shabbat after Simchat Torah, the synagogue was overfull, all members of the congregation fixing their attention, sad to say, more on the Rav himself than on the prayers they were addressing to their Maker. Throughout that morning, they watched him anxiously. It was true that Dovid was by his uncle's side, holding the siddur for him, supporting him by his right elbow. But, one murmured to another, perhaps the presence of such a man would hinder rather than help his recovery? Dovid was a Rabbi, this much was admitted, but he was not a Rav. The distinction was subtle, for one may become a Rabbi simply through study and achievement, but the title Rav is given by a community to a beloved leader, a guiding light, a scholar of unsurpassed wisdom. Rav Krushka was all these things without doubt. But had Dovid ever spoken in public or given a magnificent d'var Torah, let alone written a book of inspiration and power, as the Rav had? No, no, and no. Dovid was unprepossessing to the sight: short, balding, a little overweight, but more than that, he had none of the Rav's spirit, none of his fire. Not a single member of the congregation, down to the tiniest child, would address Dovid Kuperman as "Rabbi." He was "Dovid," or sometimes, simply, "that nephew of the Rav, that *assistant*." And as for his wife! It was understood that all was not well with Esti Kuperman, that there was some problem there, some trouble. But such matters fall under the name of lashon hara—an evil tongue—and should not even be whispered in the holy house of the Lord.

In any case, Dovid was agreed to be no fitting support for the Rav. The Rav should be surrounded by men of great Torah learning, who might study night and day, and thus avert the evil decree. A pity, said some, that the Rav had no son to learn in his name and thus merit him a longer life. A pity, too, said others, more quietly, that the Rav had no son to be Rav when he was gone. For who would take his place? These thoughts had circulated for months, becoming more distinct in the synagogue's dry heat. And as the Rav's energy had drained from him, Dovid, too, had become a little more bowed with every passing week, as though he felt the weight of their stares upon his shoulders, and the force of their disappointment crushing his chest. He rarely looked up during the service now, and said nothing, continuing to turn the pages of the siddur, focusing only on the words of prayer.

By midmorning, it was clear to all the men that the Rav was worse than they had seen him before. They bent their necks around the corners where fireplaces and built-in larders had once stood and shuffled their plastic chairs a little closer to him, to observe him more exactly, to will him on. Through the morning service of Shacharit, the room grew warmer and warmer, and each man became aware that, even through his suit trousers, he had begun to stick to his seat. The Rav bowed low during Modim, then straightened again, but they could see that his hand gripping the bench in front of him was white and trembled. And his face, though determined, faltered into a grimace with every movement.

Even the women, observing the service from the upper gallery built around three sides of the room, peering through the net curtain, could see that the Rav's strength was almost gone. When the aron was opened, the Torah scrolls exhaled a fragrant cedar breath into the faces of the congregation, which seemed to rouse him, and he stood. But when the cabinet was closed his sitting seemed a surrender to gravity rather than a decided motion. He released the energy that had supported him and fell into his seat. By the time the Torah portion was half read, every member of the congregation was willing Rav Krushka to take each rasping, painful breath. If Dovid had not been there, the Rav would have slumped over in his place. Even the women could see that.

Esti Kuperman watched the service from the women's gallery. Each week a place of honor was reserved for her, in the front row, by the net curtain. In truth, the front row was never occupied at all, even at such times as these, when every seat was needed. Women would stand at the back of the gallery, rather than take one of those front-row seats. Each week Esti sat alone, never bending her thin neck, not showing by any word or glance that she had noted the empty seats on either side of her. She took the position in the front row because it was expected. She was Dovid's wife. Dovid sat next to the Rav. If the Rav's wife had not passed on, Esti would have been at her side. When, God willing, they were blessed with children, they would accompany her. As it was, she sat alone.

Farther back in the women's section nothing could be seen of the service at all. For the women in those seats only the melodies penetrated, as in the chambers of Heaven, whose doors open only to voices raised in song. Esti, though, could observe the crowns of the heads below, each covered by an oval of hat or decorated with a round circle of kippah. Over time the hats and kippot had become individual to her, each blotch of color representing a different personality. There was Hartog, the president of the board, solidly built and muscular, walking up and down even while the prayers continued, occasionally exchanging a word with another congregant. There was Levitsky, the synagogue treasurer, swaying in a nervous pecking motion as he prayed. There was Kirschbaum, one of the executive officers, leaning against the wall and constantly dozing off and waking with a jerk. She watched them come and go, ascend the steps to the bimah, and return to their places, where they'd stand and rock gently in place. She felt a strange sort of disconnection. At times, when she was staring down, the movements seemed like some game played on a checkerboard—round pieces advancing purposefully but without meaning. In the past she had often found herself becoming lulled into a trancelike state by the familiar melodies, the unchanging pattern of movement below, so that she would scarcely notice when the service was over and would be shocked to find the women around her already wishing her a Good Shabbos, the men below already drifting from view. Once or twice she had found herself standing in what seemed to be an empty synagogue, afraid to turn around for fear that some of the women might remain, behind her, whispering.

On this Shabbat, though, she restrained herself. Like the rest of the congregation, she sat when the Torah scrolls, clothed in regal velvet, were returned to the aron at the front. Like the rest, she waited patiently for the leader of the Shacharit service to step down from the bimah and the leader of the next service, Mussaf, to step up. Like the rest, she was puzzled when, after five minutes had passed, Mussaf had not yet started. She peered through the net curtain, trying to discern what was happening below. She blinked. On her husband's arm, the hunched figure of the Rav, clad in his black overcoat, was making his way slowly to the bimah.

In earlier times, the Rav would have addressed them at this point in the service, taking the Torah portion they had just read and weaving it, with other sources, into an intricate and beautiful lesson. But it had been many months since he had spoken to them like that. This week, as for so many weeks now, a copy of one of his previous sermons had been left on each seat. The Rav was not well enough to speak. And yet, in the men's section beneath her, he was ascending the three steps to the podium. A rustle of voices rose up around the synagogue and fell silent. The Rav would speak.

The Rav raised his arm, thin and pale in the sleeve of the coat. When he spoke, his voice was unexpectedly strong. He had been an orator all his life; the people did not need to strain to catch his words. "I will speak," he said, "only for a moment. I have not been well. With Hashem's help, I will recover." There was a vigorous burst of nodding around the room; several people clapped and were swiftly quieted, for theater applause has no place in a synagogue.

"Speech," he said. "If the created world were a piece of music, speech would be its refrain, its recurring theme. In the Torah, we read that Hashem created the world through speech. He could have willed it into existence. We might read: 'And God thought of light, and there was light.' No. He could have hummed it. Or formed it from clay in His hands. Or breathed it out. Hashem, our King, the Holy One Blessed Be He, did none of these things. To create the world, He spoke. 'And God said, let there be light, and there was light.' Exactly as He spoke, so it was."

The Rav broke off, coughing violently, a sickly bubbling sound in his chest. Several of the men strained to move to him, but he waved them back. He supported himself on Dovid's shoulder, gave three sharp coughs, and fell silent. He breathed heavily and continued.

"The Torah itself. A book. Hashem could have given us a painting, or a sculpture, a forest, a creature, an idea in our minds to explain His world. But He gave us a book. Words."

He paused and looked around the hall, scanning the silent faces. When the pause had gone on just a little too long, the Rav raised his hand and banged it loudly on the lectern.

"What a great power the Almighty has given us! To speak, as He speaks! Astonishing! Of all the creatures on earth, only *we* can speak. What does this mean?"

He smiled faintly and looked around the room once more.

"It means we have a hint of Hashem's power. Our words are, in a sense, real. They can create worlds and destroy them. They have edges, like a knife." The Rav brought his arm around in a sweeping motion, as though wielding a scythe. He smiled. "Of course, our power is not Hashem's power. Let us not forget that, either. Our words are more than empty breath, but they are not Torah. Torah contains the world. Torah is the world. Do not forget, my children, that all of our words, all of our stories, can only, at best, amount to a commentary on a single verse of the Torah."

The Rav turned to Dovid and whispered a few words. Together, the two men walked down from the bimah and back to their seats. The congregation was silent. At last, gathering himself, the chazzan began to pray the Mussaf service.

The Rav's words had clearly weighed with the chazzan leading the prayers, for the man seemed to be paying peculiar attention to each letter, each syllable of every word. He spoke slowly, but clearly and with power, as though he were hearing and appreciating the words for the first time. *"Mechalkel chayim b'chesed,"* he said. ("He sustains all living things with kindness, He gives the dead life with abundant mercy.") The congregation responded in kind, their responses becoming louder and clearer until they were speaking with one great voice.

As the chazzan reached the kedushah, he began to sweat, his face was pale. *"Na'aritzecha v'Nakdishecha . . ."* he declared.

"Kadosh, kadosh, kadosh," ("Holy, holy holy is the Lord") the people responded, raising themselves onto the balls of their feet, many feeling a little light-headed, perhaps through the heat.

And it was at that moment, when all were reaching up on their tiptoes to the Almighty, that a crash resounded in the hall, as though one of the mighty cedars of Lebanon had fallen. The men turned and the women craned. The congregation saw Rav Krushka, lying on his side, by his seat. He let out a long moan, but there was no movement in him except his left leg, twitching against the wooden bench, the knocks sounding loud and hollow around the synagogue.

There was a moment of quiet and a sensation of pressure beating at the temples.

Hartog was the first to recover. He ran to the Rav, pushing Dovid to one side. He loosened the Rav's tie and took his arm, shouting, "Call an ambulance and bring blankets!" The other men looked confused for a moment. The very words "call an ambulance," uttered in the Rav's synagogue, on the Sabbath, seemed unreal; it was as though they'd been asked for a slice of bacon, a pint of prawns. After a long moment, two of the young men started up and dashed toward the door, racing for the telephone.

High above, Esti Kuperman stood still, although some of the other women were already making their way downstairs to see what should be done.

Esti watched her husband take his uncle's hand and pat it, as though to comfort the old man. She noticed that Dovid's hair was thinner, seen from this angle, than she had thought. Some part of her noted, almost without intending to, that Hartog had already left the Rav's side, leaving his care to the other medical members of the congregation. That he had pulled three or four men of the synagogue board to one side, that they were in conversation. She looked at her own bony fingers, curled around her siddur, the nails very white.

And for an instant, she felt heavy damask wings stirring the air against her face. The beating wings might have surrounded her, moving more slowly, more heavily, circling and ascending infinitely slowly, bearing a far greater burden than the soul of one old, tired man with a shadow on his lung. The breath had gone out of the room, and the beating wings were a pulse, growing fainter and fainter.

Esti felt exhausted, unable to move. Dovid raised his head to the women's gallery, looked to her accustomed place, and shouted out, "Esti!" plaintive, frightened. Esti started back from the rail and turned to stumble to the door of the stairwell. She was faintly aware that some of the women were touching her, reaching out their arms to . . . stroke her? Support her? She wasn't sure. She continued toward the exit thinking only that she must go now, that there would be something she should do.

And it was only when she was running down the stairs toward the men's section that a thought awakened in her mind—a thought at once shocking and joyful, a thought of which she felt instantly ashamed. As she raced down the stairs, the rhythm of her steps echoed to the beat of her repeated thought: "If this is so, then Ronit will be coming home. Ronit is coming home."

The night before, I dreamed about him. No, really. I knew him by his words. I dreamed about a huge room filled with books, floor to ceiling, the shelves stretching on and on farther and farther out, so that the harder I looked, the more that became visible at the limits of my sight. I realized that the books, and the words, were everything that was and everything that had ever been or would ever be. I started walking; my steps were silent, and when I looked down I saw that I was walking on words, that the walls and the ceiling and the tables and the lamps and the chairs were all words.

So I walked on, and I knew where I was going and I knew what I would find. I came to a long, wide table. Table, it said. I am a table. All that I have ever been or ever will be is a table. And on the table was a book. And the book was him. I knew him by his words. Truthfully, I would have known him if he'd been a lamp, or a pot plant, or a scale model of the Long Island Expressway. But, appropriately enough, he was a book. The words on the cover were simple, good words. I don't remember what they were.

And, like you do in a dream, I knew I should open the book. I put out my hand and opened it and read the first line. As I read it, the words echoed around the library. They said, like God said to Abraham: "You are my chosen one. Leave this land and go to another place which I shall show you!"

Okay, so, I made that last part up. But the other stuff was genuine. I woke up with a headache, which I never get, but it was as if someone had dropped a dictionary on my skull during the night. I had to take a long, really hot shower to ease the words out of my brain and the tension out of my shoulders, and when I was done, of course then I was late for work, so I was walking, no, make that marching down Broadway in search of a cab, which you can only ever find when you don't need one, when suddenly I heard a voice say, as though it'd spoken right in my ear:

"Excuse me, are you Jewish?"

And I stopped, almost jumped, because it was so close, and so unexpected. I mean, particularly in New York, where everyone's Jewish anyway. So I turned to see who it was and lo, I had fallen for the oldest trick in the book, because there was a guy with a smart suit, a neatly trimmed beard, and a stack of flyers, clearly out to sign up some Jews for his one hundred percent top-quality religion.

Poor guy. Really. Because I was late, so in a bad mood to start off with. And I'd had that dream. Usually, I would have just walked on by. But some mornings you just want to fight with someone.

I said, "I'm Jewish. Why?"

Except, of course, I said it in a British accent, which I could see puzzled him straightaway. On the one hand, he wanted to say, "Hey, you're British!" because he's American, and they like to tell me that. But on the other hand, he had God whispering encouragingly in his ear, saying here, here is a woman whom you, my friend, can win for righteousness. The guy pulled himself together. Souls to save, worlds to conquer:

"May I interest you in a free seminar on Jewish history?"

Right. Of course. He was one of these guys. Not selling a new religion, but the old one; winning people back to the faith. Free seminars on Jewish history, Friday night dinners, a bit of Bible code thrown in. Well, I guess it works for people who've never had that experience. But that's not me. Hell, I could be leading one of these things.

I said: "No, thanks, I'm really busy right now."

And I was about to turn and walk away when he touched my sleeve, just brushed it with the palm of his hand, as though he wanted to feel the material of my coat, but it was enough to freak me out slightly. It made me almost long for a Lubavitch boy, whose sweat and desperation you can smell from three feet away, and who would never touch a woman. Anyway, my guy held out a leaflet and said:

"We're all very busy. These are fast-moving times. But our ancient heritage is worth making time for. Take a flyer. Our programs run all over the city; you can join anytime you like."

I took the flyer. And I glanced at it for a second, intending to walk on. And then I looked for a bit longer, just standing there. I had to read it over and over, trying to understand what I was looking at. A bright yellow sticker on the front read: "Monday night special seminar—Rabbi Tony will talk on Rav Krushka's book, *Day by Day*, and how to apply its lessons in our lives." I mean, I knew he wrote a book, but when did it come over here? When did he produce lessons to help us in our lives? When did people who call themselves "Rabbi Tony" start being interested?

I pointed at the yellow sticker and said: "What's this?"

"Are you interested in Rav Krushka? That's a wonderful presentation. Gets right to the heart of his teachings. It's very inspiring."

Poor guy. It wasn't his fault. Not really.

I said: "What's your name?"

He smiled broadly. "Chaim. Chaim Weisenburg."

"Well, Chaim. What exactly are you doing this for?"

"This?"

"This, standing on the street corner, handing out flyers to passersby. Are you being paid for it? You owe some money? They threaten to break your legs?"

Chaim blinked. "No. No, I'm a volunteer."

I nodded. "So you're doing this out of the goodness of your heart?"

"I'm doing it because I believe it's the right thing to do. Our heritage—"

I spoke over him. "Right. Heritage. Only it's not heritage you're selling here, is it, Chaim? It's religion."

He spread his arms wide, a little flustered.

"I wouldn't say *selling* exactly, it's more—"

"You wouldn't say selling? But don't you get something in return for handing out all this religion?" He tried to speak, but I just barreled on. "Don't you, Chaim Weisenburg, get a special seat in the world to come if you get a few straying Jews signed up? Isn't that why you're doing it? Profit? Face it, Chaim, you're just in it for yourself, aren't you?"

He was angry now.

"No. No, that's not it at all. That's not how it is. God has commanded us—"

"Ah. Okay. Now we're getting to it. *God* commanded you. God tells you what to do and you jump to it. You're doing this because you think God wants you to, right? God wants you to find the straying Jews and bring them back to the fold?"

Chaim nodded. A few people turned their heads as they walked past, but no one stopped.

"Well, let's say God did command you to do that. Has it ever occurred to you, Chaim, that some of us don't want to be brought back? Some of us don't want to be found? Some of us have been in that fold and found it narrow, and limiting, and more like a prison than a safe harbor. Has it ever occurred to you that God might be *wrong*?"

Chaim opened his mouth and closed it again. I guess it was obvious I wasn't going to be attending any seminar. I ripped up the flyer and threw it at him in confetti pieces. I admit it, I'm a drama queen.

When I got to the subway station, I turned back to look at him, and he was still staring at me, his flyers hanging limp in his hand.

Dr. Feingold tells me that I need to work on "feeling my feelings," in the interests of which I have to admit that ol' Chaim got to me more than I'd expected. I was still thinking about him, and about all those saps lining up to take seminars in "the lessons of Rav Krushka," when I got into work. I carried on thinking about it through the working day, which is pretty unusual for me. I usually enjoy the way work forces everything else out of your head. I work in corporate finance; I'm an analyst. It's a full-on job, it takes all the brains I have in my head. I think that's what most of us want, really, isn't it? A challenge that's just hard enough that we *can* accomplish it, but it'll take everything we've got. So that there's no room left in us for the doubt, the worry, the internal crises. We have to let it fill us up because that's the only way to get the job done. Dr. Feingold says, "So you won't have time to think, Ronit?" and she's probably right, but maybe introspection is overrated. Anyway, I like my job, and I'm good at it. I had a new contract to work on, which demands full concentration if you're not going to misplace a million dollars, and yet somehow there Chaim was, all day. I kept imagining him on the street, handing out his flyers. Some people would walk on, but some people would take one. And of those, some people would call, and of those, some people would end up attending that seminar. Chaim was wearing a sharp suit. The flyers were glossy. They're probably doing well. Hundreds of sheep are probably stumbling back to the fold right now. It unsettles me, just a bit, to think about the business of it, about the expenditure-to-sales ratio and the probable returns. If you can put a value on a soul, there's probably someone out there just like me, crunching the numbers on the religious-zeal biz.

And, yes, yes, Dr. Feingold would probably say that even thinking about *that* was a way to stop thinking about *other* things, but you know, sometimes I'm just too clever even for myself.

I stayed late at work, trying to make up for the things I hadn't got done during the day, but of course that never happens because you get more and more tired as the evening goes on, and the amount of time the work's going to take gets longer and longer. Eventually, I noticed Scott and I were the only two people left in our section, and I thought it wouldn't be long before he came over and tried to *talk* to me—or didn't. Didn't would have been even more uncomfortable, so at nine o'clock I went home. Without wishing him good night.

Inevitably, because journeys are so good for brooding, thoughts of Chaim and Rabbi Tony led to thoughts of London, which are never good thoughts to have. And when I got back, after dark, I realized, of course, that it was Friday night, which is never a good thing to realize. And I started to think about my mother, one of the only distinct memories I have of her, which must have been because it was of something that happened so often: on Friday night, lighting her candles in those huge silver candlesticks covered in silver leaves and flowers.

And I knew it wasn't going to get any less maudlin from then on. And I really wasn't up for one of those fun evenings contemplating how no one else in my life has ever truly loved me, so I poured myself a large one and went to bed with a book.

That night, I dreamed of nothing and no one, which was perfect. When I woke, it was late. I walked to the Museum of Natural History on Seventy-ninth Street, but by the time I'd got there it was closed, and it was too cold to sit in the park. I could have called someone, made dinner plans, gone to the movies, but I didn't; I watched the rest of the day pass by, the hours chasing each other to sunset.

At eight o'clock it'd been dark for about an hour, and I was thinking of ordering takeout when the phone rang. I picked it up and there was a silence on the other end, then the sound of drawn-in breath. I knew it was Dovid before he spoke a word. He's always done that on the phone—a silence. Like he's trying to decide whether, after all, you'll be glad to hear his voice.

So while he was saying "Hello, is that Ronit?" I was already thinking of witty remarks to make, of ways to point out how unusual this call was, how unexpected. I was already gathering my armor around me, so that no message he could give would hurt me.

"Ronit? Is that you?"

I realized I hadn't spoken. "This is she." God. So American.

"Ronit?"

He wasn't convinced.

"Yes, this is Ronit. Who's calling?" I wasn't going to make it easy for him.

"Ronit, it's Dovid."

"Hi, Dovid—what can I do for you?" I sounded so cheerful, like it was six weeks, not six years, since we'd last spoken.

"Ronit," he said again. "Ronit . . ."

And it was only then, listening to Dovid unable to do more than say my name over and over, that I began to think about what earthquake could have shaken that little world and produced this aftershock several thousand miles away; an unexpected call. Not a call before New Year, or at Passover, but a call on a regular Saturday night. And I thought, of course. Because there are no coincidences.

"Ronit," Dovid repeated.

"What's wrong, Dovid?"

And Dovid took a breath and told me that my father was dead.

Chapter Two

He makes the wind blow and He makes the rain descend. He sustains the living with kindness, and resurrects the dead with abundant mercy.

From the Amidah, recited in the evening, morning, and afternoon of every day

Torah, we are told, is compared to water.

Without water, the earth would be but a thirsty husk, a parched and aching desert. Without Torah, man, too, would be only a shell, knowing neither light nor mercy. As water is life-giving, so Torah brings life to the world. Without water, our limbs would never know freshness or balm. Without Torah, our spirits would never know tranquility. As water is purifying, so Torah cleanses those it touches.

Water comes only and forever from the Almighty; it is a symbol of our utter dependence on Him. Should He withhold rain for but a season, we could no longer stand before Him. Just so, Torah is a gift that the Holy One Blessed Be He has given the world; Torah, in a sense, contains the world, it is the blueprint from which the world was created. Should Torah be withheld only for a moment, the world not only would vanish, but would never even have been.

We should not separate ourselves from Torah, as we would not deny ourselves water. For those who have drunk of it will, in the sum of things, live.

By nine o'clock on Saturday night, Shabbat had been over for an hour, and the gray-faced doctor had released the Rav's body.

In the synagogue's entrance hall, an urgent, whispered congress was taking place among the members of the synagogue board: Hartog the president, Levitsky the treasurer, Kirschbaum the secretary, Newman, and Rigler. There were important matters to discuss: the issue of who would undertake to prepare the Rav's body for burial the most pressing of them.

"Dovid is head of the Chevra Kadisha," said Levitsky. "It is right that he should continue his duties. It is not forbidden. A nephew may perform taharah for an uncle."

"Dovid will not want to perform this duty," declared Rigler. "It is unthinkable. We will undertake the work."

"No—it is right." Levitsky's face trembled with the excitement of having a position, of taking a stand. "It is more dignified. We must think of the Rav's dignity."

Newman remained silent, glancing from one face to another, attempting, as was his way, to discover where the consensus would fall.

After the argument had raged for a few minutes, and Rigler had begun to gleam with sweat, Hartog drew himself up. He said:

"Do you not think, gentlemen, that we should ask Dovid? I am sure that he will have an opinion in the matter." The other men fell silent. They stood contemplating the quiet of the synagogue. When Newman spoke his voice seemed loud.

"What will happen now?"

Hartog looked at him. "Now? Now we must prepare the Rav for burial."

"No," said Newman. "What will happen now? Now that he is gone."

Hartog nodded. "There's nothing to fear," he said. "The Rav's work will continue. His book will still be read, his thoughts will live within our minds. The shul will continue its work. Everything will remain as it has been. Nothing need change."

A question remained unspoken. Each of them knew it; it was the same question that had been raised among the men on many other occasions. In quiet meetings, over Sabbath tables, and in whispered telephone conversations, the question had been asked and then abandoned. It was too difficult to address, an impiety while the Rav yet lived. And yet now, each of them wished he had had the courage to voice it strongly, to solicit opinions, even to ask the Rav what he himself thought. It was too late for this indecision. The question ought to have been answered months earlier.

Levitsky bent his head and looked at his shoes:

"Who will lead us now that our pillar of fire is gone?"

The men looked at one another. This was the heart of it. There was no answer, none at least that made itself apparent to them. They looked at one another in silence, lips pursed, eyes narrow.

Only Hartog smiled. He brought his hand down on Levitsky's shoulder.

"Dovid," he said. "Dovid will lead us. We will not ask him today, of course. But I shall speak with him. He will lead us. Today, though, we concern ourselves only with the taharah."

If he saw the glances exchanged by the other men at this, Hartog gave no sign of it. He strode through the double doors into the main shul. Behind him, Kirschbaum muttered, "Dovid?"

Rigler nodded and replied, "But his wife . . ."

Esti received the message that her husband would not return that night, that he would wait the night with the Rav and in the morning complete the taharah. She found herself packing her things for the mikvah, just as she had planned. She felt oddly proud that her actions continued in their intended path, even though she had not willed them. She felt it boded well. Nothing had changed, the pattern of her life remained the same. This indicated that nothing need change. Like any normal woman, she was preparing herself to return to her husband's bed.

Each month, when a woman is bleeding, she is forbidden to her husband. They may not have marital relations, may not touch, may not even sleep in the same bed. And when her flow ceases, the wife must count seven clean days, as is written in the Torah. And at the end of those clean days, she must visit the mikvah to immerse herself completely in natural water: rainwater or river water or seawater. And once she has immersed herself, she may return to her husband's bed.

The mikvah is a sacred place, a holy place. More holy, perhaps, than a synagogue, for we learn that when a new community is founded, the mikvah should be built first, the synagogue second. Like so many holy things, mikvah is private. For this reason, women do not disclose their day of visiting its cleansing waters. For this reason, the building itself will be arranged so that no woman has to see another at the mikvah. Several comfortable bathrooms lead off the central chamber with its pool of deep water. In each bathroom, a woman washes herself privately, summoning the attendant only when she is ready to immerse herself in the mikvah. Thus, the mikvah remains a hidden thing, between the woman, her husband, and the Almighty.

In the bathroom at the mikvah, Esti emerged from her bath and stood before the mirror, observing her naked body critically. She was, she decided, too thin. She was growing thinner, year by year. Something must be done. She had decided this before, and determined to eat more; it was almost a weekly resolution. She glossed her vegetables with butter and her roast potatoes with schmaltz. She doused rice dishes with oil, and fried her fish in batter. During one particularly concerted attempt, she had even tried to eat her breakfast cereals with cream instead of milk. But no matter how decadent the meal, her appetite would dissolve as she reached the table. If she forced herself to eat, her stomach rewarded her with wrenching guts and miserable nausea.

But, she decided, it must be attempted again. She was sure she had become thinner, even since last month. Her breasts, she thought, hung unexpectedly on her chest as though she had slung them in a hurry from her neck. She twisted her arm. Her elbow seemed a bare hinge, jutting and forlorn. She ran her thumb along her torso, feeling the undulating ribs just below the surface. It would not do.

She trimmed her nails hard, so that her fingertips ached. She collected the clippings and brushed them into the dustbin. Wrapping herself in her robe, she summoned the attendant and proceeded along the short passage to the pool of still water. She hung the robe on a hook and, naked, walked down the steps into the water.

When she was first married Esti had entered the mikvah with a sense of awe. On the day before her wedding, her mother accompanied her to the mikvah for the first time. It is a mother's role, a mother's duty to guide her daughter in the complicated and delicate matters of family purity, that is to say, matters concerning menstruation. Esti, the youngest of three daughters, had witnessed both her sisters accompany their mother on their own prewedding journeys, leaving pale and nervous for the mikvah, returning two hours later wet-haired and smiling softly. She had imagined that perhaps it would be a secret female ritual, a celebration. And, in a way, it had been. Her mother, a small, slight woman yet a person of tremendous force, had shown her how to trim her nails and clean under them to ensure that not a particle of dirt remained. She had done so with a wooden point; the cleaning was painful but Esti had not complained. She watched her mother take each finger, one by one, and make them pure and holy once more.

In the bathroom, while they waited for the attendant to take them to the pool of cleansing water, Esti's mother had run through the many tasks that still needed to be completed, ticking them off one by one on her fingers: final check of the flowers, final conversation with the caterers, a hem to be sewn up, the floral barrier between the men and women at the reception to be erected. Esti wished, and felt guilty for wishing, that her mother would stop talking about these tiny concerns. There seemed to her to be a larger matter here. At last, her mother seemed to notice her failure to respond to each issue and she, too, became quiet.

Esti's mother took her hand and stroked its back with a fingertip. She smiled to herself, a secret mother-smile in which Esti knew she could have no part. Still holding Esti's hand, she said:

"You may not like it at first." Esti remained silent. Her mother continued. "It's different, for men and women. But Dovid . . . he's a kind man. You'll be surprised; in the end you might quite enjoy it. Just"—her mother looked up at her—"try to be kind to him. It's more important for men than it is for us. Don't push him away."

Esti thought she understood. She was twenty-one years old and the words had weighed on her, the delineation of the duties of a wife. At this moment, at the point of marriage, she had imagined that she understood all that would be required of her, and that she knew where the pitfalls lay. She nodded solemnly at her mother's words.

When the attendant took them down to the mikvah pool, Esti had spoken secretly with the Almighty. She had said: "Please, Lord, cleanse me and make me whole. Remove that in me which is displeasing to you. I will forget all that I have done. I will be different. Sanctify my marriage and allow me to be as other women." She remembered entering the mikvah and feeling that her skin was porous, that she was infused with the water, which is Torah, which is life. She remembered knowing that all would be well.

In recent years, though, she was only able to utter the first word of her prayer. "Please," she would say in her heart as she entered the water, "please." Each time, she wanted to continue the prayer, but did not know what to request.

Esti realized that she had been standing in the water, unmoving, for a little too long. The attendant, a woman in her late fifties, was looking at her curiously. She took a breath and ducked under the water, lifting her feet. She bobbed upward, pulling in her knees to her stomach, lifting her feet up from the smooth tiles beneath. She felt her hair stream out, washing around her face. She counted one, two, three and then rose again, gulping air, water pouring down her face.

Walking back to the house, wet-haired and warm, Esti thought of Dovid, watching the night with the Rav, reciting psalms as he had done so often in prayer for the old man's recovery. She saw that she had been mistaken in thinking that nothing had changed; everything was the same, but everything was different. Dovid was reciting the same psalms, but for the dead and not the living. She had visited the mikvah to purify herself for her husband, but now Ronit was coming home. Walking home, under the waning moon, Esti felt, faintly, the turn of the tide.

In the morning the men of the Chevra Kadisha began their work on the Rav. They met in the small antechamber at the burial grounds. They were four: Levitsky, Rigler, Newman, and Dovid himself.

Dovid had watched the night by the body, reciting psalms. A small headache began to pulse at his temples. He spoke to the headache, asking its nature. The headache answered with a single, light touch. Very well, not serious then, merely a symptom of fatigue. He sat, watching as the men began to strip the body and clean it.

Levitsky was a small man, with a mustache and thick glasses. He and his wife, Sara, had four sons, each as blinking and molelike as Levitsky himself. But the man had deft, quick fingers and a lightness of touch. Newman, in his late thirties, was rotund, thoughtful, and calm. He was strong; it fell to him often to lift and carry, to support the dead or to move them. Rigler was taller, thinner, and easily angered. His cheeks were perpetually red, his eyes darting here and there. He was observant, though, and had often accomplished a task before the others saw that it was necessary.

They had worked on many taharahs before; these men and the

five or six others who volunteered for the solemn task. They each knew the jobs that were to be done. The men worked in almost complete silence, but the little room at the burial grounds rang with a certain music of order, audible only in small, confident movements, as each one took up his place.

Rigler combed the Rav's hair, collecting every strand that fell. Levitsky held each finger gently—for it is forbidden to hold hands with the dead—and trimmed the nails, before beginning on the toenails. Dovid watched. He was not unfamiliar with the task. Many times, the old man had been unable to hold the scissors steadily. Dovid noted that although the Rav's fingers were a little stiff, his yellowed, ridged nails were the same. Levitsky collected the spiky parings in his hand. When Rigler had finished combing the hair, they laid these human shavings onto the soft earth lining the coffin. Every piece of the body must be buried. Not a hair, not a nail, is to be defiled.

It was time to pour the water. Dovid rose from his place and, with Newman, began to fill the large enamel jugs. They would each take a jug and pour, one after the other. The water would have to be continuous, one jug beginning before the previous one ended. If there was a break, even an instant, between the first jug and the second, they would have to begin again. The job took a certain amount of physical stamina. As Dovid lifted his jug, hefting it to the level of his shoulder, he felt the headache pulse once, loudly, above his right eye.

"Okay?" said Newman.

"I'm ready," Dovid replied, and nodded slowly, so as not to disturb his pain.

Rigler raised the metal slab a little, at the head, so that the water would drain away. And they began. Newman poured evenly, the water streaming across the face, the chest, down the arms and legs. Dovid looked at the old man's face, beneath the living water. It seemed almost grave, as though he were experiencing troubling thoughts.

"Dovid!"

Newman spoke sharply. Dovid looked up, startled, and realized that the other man's jug was poured out, only a few drops remaining. He had no time to position his own jug, to begin to pour. The water cascading down the Rav's face and body ceased. The room was silent.

Newman said: "No matter, no matter, Dovid. You're tired. We'll start again. Reuven and I will pour."

Feeling foolish, Dovid paused. He looked at the faces of the men around him. They were all pinched and yellowed, but less tired than his; they had not watched the night with the Rav. It would be so easy simply to say yes, I will go home to sleep for an hour or two. He would return to the burial grounds for the funeral later that day. Esti would be at home, she would make him some chicken broth. What husband would refuse an hour or two with his wife at a time such as this?

"No," he said. "No. We'll begin again."

They poured the water. This time, Dovid poured first. Newman was ready as his jug emptied, and began to pour exactly as the flow dwindled to a trickle. And as the water played across the Rav's face and naked body, Dovid felt his headache pulse softly, quieter with each beat, until finally it had melted away and he was, like the Rav, silent and at rest.

The men dried the Rav's body with large, thin towels and began to dress him. The linen garments had been prepared and lay, orderly, waiting to be worn for the first and final time. First, they placed the linen headdress on the Rav's head, pulled it down over his face, and fastened it at the neck.

When he had first attended a taharah, Dovid remembered feeling that the body, clad only in its headdress, had an uncanny look, a dreadful anonymity. Now, however, he saw the beauty in the order of dressing. Once the head was covered, the body lost its force of personality; it was transformed into a holy object, to be disposed of with respect and honor, as ancient Torah scrolls are buried in the ground once they become unreadable. Covering the head was the proper place to begin; after it was done, everything became easier.

Newman helped to raise the body a little, at the hips, while Rigler slid the linen trousers up. Without a word being said, Levitsky moved to tie the special knot in the band at the top of the trousers. Gently, Rigler fitted the Rav's feet into the sealed ends of the trousers, as though ensuring that they rested comfortably. Rigler and Newman lifted the body a little, to pull over the white shirt and jacket.

As they did so, bending the body at the waist, a little moan emerged from the hooded head, a groan that an old man might make when his movements gave him pain. The men stopped, looked at one another. Newman, his hands clasped around the body's abdomen, pursed his lips. He readjusted his grip and another smaller sigh came from beneath the white headdress.

"Perhaps," said Levitsky softly, "you should not press on the chest so firmly, Asher."

Newman nodded and carefully moved his hands, so that he was supporting the body from under the arms. The dead man made no more sounds as he was clothed in his white shirt and jacket, each tied with the same special knot.

By now the body was completely covered. The jacket's sleeves were closed, like the trousers, so both hands and feet were hidden from view. It only remained to wind the linen belt around the waist. The men did so slowly, to avoid expelling more air from the body. Levitsky bent to tie the last knot in the belt. He paused. His fingers hovered, trembling, over the final fastening. Still bent over, he raised his head to look at Dovid.

"Dovid," he said, his voice clipped, "it would be right for you to fasten the belt. You are his nearest family here."

Levitsky moved away from the white-clad body, and Dovid moved toward it. He took the ends of the white linen belt in his hands. This was the final knot, in the shape of the three-pronged letter *shin,* the first letter of one of the names of the Almighty. Once this knot was made, it could not be undone. He had tied such knots many times before, for many men, but felt oddly unwilling to begin this time. This knot would be the end of it, this knot that could never be untied, this thing that could not be undone. Once this was done, there could be no denying it; something would change. Well, he said in his heart, so be it. Nothing could remain the same forever. He tied the belt.

Together the men moved the body from the table into the waiting coffin. As they rose, the four men found themselves suddenly a little dizzy. Simultaneously, they reached out their hands to steady themselves, resting the flats of their palms on the wall, or gripping the edge of the central table. As one, they looked up and, each seeing the others, began to smile. A chuckle rippled among them, like the sound of running water.

"Have we done all that is needed?" asked Levitsky.

There were nods, closed-mouthed smiles of agreement.

"Then it only remains," he continued, "to ask the forgiveness of the Rav."

The men turned to the coffin, and each spoke quietly in his own words asking for the Rav's forgiveness if they had, in any way, behaved without proper respect to his body.

After a pause, Rigler began to screw down the lid of the coffin. Dovid turned and walked from the small room. He was unsurprised to find that the world beyond was suffused with early-morning sunlight.

It's difficult to work out the meaning of life in Hendon. I mean, it's difficult to work it out for yourself, rather than allowing other people to tell you. Because in Hendon there are plenty of people just dying to explain the meaning of life to you. I guess that's true in New York, too, but in New York, everyone seems to disagree with everyone else about what the meaning of life *is*. In Hendon, at least the Hendon I grew up in, everything faced in one direction, there was nowhere to get a grip. You need that disagreement, we all do, so that we can realize that the world isn't smooth and even, not everyone agrees with everyone else. You need a window into another world to work out what you think of your own.

For me, growing up, it was magazines. I used to sneak into WH Smith on my way home from the Sara Rifka Hartog Memorial Day School and read magazines. It didn't much matter what. I'd pick something at random off the shelf. I didn't properly understand the differences. I couldn't have told you about their target audiences or demographics. I read *Loaded* and *Vogue*, *Woman's Own* and *Rolling Stone*, *PC World* and *The Tablet*. In my mind, they became jumbled, those scraps of other lives. There seemed to be so many different things to know about: music, films, TV, fashion, celebrities, and sex.

These days, I buy magazines all the time; I go into Barnes & Noble, choose one I want, and take it home. There are stacks of them all over the house, covering half the surfaces, and yeah, I know I'm proving something to myself, but it's something worth proving, so I go on accumulating piles of glossy paper.

Strangely, though, I find there's no magazine called *Death*. You'd think one of them would at least run an article. Some helpful household magazine could do a feature: "Homemade Coffins: A Cheaper Alternative." *Cosmo* could do: "Grieving: Do It Better, Faster, and More Often." Even a *Vogue* special on funeral outfits would be some help. But no, nothing. It's like this essential feature of human beings simply doesn't exist in the full-color magazine world.

So, there's always therapy. I thought of calling Dr. Feingold, but I didn't want to listen to her answers masquerading as questions. Not then, anyway.

I thought of saying okay, he's dead, but I never liked the old sod anyway. I'll call some friends, go dancing, get drunk.

And then I thought of the garments that they would be dressing my father in: white linen with closed arms and legs. Every human being, whoever you are, whoever you had been, gets the same. And I thought: in my father's house, they would know what to do. In my father's house, they wouldn't need any magazine to tell them.

* * *

So, this is what you do, this is what *I* ought to be doing, the Jewish mourning ritual for close relatives: parents, children, siblings, husband or wife. In the first week, you tear your clothes, you don't cut your hair or wash in hot water, and you cover your mirrors (because this is no time for vanity). You sit on a low stool and you don't leave the house, unless you really have to (because grief needs space and time). And you don't listen to music (because music will remind you that somewhere in the world, someone is happy).

That's the first week. Then, in the first thirty days, you can leave your house and wash, but you don't listen to music or buy new clothes or attend parties. Then, after the first thirty days but still in the first year, you don't buy new clothes.

And at the end of the first year, they set the tombstone at the grave and you go, and you pray. And every year from then on, you light a candle on the anniversary of the death. It's very orderly, very precise. I could map out the whole of my next year, or next month. It's supposed to make everything simpler.

Except that for me, now, it makes nothing simpler. Because this stuff only works if everyone else knows what you're doing. It works if you're sitting on your low stool, in your torn clothes, and your friends and family come to visit. They bring food, they talk in low voices, they pray. But I'm here, and I'm not that anymore. And somehow it wouldn't work to call up a friend and say: "I would now like to participate in the ancient Jewish grieving ritual. For this, I will need some volunteers."

I sat for a while. I thought about what would be happening now, in England. I thought about the end of the world, and what's supposed to come after. I thought about eternal life in the next world. I couldn't bear that anymore. I fished a pair of nail scissors out of my makeup bag and sawed through the hem of the jogging top I was wearing. It ripped with a fairly satisfying noise, scattering little gray fibers in the air. It felt good, I'll admit it. It felt like I was *doing* something, which I suppose is the point. And then it felt like nothing again, like I'd ruined a perfectly useful item of clothing.

So I called Scott. Late at night, but hey, he did always say: "Call me anytime." "If you really need to," he'd add. "If you have to."

I called him, not because I need him, or want him back, or any of that bullshit, but because I knew, I just knew, that he'd understand. While the phone was ringing, I almost convinced myself to hang up, because maybe even calling made me weak, when I should be trying to be strong. And then he answered.

I said, "Hi, it's me."

He said, "Oh. Okay."

"Scott, I wouldn't call, only . . ."

I paused for dramatic effect. I did. I admit it. I paused so he'd think I was going to tell him I loved him, or wanted him back. So that he'd feel really lousy, really small-minded and petty when I said:

"I've just heard, my father's died."

An intake of breath.

"I'm so sorry." He sounded sorry. A pause, then: "I'll come over."

"No, no, you shouldn't. I'll be fine."

"I'll come."

"Are you sure? Can you get away?"

"Yes," he said loudly. "Yes, I'll come now and take that conference call."

I remember one drunken evening in some bar downtown. It was a team-building night, so it was the six of us: Anna, the trainee, big eyes, short skirts; Martin, account manager, hoping Scott would go home, so he'd be alpha male; Bernice, quiet, husband called at least twice a day; Carla, the boss, wool suit, wanting to be generous but looking nervously at the menu every time one of us ordered a drink; and Scott, the big boss, fraternizing with the troops. And me.

Martin, as usual, was trying to put his arm around Anna and talking too loudly. He stabbed the table with his finger and said, "You know what the problem with this country is?"

We shook our heads. Bernice and I exchanged a look.

"Too. Much. Religion. That's the problem. It's the religious rednecks, in Iowa, who are destroying this country. With censorship. That's what's ripping this country apart: censorship. You know, Ronit, you guys have got the right idea in Europe." He pronounced my name wrong, as usual, putting the stress on the first syllable, *Ro*nit, instead of the second: Ro*nit*.

"Oh, yes?" I said.

Disobedience

"Yeah. God. Is. Dead. I mean, what's the point, right? Am I right?" I kept silent. Martin looked around the group and repeated, "Am I right, guys?"

Carla glanced at Scott. He gave her an encouraging smile. It was his I'm-here-for-you-as-a-mentor-but-you-have-to-deal-with-your-own-team smile. She said:

"Well, I guess it does seem kind of irrelevant . . ."

"Yeah!" said Martin. "Yeah! I mean who the hell remembers the catechism, or the twelve apostles—"

"Or the Ten Commandments," Carla chimed in.

"Yeah, who the hell knows what the Ten Commandments are, anyway? Aren't they like, don't litter, don't smoke, and buy American, or something?"

Everyone laughed. Even quiet little Bernice giggled, silently, shoulders shaking. Except Scott, I remember.

Anna, finally catching up to the conversation, said:

"Yeah, I bet not a person in this room knows the Ten Commandments."

I could have laughed then. I could have faked a little mirth. Martin would have gone on to some other rant. But I said, "I do."

Silence. They looked at me. It wasn't *absolutely* the best thing to say in a downtown bar on a Friday night.

Carla said, "Bet you don't."

I held up my fingers to count as I said:

"One. I am the Lord your God. Two. You shall have no other God before me. Three. Do not take the Lord's name in vain. Four. Honor your father and your mother. Five. Remember the Sabbath day to keep it holy. Six. Don't murder. Seven. Don't commit adultery. Eight. Don't steal. Nine. Don't bear false witness. Ten. Don't covet."

They looked at me, openmouthed. Scott's eyes met mine, a good blue, a bright, good look of respect and I thought: I should have done it in Hebrew.

Martin said, "Yeah, well, who keeps them, anyway?"

And, I must admit, he had a point. Because it was that night that Scott offered to share a cab home with me.

I looked around the apartment, trying to remember if any of the things belonged to him, or to the time we were together. And would it be better or

31

worse if I put them away. Better that he shouldn't think I was keeping reminders of him around. Worse that he might notice their absence and realize
I'd put them away. Crap.

I stood, holding a wooden cat he'd bought me, wondering what to do with
it. It had been a makeup gift. He'd made one of his irritating remarks about how
women shouldn't live alone. I'd said something like, oh yeah? And he said,
yeah, especially not Jewish women. You guys get mean. You should at least
have a cat or something. And I said, we get *mean*? I told him he was a self-hat-
ing Jew, and he said show me a Jew who isn't, and then I threw him out.

A couple of nights later I came home late from the gym to find him skulk-
ing in the lobby of my building, holding the cat wrapped in parcel paper. That
was the first time he stayed all night. I asked him how he could, and he said
his wife had taken the kids to her parents' in Connecticut; they visit with her
family, go to church, country stuff, he said. I hit him and said, church! You
married a shiksa?! And he said, you can talk. And I said, *I* am a completely
different situation. And he said, oh really, and he leaned in, and I could smell
his skin: cedarwood, linen, and lemons, filling my nostrils.

Afterward, I told him that my father would want me to try to win him,
Scott, back for the faith. He said, wouldn't he want me to win *you* back? I
didn't answer that.

I was thinking about this, and about the smell of his skin, and the size of
his hands, which were far too big, ludicrously large, clown hands, when the
buzzer sounded, and it seemed like only half a second at most before he
came through the door, and I realized I was still holding the stupid wooden
cat.

I put it down on the hall table and said, "Hi."

And he said, "Hi. Should I be wishing you a long life or something?"

"You can if you like. But I kind of thought you wished I were dead."

He ran his hand through his hair, looking tired and irritated.

"I don't wish you were dead. Christ, Ronit, why are you always so . . ."

"Annoying?"

"Defensive."

I don't know, I nearly said, I can't *think* why I'd need to defend myself
from you.

Instead I dug my nails into the palm of my hand—hard, really hard—and said:

"I'm glad you came."

He opened his arms wide and hugged me. I didn't do anything. We stood like that, in the hallway, he with his arms around me, for a long time.

"How long can you stay?"

He took a breath and let it out. He bit his bottom lip, that thing he always does when deciding whether or not to tell the truth. He said:

"I told Cheryl I'd be gone awhile. I'm on a conference call with Tokyo. I guess I should be back before dawn. Say, two a.m.?"

"Can you make it four?"

He looked at me, calculating probabilities. How angry would I be if he said no? What might I do? Would Cheryl be asleep by two anyway? How much sleep did he need before tomorrow?

"Why?" he said.

"It's just, the funeral will be over in England by four, our time. That's all."

I'm pathetic, I thought, just pathetic.

"Okay," he said. "Four."

It was awkward. We stood in silence for such a long time that I seriously considered saying, hey, how 'bout them Yankees? Or talking about politics or even about work, because we never had a problem when there were things to talk about. Or things to do. The problem was when we were both quiet and he started to get that look on his face like he was thinking about his wife.

We sat on the couch, almost touching but not quite, and after a little while that started to get to me because I noticed how we were sitting in the exact same posture. So I offered to make some coffee, except I realized as he was accepting that I knew how he took his coffee and the idea of making it how I knew he liked it seemed so intensely personal that I thought I'd rather open a vein and bleed into the cup.

So I said something lame like I'm not sure I have any coffee, I'll check.

He gave me this really weird smile and said, "You? Not have coffee? Things have changed around here."

He said it like he was offering me a gift.

I didn't say anything. I walked into the kitchen. And that was the point when I thought, what the hell am I doing? I held on to the enamel of the sink and looked around at the food that I knew wasn't kosher and the dishes that hadn't been kept separate and the appliances that I use on Shabbat. And I had a sudden dizzy sensation that none of these things belonged to me. I felt like I'd marched in off the street into the wrong apartment, and I'd never met that man sitting on the couch before. It was all like something I'd read in a magazine a long time ago: alien, unfamiliar, and terrifying. And a little voice tickled in my ear, saying, well, this is what you get.

I knew that voice.

It said it again: this is what you get, Ronit. All you have for comfort is a married man. All you have for strength is a job. What did you think was going to happen?

And I gripped the sink tighter, drew a breath, and said, I'm not listening.

I didn't realize I'd said anything out loud until Scott said, "What was that?"

I said, because it was the first thing I could think of, "What do you think about my going back to England?"

"What do you mean, what do I think?"

"I mean, do you think I should go?"

"Why the hell not? You've got the German project under control, haven't you?"

I'd forgotten this about him, the tendency to relate all life decisions back to work. I wanted to shout, you idiot, that's not what I meant, and the anger snapped me back into focus and I remembered that I was here, now, in the middle of my own life.

I said, "Yes, it's under control. That's not the point."

I think he said something then, but the kettle started to boil, so I didn't hear it.

As I walked out with the coffee I said, "I guess I should go. That's what you do, right? I should go home, see my people, visit my father's grave. That stuff."

He looked at me.

"Sure."

I sat on the couch next to him and stared silently into my coffee.

After a while, he said:

"What is it that you're afraid of?"

And I almost laughed, almost but not quite.

I said, "Maybe that he'll still be there. Still disapproving. Still disappointed."

Scott said, softly, "And maybe that he won't?"

And I felt tears starting then, in the itching of my eyes and in the back of my throat, and to stop them I took a sip of coffee and thought about the positives, the black side of the balance sheet. I could visit England, and there'd be no awkward scenes, no difficult conversations. And I could bring home my mother's candlesticks. I could almost feel myself holding them, their heaviness in my hands. My mother's tall silver candlesticks, sinuous, wreathed in flowers and foliage. I saw them as my mother used to use them, and as I used to light them later, every Friday night. I saw their beautiful intricacy, each one as long as my forearm, gleaming silver, with a wide, claw-foot base, a slender stem that swelled into a large bulb covered in silver leaves, then on up to a smaller, similar bulb, and then another, before ending with the candleholder itself, large enough to take a candle that would burn for twenty-four hours, if that was required. The candlesticks I never could have asked my father for all these years, because he wouldn't have wanted them to reside in my heathen home. It would be good, somehow, to have them here.

I almost said that to Scott, but then I thought, actually, why do you deserve to know this? The time's passed now for you to know this sort of thing about me, so I stopped talking and looked down. Scott took my hand and said, "Ronit, will she be there, that girl who you . . ."

I smiled because he couldn't have been more wrong. The tears had passed without being shed, and I felt better. I said, "Esti? No, I don't think so. She'll be long gone by now. She was worse than me, back in the day."

He smiled. I smiled. We sat and drank coffee, just like old friends.

Later on, we talked. About England, about my dad. I tried to explain how different Jews in Britain are from Jews in America. I didn't get very far, but it was good to be talking like that, like it was business. That's one thing about

Scott—he makes everything seem simple, because in his mind everything is.

He said, "He was some big-deal Rabbi, your dad? Wrote a book, founded a synagogue. What happens now?"

I shook my head. "If I know that community"—I looked at my watch—"yep, they'll already be talking about who's going to replace my father."

"*Now*? When he's not even buried?"

"Oh, yes, especially now. This is the crucial moment. They'll want it easy and smooth. You see"—I leaned back in my chair, relaxing now that I had some lecturing to do—"the dynamics of synagogues are really very simple, like the dynamics of monarchies. It's all about succession. The simpler the succession, the happier everyone is."

"So will they have chosen a successor already?"

"Probably. Or at least the board, which means the *money*, will have someone in mind." I looked at the ceiling for a moment, thinking back. "My knowledge isn't as current as it used to be, of course, but I'm guessing my cousin Dovid's a front-runner. Although . . . he's not that confident. Doesn't really have the, y'know, va-va-voom for the job."

"A *Rabbi* needs va-va-voom?"

I smiled. "You know what I mean. Charisma. People skills. Good speaking voice. That sort of thing." I took another gulp of coffee. "Still, I think Dovid will be their man."

"How come? If he doesn't have the charisma, people skills, good speaking voice?"

I thought for a moment, staring into my coffee. "He's obedient. That's the kind of guy Dovid is: he's quiet, soft-spoken, does what he's told. They won't want another firebrand Rabbi. The board will want someone who they can boss around, tell what to do, who won't make trouble." I smiled. "I guess, even if I were a man, I wouldn't quite fit the bill."

He looked at me with a sort of smile, half sympathetic, half amused. Suddenly, I didn't want to talk about this anymore. And after all, what had I called him for in the middle of the night? It wasn't to grieve with, it wasn't to talk over memories of my father, or sit on a low stool.

I said, "Look, do you know what I need right now?"

"What?"

Disobedience

I put my hand at that place at the back of his neck where his hair is short, soft bristles and pulled him toward me. And because it was easy, I guess, or familiar or just because it put an end to the awkwardness, he kissed me back. He smelled exactly like I remembered, maybe even better. And we fell to doing other easy, familiar, forbidden things.

Chapter Three

Blessed are you, God, our Lord, King of the Universe, who distinguishes between the holy and the workaday, between light and darkness, between Israel and the nations, between the seventh day and the six days of creation. Blessed are you, God, who distinguishes between the holy and the workaday.

From the Havdalah prayer, recited at the end of Shabbat

In the beginning, the Lord created the heavens and the earth. And the earth was *tohu vavohu*. What is *tohu vavohu*? This matter is much debated among the sages. There are those who say: formless. There are those who say: void. There are those who say: astonishingly empty, as though they had stood alongside the Almighty in the time before time and had been astonished at the emptiness, had, perhaps, remarked upon it.

And there are those who say: chaotic. This interpretation seems to allow the words, which are all that we have of the beginning, their voice. *Tohu vavohu*. Higgledy-piggledy. Upside down. Inside out. Hither and thither. The Creator wanted to show us the first contraction of all-that-is. All modes of expression were open to Him, every human sense. He chose words—*tohu vavohu*. Tumble-jumble.

In the beginning, God created the heavens and the earth. And the earth was bingle-mingle.

In the beginning, therefore, the most important work is of separation. It is of pulling apart the tangled threads. It is of saying "This shall be separate from that. This shall be water, this shall be sky, and this shall be the line between them, the horizon." It is of setting a line between them.

What does it mean, that this world came into being at first through a blinding act, but then, subtly, slowly, as elements were teased away, as infinitely fine lines were drawn? It means, surely, that to understand the world, one must understand the separation.

On Wednesday night, the fifth night of the shiva, Dovid watched Esti cook. He took pleasure in this, in a simple appreciation of her skills. He enjoyed the sense of professionalism in her calm addition of seasoning or her careful reaching for a cast-iron saucepan. He imagined that she liked to cook. He had no way to know, but the fact that she continued to prepare meals seemed to indicate that she must take some pleasure in it. In any case, how else were they to communicate? She cooked and he ate—this, too, was a form of speech.

The previous year, a new member of the community—Mrs. Stone, the orthodontist's wife—had approached him at the buffet after the Shabbat service and whispered:

"Your wife, Rabbi Kuperman." She had yet to learn how to address him from the others. "Does your wife speak?"

He saw several of the women around her turn their heads and blink, like birds of prey. He almost smiled. One of these women would take her aside in the next few days and explain *how things were*, that certain things could be discussed, and certain things could not. Mrs. Stone would be brought into line.

"Of course," he said. "Of course she speaks."

And it was true. Esti often spoke. There had been a time when they spoke to each other in long, effortless conversations. They had spent nights like that, still talking when the sky grew pale.

Yet here they were, conversing through pots and pans,

through—what was she cooking? The pans simmering on the hob were the fleishig set. Meat, then. Dovid raised himself a little in his place and saw that she was stirring some minced beef. With the red-handled spoon that went with the orange fleishig pans and the burgundy plates. This, too, was a form of communication. The wordless order of the kitchen, the separation of milk and meat, which was not forced but seemed to emerge naturally from each utensil. Of course, each item seemed to say, meat will be cooked in the red pots, and dairy will be cooked in the blue. It is natural, in the same way that trees remain rooted in one spot, that water runs downhill, that the walls of a building do not dance. Such order, Dovid thought, is the simple voice of God, whispering softly in the world.

They had need of order and, in truth, they had need of silence. It had been a turbulent, nauseous week. They were not sitting shiva—the duty was not theirs, being neither parents nor siblings nor children to the Rav. Yet is it not written that a man who teaches Torah to another may be considered his father? Thus the whole community was bereaved, and Esti and Dovid's house had become a way station of grief.

Every night there had been knocks on the door, murmured words, gifts of food. The visitors blended in Dovid's mind into a single face, both solemn and demanding. Only a few individuated details remained: Levitsky, who had arrived with a tin of biscuits and had clasped it like a baby throughout his visit, while his mouth worked and his eyes watered; Frankel, who had given them copies of the Rav's sermons to "help them through this difficult time"; and Hartog, who had visited three times, dressed in his Harley Street suit and accompanied by his wife, Fruma, immaculate in navy blue. Hartog and Fruma had simply sat in silence, until that silence had become so thick, so velvety and deafening that Dovid was forced to ask about synagogue business. Hartog had been pleased to reply gravely and at length, though Dovid was in no way able to assimilate the information he received.

Yet in the face of all of this, Esti was able to retain her inner calm. She showed no signs of distress or dismay. Things with her continued as they had always done. Dovid knew what was said about his wife. It was true that she was often silent, even in company, even when directly addressed. She had an oddness of manner to her, an ability to become suddenly very still. They did not appreciate this other gift, the preservation of order in her inmost self as she stirred and chopped, seasoned and tasted.

And then, something. He had not been paying close attention, it was true, but surely. Surely, that was not right. Esti was holding a pack of butter in her hand, had peeled back the paper, and was slicing a small piece, straight into the beef. Surely it must be margarine. Surely. He hesitated, for a second. And then, seeing the gold wrapper, he was sure. He jumped up, touched her wrist, and said, "Esti . . .?" intending to begin a conciliatory sentence. But it was too late. The butter had fallen.

In the beginning, it is of separation. But it is not only of separation. It is, more correctly, of appropriate separation.

For when the Lord created the world, His work was not only an act of dividing this from that. He also commanded that certain things should mingle. He created herbage and fruit trees, sea creatures and creeping things, birds and beasts, man and woman. And the first commandment that God laid upon His creations was this: "Be fruitful and multiply." Thus, it is right for certain creatures in their season to be as one, and for others to be separate.

For us, who have been swept from the dust, who have been taken and formed out of all that is less, our work is of understanding the subtlety of the boundary. It is of tracing it, ever finer and finer. It is of accepting and learning what must be separate and what must be mingled.

The smell hit Esti first, before she even knew that Dovid had grabbed her wrist, was saying, "Stop, Stop!" The smell was wrong—the rich beef scent was mingled with something heavier, sweeter. Before Dovid spoke, Esti knew that she had erred.

She allowed Dovid to take the pack from her. He muttered that the kitchen had become disordered with all these people passing through the house, helping themselves, feeling at home. She nodded. He continued: these things would happen, there was no help for it.

And Esti grew still, because she knew that she had stopped thinking for a moment. As she'd reached for the margarine, she had ceased, for a time that seemed less than nothing, to recite the constant litany that had kept her mind occupied. For four days now, since Shabbat, she had pitched a fence in her mind, had patrolled it relentlessly, listing and relisting the work she had to do, the things to buy, to make, to cook, the people to telephone. And it had worked—she had not thought.

But, reaching for the margarine and, perhaps, feeling Dovid watching, her mind had stumbled. And while she reached, and poured, and stirred, Esti had been thinking about the things she had long ago decided to forget. She had been thinking of the change that would surely come now. Of what might happen this week, next week, the week after. And she had been thinking of her. Of the tips of her fingers, lightly brushing the back of her neck, moving around, stroking her jaw, until her thumb rested on her lips.

Staring at the pan, still bubbling its cross-breed aroma, Dovid and Esti both felt it recede from them. They could, perhaps, have called a Rav—another Rav, from some other community—asking for a way to make it kosher again. But the pan seemed scarcely theirs anymore—Esti would never cook with it; Dovid would never eat from it. Dovid wrapped the butter-beef in layers of newspaper and put the soggy bundle in the dustbin outside. Esti left the pan on the step—when it cooled, she would wrap and discard it.

She did not have the heart to begin again. Dovid brought bread from the cupboard and cheese from the refrigerator, and they ate at the kitchen table. He told a story of a similar event from his Yeshiva days. It was a humorous anecdote; a young man had mistaken his containers, and made a cheese lasagne with real beef instead of soy. It wouldn't have been so bad, but he'd invited the Rosh Yeshiva for lunch. The whole thing, of course, had to be thrown away, and the Rosh Yeshiva had made all the students spend three weeks reviewing elementary kosher food law.

Esti laughed. She took small mouthfuls of her bread and cheese, chewing slowly. Then, carefully, as though the thought were occurring to her for the first time, and it was nothing to her whether she ever heard the answer, she said:

"When is Ronit coming?"

Dovid looked at her sharply.

"You haven't mentioned her to any of the visitors?" he said.

Esti gulped, shook her head.

"I just . . . I just don't know if she'd want that," Dovid said.

Dovid looked down at his plate and watched Esti eating in silence. Esti wondered if he'd forgotten the question. Then, staring intently at a space a hand's breadth to the right of Esti's head, he said:

"Tomorrow. She's coming tomorrow. You don't have to see her if you don't want to. I can talk to her about the family things, she can stay in a hotel. This doesn't have to be complicated—it can be very simple. Business. She doesn't need to know you're here if you don't want her to."

If Dovid had been looking at Esti's face, he would have seen the blink of surprise, the visible start. As it was, he heard her say in a voice a little choked:

"She should stay here."

He looked at her, as though weighing her resolve. He nodded, said:

"It's your decision."

They ate for another few moments in silence. Then Esti asked:

"Does she know about us?"

"She knows I'm married."

"But to me?"

"No." Dovid looked down at the empty plate before him, pushed it away slightly, swept a few crumbs from the table into his hand, and then brushed them onto the plate. "No," he said, looking back up at Esti, "I had no words."

I told myself it would be easy. How hard could it be? Go back to London for a little while, pick up some family knickknacks, make nice with my cousin Dovid and his wife, come back home. And after all, even if it turned out not to be easy, it was the right thing to do, the grown-up thing to do. Dr. Feingold approved of spending some time in London, not that she *said* so, but I could tell in the way she didn't question, didn't ask me why I felt I had to. Getting the time off work was no problem. Scott had obviously primed Carla about my loss, because she was all ready with the sympathetic face and the offer of however much time I needed, which so isn't her style. In fact, she offered me a month:

"That's the Jewish period of mourning, isn't it, Ronit? A month?"

I didn't want to go into it, so I just said:

"Yes, a month."

And, like that, it was done. I guess sleeping with your boss's boss really does have some advantages. I booked my ticket. So far, so easy. Just like planning a vacation.

Only, then came the insoluble, irreducible, unavoidable problem: what to wear. Eight hours before my flight, I was standing in front of my closet, still looking. I'd gone through to find the long skirts. I had thirteen, but all of them were wrong. Half had slits—impossible. Most of the others were tailored or clingy or rode below the navel. Absolutely impossible. So I was left with a gray skirt that I sometimes wear around the house if I'm feeling bloated. It's elasticized.

And then, a shirt? Pulling out every item of clothing in my possession, I discovered that I own over three dozen shirts and blouses, including eight white ones. But not a single one buttoned right up to the neck, with sleeves that reached the wrists. And my sweaters, again, clung. In the end, I found a blue turtleneck, loose and baggy, that had fallen to the back of the closet.

I put this outfit on and stood looking at myself in the mirror. I knew I couldn't wear it. Not only because I looked like the "before" picture in some style magazine, but also because I looked nothing like *them*—those *frum*, respectable women who spend their lives driving Volvos between Kosher King and Hasmonean or Bais Ya'akov School. I looked like an unhappy parody of them. The thing is, you see, it's not just about covering up the right bits—it's also about their *style*.

For one bizarre moment, I seriously considered taking the subway to Brooklyn and buying myself a whole new wardrobe: pinafore dresses and loose long-sleeve T-shirts, velvet hair bands, white tights and brown lace-up shoes. I even imagined getting a sheitel, one of those long blond ones with a deep fringe that so many of those women wear on festivals—so that I could arrive in London pretending to be married. I could invent some kids, Breinde, Chanale, Yisroel, and Meir, whom I'd left with my husband, Avrami Moishe, in Crown Heights. Yes, I'd say, I work as a speech therapist while Avrami Moishe learns Torah, of course. I could question how kosher their kitchens are. I could say—you know, you were right, it *was* just a phase. Look, now I'm all cured.

I found something shockingly delightful in this idea—I played around with it, called a friend to share. We made the fantasy wilder and wilder. What if I shaved my head, because even my husband shouldn't be allowed to see my hair? What if I wrote on a chalkboard, rather than talking, so as not to speak in front of men? What if I told them I'd only eat meat that had been slaughtered by my own Rabbi? We laughed. I didn't go to Brooklyn.

Which left me still in front of the closet. I pulled out everything and laid it on the bed again. I considered going as Ronit, independent career woman of New York. They wouldn't be surprised, but maybe intimidated. I'd wear one of my somber, serious trouser suits, with a pair of high-heeled boots. I'd take my business cards, offer to shake hands with the men, pretend I'd forgotten absolutely everything. I'd make out that I was puzzled, and faintly amused, by their quaint ways. I imagined myself standing in the synagogue, making a cell-phone call on Shabbat. I imagined the shocked faces.

Dr. Feingold said this obsession with clothing is a displacement activity. She told me I need a grieving ritual, and the obsessive choosing of costumes is standing, in my mind, in place of a more profound expression of my loss.

I wanted to ask her, "And what does it say about you, Dr. Feingold, that you live by yourself in an immaculate white apartment, with a pristine cat you call Baby?" Of course, I listened and nodded instead, because I *so* didn't want to get into another conversation about aggression, my boundary issues, and my habit of what she calls "resisting the process." What she doesn't know is, I've built my life on resisting the process.

At four hours to go, I was still no closer to a decision. I thought of calling Dovid for advice, but he wouldn't even have understood the question. Besides, when I'd spoken to him earlier he didn't seem to have the firmest grasp on reality. I'd been thinking through people to contact in England—people I might actually want to see. I asked him about a few: his brothers, a couple of girls I went to school with, and Esti. He didn't even seem to hear when I said Esti's name, barreled straight on past her. I didn't push it—I figured she must've left soon after I did.

He filled me in on some of the details of his life. He's been working as my father's assistant for the past few years, which means, as I suspected, that he's been groomed for greatness.

I said, "So, you'll be the next Rav then, Dovid?"

There was a long pause.

"No," he said. "No, I can't. I mean, it's not. We don't want that."

"We?" I said. "Your wife doesn't want it either?"

"My wife?" As if he'd never heard of such a thing. "No, it's not. I don't. I don't want that."

He turned the conversation to family news. I think he was just being coy. It's too early for him to voice his ambition. Over there, people who hardly knew my father will still be lamenting his passing vocally. Whereas I . . . I find it hard even to bring his face properly into my mind. It's been six years since I last spoke to him and that was only a brief Happy Rosh Hashanah call; it's not like I miss his company.

Dovid told me about his last few months. Months of coughing and retching, he said, bringing up mucus and blood, months of blackouts and dizzy spells. He was always thin, never strong, even when I was young. Sometimes, after a difficult day, he'd sit in the tapestry chair in our living room, finger and thumb pressing the bridge of his nose, where his glasses sat. He would become so still, almost as if he weren't breathing at all. And his hands were so white, and the veins in his wrists were so blue. Sometimes, finding him like this, I'd almost convince myself he *was* dead, so I'd tug on his coat and he'd open his eyes and mutter something in Yiddish, which I didn't understand, but which didn't sound angry, at least.

Even once I was a teenager, even once we'd started arguing about so many petty things—the way I wore my skirt, or my habit of watching the televisions in our local Dixons when I thought no one would see me, or when I started waiting three hours and not six between meat and milk—even then, I was always so relieved to see his eyes open. I think of this, and I do feel sad, and I do feel sorry. And then I think about how those slow-dying months were also months of waiting. And he didn't call for me. And he didn't ask me to come. It's when I think about these things that I start to feel a tight pain in the back of my throat, a stinging in my nose. And that's when I call someone else to tell them the Fantastic Brooklyn Wardrobe Stratagem. Because I refuse to cry over him.

In the end, I took it all—skirts, blouses, sweaters, sneakers, boots, trouser suits, sweatpants, and a formal evening dress. I thought: better to leave my options open, better not to tie myself down. Better to have both the outfits that say "I come in peace" and the ones that say "screw you." Because, really, who knows what I might need to say in this situation? It meant I had three giant suitcases to check in at JFK, but hey, I spent eighteen years of my life arguing with one of the Torah giants of our generation. Staring down airline employees comes naturally to me.

On the flight, I slept. I had a strange dream, a jumble of images, only one part of which remained vivid when I woke. I dreamed of Dovid, as I'd known him when I was little and he used to stay at our house in the summer holidays. I dreamed of him sitting at the falling-apart desk in his bedroom, studying. The desk slanted to one side unless you braced it against the wall and kept holding it with one hand as you worked. I dreamed of that desk, which I hadn't thought of for years. I dreamed Dovid was working at the desk and we were arguing, he and I. Some old argument, though I don't remember ever arguing with Dovid in my life. I was shouting and shouting, but he just kept on speaking softly; I couldn't catch what he was saying. And I knew suddenly that if I could just open the desk drawers, I'd understand everything. He tried to stop me but I pushed past him. And when I opened the drawers, I found they were filled with hydrangeas, pile upon pile of them, spilling out onto the floor. I woke up as we were landing, with a sensation in the back of my throat like the end of a smell, the tail of it. As if someone had wafted a bunch of hydrangeas past my nose. And I was in London.

Scott once said to me that you belong in three places: the place you grew up, the place where you went to college, and the place where the person you love is. I'd add a fourth component to that: the place where you first sought professional psychological help. Therapy has a way of tying you to a location, of fastening you to its way of thinking. In any case, by either reckoning, I now belong in New York more than I belong in London. I went to college here, Dr. Feingold is here. If you can stretch "person you love" to "person you like to have sex with," then Scott's here, too. Of course, this doesn't stop Americans from offering me "a spot of tea" whenever they hear my accent, but still, it *feels* true. I'm a New Yorker.

According to that calculation, though, I still belong in London as well. Which doesn't feel true at all. I took a cab to Dovid's house and, as we entered the heartlands of northwest London—Finchley Road, Hampstead, Golders Green—I spotted more and more familiar places. A bakery where they made the best iced cakes in the world: pink and yellow and white. The WH Smith where I spent hours after school reading forbidden magazines. The Sara Rifka Hartog Memorial Day School itself—hiding behind a thick screen of pine trees, but I knew it was there, another one of these public spaces cobbled together from hollowed-out houses. I didn't feel any pleasure, though, no nostalgia. I felt more like a jaundiced tourist, gazing at England with a cold and unforgiving eye, than a native coming home. No, I wasn't looking at *England* in that way. It was the English Jews. I don't really mind England so much, not that I ever saw a lot of it when I was here. But the way Jews are here . . . it just makes me want to kick over tables and shout.

I'm friends with Jews in New York. Not *Orthodox* Jews, but some knowledgeable, articulate, highly identifying Jews. The kind of people who boycott the *New York Times* because they think it's anti-Israel, or who argue violently against boycotting the *New York Times* for precisely opposite reasons, or stage Jewish rallies against France or write Jewish poetry or talk intelligently on television about the Jewish perspective on things. Who would never dream of apologizing for, let alone denying, having a Jewish perspective on things.

By and large, you don't get people like that in England. Sure, you get the odd participant in *Thought for the Day* on BBC radio, producing some platitude "from our sages." And of course you get the self-haters, the "Israel is evil" brigade. Self-loathing is an equal-opportunity employer, after all. But you don't get the vast participation in the cultural and intellectual life of the country of people who want to talk about, write about, think about Jewish things. And who know, confidently, that people who aren't Jewish will be interested in what they have to say, too. Who aren't afraid to use Jewish words, or refer to Jewish holidays or Jewish customs, because they trust their readers to understand what they're talking about. You don't get that here. It's as though Jews in this country have made an *investment* in silence. There's a vicious circle here, in which the Jewish fear of being noticed and the natural British reticence interact. They feed off each other so that British Jews cannot speak, cannot be seen, value *absolute invisibility* above all other virtues. Which bothers me, because while I can give up being Orthodox, I can't give up being a Jew.

Thinking about this reminded me of some of the male members of my dad's synagogue. Professional men, mostly, doctors, lawyers, accountants. I remembered the way they used to talk about their non-Jewish colleagues. Some of them, anyway. They'd say, "They don't understand about Shabbat, those goyim," or "They think kosher food just means not eating bacon," or "A new secretary asked if I wore a kippah to cover my bald spot!" They used to laugh at these mistakes, but never tried to correct them. They'd say, "You can't make them understand, you can't explain. They don't have the capacity." As though they were discussing children or the mentally disabled.

They'd say wider things. They'd say that such and such a person was "bad for Jews," because she wrote in a negative way about mikvah. Or that such and such a person was "good for Jews," because he gave a bland talk on "Jewish ideals" on a Sunday morning BBC television program. They believed, without question, that debate about Jewish issues was bad, that unadulterated praise was all right but silence was best of all. I can't stand them. I'd forgotten it was these people I was coming back to: these views, that synagogue full of small, cramped minds, grown twisted through lack of sunlight. That world of silence, where Jews must remain more quiet than non-Jews, and women more silent than men.

And thinking this, picturing the airless interior of the synagogue, I looked out of the window and saw it there. Standing behind its fence but still visible. My father's synagogue. It was as though I'd summoned the building forth from my mind. Two semidetached houses, glued together and scooped out. I've never understood why they did that: presumably it must be cheaper than building something new, but given property prices in Hendon, probably not by much. I feel like it might have to do with faith: the idea that we won't be here long, that the Messiah will be here any day, so we shouldn't build anything long-lasting. I remember when they bought them—Hartog took us round before any work had been done, crouched down, breathing heavily into my face, and told me, "This will be your daddy's new synagogue. " I couldn't imagine it—they were just two houses. In one of the bedrooms, the wallpaper was decorated with rockets and moons. Even once half the floors and ceilings had been stripped out, the walls painted white, the ladies' gallery created, I still imagined the rockets and moons were there somewhere. I used to pick at the corners of the wallpaper and paint, hoping to find them.

The cab made one turn, then another, past houses that were suddenly absurdly familiar. And there we were. A semidetached house with a pale yellow door, paint flaking from the window frames, the garden a tangle of long grass. Condensation was collecting at the corners of the windows, and one gutter dangled loose, like a broken limb. I rang the bell.

Dovid answered a fraction too quickly. He looked tired, and though I knew he was only thirty-eight, he looked about fifty to me. He was wearing that Yeshiva-boy costume of black trousers and white shirt, but his skin was sallow and he was unshaven. He smiled and immediately blinked and looked down. I wondered if he'd noticed that the skirt I'd chosen had a slit.

He said, "Ronit, it's good to see you."

I said, "Hey, Dovid," and moved forward to kiss him on the cheek. He took a step backward, shaking his head slightly. I'd forgotten. It's not allowed. To touch a woman who's not your wife. Even shaking hands isn't allowed. I bit back the apology rising to my lips, because the last thing I wanted to do was start apologizing for not being like them anymore.

He showed me into the front room and asked, tripping over his words, whether I'd like anything—a drink, some food? And I said sure, actually, I'd love a Coke. He half ran into the kitchen. I looked around the living room. Decorated in the blandest possible colors—pale yellow walls, beige carpet. No pictures apart from a large Mizrach on one wall, and a wedding picture on the mantelpiece. Right, wedding picture. Okay, let's take a look at the wife.

I picked up the picture, heavy in its silver frame. Nothing unexpected: Dovid in his hat and suit, looking younger and happier, with his hand resting on the shoulder of a smiling woman in a white dress. And I thought, the wife looks a lot like Esti—how creepy. It occurred to me, almost as a joke, that maybe Dovid married one of Esti's sisters. Even creepier. And I looked more closely. And I knew. Dovid came bustling back in with my drink. He saw me looking at the picture and he stopped. He said:

"Ronit, do you . . ." and broke off.

There was an awkward silence. Usually, I'd have filled it. But I couldn't think of a single thing to say.

Chapter Four

All say:
Blessed are you, Lord, our God, King of the Universe,
who did not make me a slave.
Men say:
Blessed are you, Lord, our God, King of the Universe,
Who did not make me a woman.
Women say:
Blessed are you, Lord, our God, King of the Universe,
Who made me according to His will.

From Shacharit, the morning prayer

A tale is told by our sages that, when Hashem created the sun and the moon on the fourth day, he made them equal in size. (Just as, we learn, man and woman were first created in perfect equality.) For it is written, "And God made the two great lights." But the moon complained at this, saying, "Two rulers may not use one crown." And Hashem replied, saying, "Very well, since you ask for one to be lesser and one to be greater, your size shall be diminished, and the size of the sun increased. Your light shall be one-sixtieth of its previous strength." The moon complained to Hashem at her plight and, so that she should not remain utterly without comfort, Hashem gave her companions—the stars. Now our sages tell us that at the end of days, when all things will be put to rights, the moon will once more be equal with the sun. Her demotion is only temporary; in time her full glory will be restored.

And what do we learn from this? In the first place, we learn that the moon was correct, for Hashem hearkened to her words. In this imperfect world two rulers cannot use one crown. One must always be lesser, and one greater. And so it is between man and woman. And so it will be until that time of perfection that we believe with complete faith will come soon and in our days. And yet, we learn that Hashem is merciful. That He recognizes the plight of the lesser of two. That He gives comfort to those in need. We learn that the stars are His gift to the moon.

At the Sara Rifka Hartog Memorial Day School, lessons were over. The girls had clumped downstairs and out to the bus stop or tube station, the noise of them on the staircases had ceased—why, wondered Esti, did they all wear such heavy shoes? Why did they stamp, rather than stepping lightly? It was a matter that Mrs. Mannheim, the headmistress, had often mentioned in assembly, entreating the girls to walk gently, to make less noise. Esti was unsure what she thought about this constant pleading; she valued quiet and yet she felt there was something vital in the noise the girls made.

In any case, the school was quiet now. There was no reason for her to wait any longer. She should go home. And yet she did not.

Esti was aware that her lessons had lacked somewhat today. She had managed to keep order in the classroom, but doubted whether she had actually imparted any Torah knowledge to the girls. Of course, this was understood; she was grieving. Mrs. Mannheim had called her at home to emphasize that she need not come in at all this week, or next week, if she desired. And yet, today, she had decided to return. It was strange, she thought. Returning to work today, rather than remaining at home. Remaining in her classroom now, sitting at her desk marking books instead of returning to the house. Everything at the wrong time. She was unable to make sense of these facts, however, and contented herself with observing them from a distance.

Another interesting development. She completed her marking, and yet she remained sitting at her desk. There was nothing for her to do. It was time to go home. Strange, then, that she was still sitting in school. She packed her bag and locked the exercise books in her desk drawer. Yes. This was appropriate, rational behavior. She picked up her bag. She began to walk, very slowly, along the corridor. She found herself examining minutely the work pinned up on the walls: an art display of the girls' paintings of a Shabbat table, seventeen sets of challot, wine, candlesticks, and goblet; a Jewish history display by some of the older girls demonstrating their studies of the Hasmonean period; a math display of twenty-three perfectly formed Venn diagrams illustrating how many girls liked hockey, how many liked netball, and how many liked both. Esti paid particular attention to the Venn diagrams. She enjoyed their simplicity and orderliness. Perhaps all characteristics could be broken down in this way, leading to a perfect understanding of human nature. People could be classified according to what they liked: some netball, some hockey, some both.

She continued to walk along the corridor. She found that it was, for some reason, necessary for her to look in every classroom, to admire the pictures on the wall or shake her head over a mislaid book or scarf or pencil case or elastic belt joined together with keys. If she had to examine every room in this way, she was aware it would be a long time before she was able to return home. She did not feel unhappy at this thought. She continued her progression, thinking herself alone in the school. She was surprised when, several classrooms down the corridor, she found a teacher still at work.

Miss Schnitzler, the geography teacher, was stapling pieces of work and what looked like black, circular maps to the back wall of her classroom. She was absorbed in her task. She did not hear Esti walking up to the door. Esti paused in the doorway, observing.

Miss Schnitzler was young—only twenty-four—and beautiful, with long curly red hair, very pale skin, and translucent eyelashes. The girls liked her for this, as children often love beautiful people, especially if they are also a little kind. Esti had spoken to Miss Schnitzler on several occasions, but did not know her well. She had heard that Miss Schnitzler was engaged to be married later in the year, and then, of course, there would be no more teaching, not for a number of years, while she bore children and raised them. Esti had seen this before: the young women would arrive, work for three or four years, and then marry and depart.

Esti watched Miss Schnitzler bend to the box of drawing pins, take up a handful, and wrestle a poster into position—one of the round, dark, circular maps. She tried to hold it steady with one hand while she pinned it with the other. She was finding the task difficult. However she placed her hands, one corner of the chart flopped over, so that she could not tell whether it was level or not.

Esti said, "Can I help?"

Startled, Miss Schnitzler whirled around, but she had kept hold of the poster with one hand so that, as she turned, the poster ripped across its center.

Both women said, "Oh!" almost simultaneously. Miss Schnitzler looked down at the piece of paper in her hand, then back up at Esti. She smiled.

"Never mind. Let's mend it together," Miss Schnitzler said.

Esti understood that she should go home. It was past time. Dovid might be worried. She observed with interest that she did not go home at all, that, in fact, she stood waiting in the classroom while Miss Schnitzler fetched a roll of sticky tape. As Esti watched in fascination, Miss Schnitzler cut short pieces of tape and then stuck each firmly to the inside of her wrist, sticking them down and pulling them off several times, puckering the white skin, then smoothing it. She demonstrated how Esti should hold the poster in position, while she stuck the only slightly sticky pieces of tape along the tear on the front. They then carefully flipped the poster over, so that Miss Schnitzler could tape the back firmly along the tear with new tape. Esti watched Miss Schnitzler as they worked, enjoying her gentle concentration, noticing the deep furrow between her eyes as she stuck down each piece of tape. Finally, they turned the poster back, Miss Schnitzler removed the unsticky tape, and Esti held the poster against the wall while Miss Schnitzler pinned it in place.

Esti looked up at the finished product. The tear was barely visible; she could only see it because she knew where to look. Stepping back, Esti looked at the entire poster, still as incomprehensible to her as it had been before. The map was round, a dark circle marked with white points. It looked like a handful of flour, flung onto a black ground. Some points were large, some tiny.

"What is it?" she said. "What does it show?"

Miss Schnitzler took a step closer to her and smiled. "It's a star chart. It shows the positions of all the stars in our galaxy."

"It's beautiful."

"Yes. It's Hashem's creation. Do you remember the story? He gave the stars to the moon as a gift, to be her sisters and companions."

Esti nodded. She was breathing slowly.

"These," said Miss Schnitzler, "are the stars we can see from where we are, at night. They all have names."

Miss Schnitzler stood close behind her. Esti could feel the woman's light breath on her neck as she spoke the names of the stars. "This," she said, "is Sirius, the dog star." Esti nodded, not daring to move or reply.

"And this is Proxima Centauri, the nearest star to earth. Apart from the sun, of course."

Esti whispered, "The sun is a star?"

"Oh, yes. It's so close, we feel it's more than it really is, something unique. But actually it's just one of the many sisters to the moon. It's not even the brightest kind. The polestar, here, is much brighter."

Miss Schnitzler moved her arm around to point. She brushed Esti's sleeve lightly. Her arm was in front of Esti's face, pointing to a star in the center of the map. Her nail was very white, a perfect crescent moon extending past the nail bed. Esti found herself suddenly filled with various unexpected desires. She wanted to blow along Miss Schnitzler's arm, to see the tiny hairs rise, or to touch the inside of her wrist with the very tip of her tongue. Esti wanted to grasp Miss Schnitzler's arm, to pull her forward and against her, to whisper in her ear, "You don't have to do it this way, you know. You don't have to get married. You don't have to leave the school. No one will force you if you simply go on saying no."

A moment hung. Esti could smell the scent of Miss Schnitzler's skin: dry like sandy soil, salt like the sea.

Esti stepped to the side and away, sharply.

"I have to go," she said. "I'll be late, I'm sorry, I have to go."

She gathered her books and left, hugging them to her. She looked down, firmly down, not at Miss Schnitzler at all.

Esti walked home. Her house was half a mile from the school; it was a pleasant walk. The day was warm, achingly so, despite the lateness of the season. Esti wanted to take off her cardigan but remembered just in time that she was wearing a short-sleeve blouse underneath. Impossible. She did not know why she even bought such ridiculous garments. If she took off her cardigan, her elbows would be exposed as she walked along the street; anyone might see her and comment. Still, it was too warm and she was walking too quickly. She did not understand why she was walking so quickly, she did not understand why she felt she should be walking more slowly. She did not allow herself to examine either of these thoughts too carefully.

She arrived at her house too soon, she felt. She walked slowly up toward it, noticing each footstep on the broken paving stones. Heel toe, heel toe. She observed her shoes: sensible brown leather lace-ups. One of the toes was scuffed. She would have to polish it.

And the pavement; so fascinating. When had she last noticed the vivid green moss and grass growing where the stones were cracked? Had she ever noted before that some of the stones were a different color than the others: a sandy brown rather than a gray? She stood in front of her home, eyeing the house with suspicion. Was anything different? Hadn't it shifted its position since she left for school in the morning? Surely it had shaken its shoulders in the meantime, and settled into a new shape, not discernible by any measurement but only by the keenest, best-accustomed eyes? To be sure, she should walk once more around the block and try to take it by surprise.

She began to walk. And stopped. She looked around. Was she being observed? By one of the neighbors or by someone inside her own house? She walked a few steps back until she was standing in front of her house. She stopped again. She had the urge to run from the house, the feeling that it might swallow her. She rubbed her knuckles into her eyes until she saw paisley in red and green.

"I am tired of you," she said to herself, pushed open the gate, and walked to her front door.

Oh, she had forgotten. Until she saw, in the hallway, the tangle of sports bag, suit carrier, raincoat, suitcases, duffel bag, and three airport carrier bags, bursting so that their sides were starting to split, she had forgotten that along with Ronit came objects, thousands of things, each with its own significance and life. That for each thing Ronit would have a story, or an opinion, loud and vivid. Esti stood, smiling, in the hallway, soaking up the Ronit-ness of everything around her. She looked at the magazines, jumpers, books, pencils poking out of the bags and tried to examine and remember each one separately. She felt it was important to note every moment.

The sound of movement came from the living room. A glass being put down, a quiet laugh. The sound of chairs being pushed back from the table. It was too soon, she wasn't ready. Did she have time to run? No. The door of the living room opened.

And there was Ronit. She was as Esti had remembered her and more. At a single glance, one could tell that she did not live here anymore; she was like an exotic bloom found unexpectedly pushing its way between paving stones. She was rosily magnificent, dressed like a woman from a magazine or a poster: large bosom straining at the buttons of a red shirt, the curve of her rounded belly and backside accentuated by a long black skirt. Esti looked, simply absorbing the sight of her, focusing first on one element, then another. Yes, this was Ronit. Black eyes, black bobbed hair, dark skin, a slash of red lipstick, and a disapproving smile.

"Esti," she said, "it's good to see you."

Esti felt suddenly overwhelmed by this immensity of experience. She was here. After so long. Here. A pressure weighed on her forehead and around her scalp, a hum like an electrical device. Ronit had seen Dovid, knew that she was married. Something should be said about that, some explanation given. She felt distracted. Ronit was looking at her. Ronit, here, was looking at her and she was aware that she was crinkling her forehead and moving her shoulders as though trying to rid herself of a skin irritation. It really was time for her to say something now. The whole of her life needed explanation. Reasons should be given for the past eight years. What could she find to say that would explain all of this? At last, she had it.

"Ronit," she said. "I'm sorry. I'm so sorry." Skin-drenching regret, blisters of misery.

Ronit said, "What?"

It was Dovid who rescued her. She had forgotten his presence entirely. He suggested they eat dinner together. Was there, perhaps, something that could be warmed up? This was utterly wrong, she saw suddenly. There should have been a sumptuous feast, thirty courses, garlands of flowers, finger bowls, palate-cleansing sorbets between dishes, twenty kinds of chicken and forty different fish. She reheated a beef stew from the freezer and served it with vegetables and rice.

"I'm sorry," she said again.

"Esti," said Ronit, mouth already full, "will you stop apologizing, sit down, and eat? This is delicious."

She was lost. Beyond apology, she could not think of anything else to say. She noted that the water jug was empty and took it into the kitchen.

"You don't have to serve us, you know!" Ronit called after her, remaining seated.

Ronit and Dovid spoke about the synagogue, about the plans for the future.

"Now, I know what you said, Dovid, but just between us," said Ronit, helping herself to more stew, "they want *you* to be the new Rav, don't they?" She smiled at the side of her mouth. "Whaddaya say, Dovid, wanna be a leader of men?"

"What?" Dovid seemed startled. "No, no. That's not. I mean, that won't. I mean"—he shook his head violently—"they'll find someone more suitable for the role. We wouldn't, you know, would we, Esti?"

Esti remained silent.

Ronit smiled. "You mark my words, Dovid. You'll be their prime candidate."

Esti pushed her food around her plate. She could not bring herself to eat any, but hoped that the others would not notice. She knew she should say something. She was picking up and discarding topics in her mind. Could she discuss the food? No, Ronit would not be interested in household matters. The synagogue? Dovid was more expert than she. The schoolteachers? No, no, certainly not that, but maybe the school?

Dovid said, "I hear talk of a young man from Gateshead, in fact, a talented bocher . . ."

Esti broke in. "Ronit, do you remember the old science rooms in school?"

Ronit and Dovid looked at her.

Ronit said, "Umm. Yes."

Esti said, "They're tearing the building down, that's all I wanted to say, just that they're pulling it down; Dr. Hartog's raised funds for a new building, across the road. Won't that be funny? The girls will have to cross the road to get to their science lessons."

Ronit and Dovid looked at her some more.

Esti stood up quickly, almost knocking her chair to the floor. She picked up her plate and held out her hand to take Ronit's.

"I'm not quite finished yet, actually."

Esti blinked and passed her hand across her forehead.

"No, no, of course not."

She took her own plate into the kitchen. Out of sight, she listened to the murmur of conversation between Ronit and Dovid. She put her plate into the left-hand sink—the sink for meat dishes—and ran hot water on it, observing the oily residue start to lift from the plate. She put her right hand under the water. It was far too hot. She held her hand there for a little while. After some time had passed, she returned to the dining room and served dessert.

Dovid and Esti had not shared the same bed for some time. The two single beds in their room had remained separated for several months, although no objects had accumulated in the space between. Dovid, in any case, had mostly slept in the Rav's house in recent months; to be there, if needed, to help the old man in the night. They did not talk about these things.

Esti often found it difficult to sleep. Regularly, she would lie awake, watching the patterns of light on the bedroom ceiling made by the occasional car driving past, creating shapes and forms out of the wallpaper patterns. This night, she could not sleep. She considered Ronit, who was sleeping just the other side of the wall to them. She thought, over and over, of how she looked now, how much better now than in memory, how she had ripened while Esti herself had shrunk. She found herself breathing heavily. She did not know whether she was about to cry or laugh or do something other, something entirely unexpected. She considered Ronit, in the very next room. She acknowledged in her own mind that she desired certain things that she could not have.

She sat up slowly in bed and swung her legs to the ground. She padded across the room. She spoke Dovid's name softly. And when she lifted the covers, climbed in next to him, and sought him, he sought her in return.

All in all I was feeling quietly self-congratulatory when I went to bed. No sudden movements from *me*, certainly not. No panic attacks, no weird silences, no shouts of "Esti! You're married! To a man!" Which is not to say I wasn't shocked. Esti and I hadn't parted on the best of terms, but things had been different between us then, sweeter. She had been different then, not so strange. To see her this evening, it was almost impossible to glimpse the girl she had once been in the thin, awkward woman she'd become. Only once or twice, as she sat listening to my conversation with Dovid, did I suddenly see her as the young woman I'd known. It was strange. For the most part she seemed just another exhausted, drained-dry Hendon housewife, and then, suddenly, not in her motion but in her stillness I would see the Esti I remembered. Observing her calm, I found myself remembering intensely the way she used to look up at me when I leaned over her, how her looks were more than my words. As if I could taste her sweetness still, and everything that had been between us.

I fell asleep early, jet lag–exhausted, into a honeyed sleep, stretching my limbs against cool sheets and leaving the world happy. I dreamed something bright and shimmering. Something to do with closed boxes and locked doors, twisted keys, screwdrivers, axes, and lock picks. I dreamed about decades-old rust flaking from hinges and shrieking latches being pulled back. It made very little sense, just a series of confused impressions.

I woke up, gasping, far too warm. My watch told me it was three a.m., my body thought it was ten p.m., and my brain was just wondering where the hell I was. I turned on the light and looked around. I hadn't taken anything in before I went to sleep, just registered a welcoming bed and sank into it. Everything was old and shabby and poorly matched and patched together. The wallpaper was some 1970s pattern of brown and orange swirls, the wardrobe was brown melamine. I was sleeping in a single bed with a saggy mattress under a duvet decorated with a faded *Magic Roundabout* pattern that I was absolutely sure I'd last seen on Esti's bed when we were both children. My suitcases took up most of the available floor space, thankfully concealing the carpet: green and blue spots on a gray background. I shouldn't care about these things, I know I shouldn't. But I do.

And as I sat in silence, I noticed a sound, a very distinctive sound, coming from the room next door. Just the other side of the wall to me, a bed was making a slight, rhythmic *squeak, squeak, squeak* sound. On and on and on.

"God Almighty," I said to the room.

"Squeak, squeak, squeak," said some old, rusty springs next door.

I needed to get out of this room, out of this house, and, potentially, out of this country. More than that, I needed a cigarette.

I pulled on some clothes, grabbed my bag, and left the house, pulling the door closed behind me. The night was cold and clear, delicious after the cloying warmth of the house. It was utterly silent, only the swoosh of an occasional car passing by a street or two away. I rummaged at the bottom of my bag, coming up with a crumpled packet of cigarettes. As I put one to my lips and fished out my lighter, I realized I was shaking. Not shivering, shaking. And I thought, shit, this is going to be harder than I thought. I lit my cigarette and inhaled.

I don't smoke, not really. Only at parties, I'll steal someone else's, and I usually have a few in my bag, in case I'm walking down the street and I want to experience that New York feeling, of being one of those women who wear high-heeled boots and smoke cigarettes.

So I went walking, like the independent woman I am. And maybe the cool air, or maybe the walking, or maybe the smoking returned me to myself. I shouldn't expect these people to make sense; they weren't my people anymore. And although I'd thought I'd known Esti better than anyone, clearly I'd been wrong. It made perfect sense. I trod out my first cigarette and lit another one. I smiled. All these years I'd been saying how insane it is here, how abnormally these people behave, and here, look, I was right. Dr. Feingold would even have an explanation for Esti: societal pressure, yada yada, normative expectations, yada yada. But that wasn't my business. Esti was a grown woman, she could work out for herself who to sleep with. I had a simple mission here, there was no need to complicate it. All I was achieving here was to upset people's lives, probably reminding Esti of things she'd rather forget. In fact, I expect that was the reason behind her oddness the previous night. Who hasn't got a few things in their past they'd rather forget? Get in, get out, get back to New York, that was the way.

The ridiculous thing is that with all the smoking and marching and thinking, I almost walked straight past it. I was only brought up short by the sight of the uneven place on the pavement, where a tree root had pushed its way through, slowly and persistently, shaking off the stones like a dog would shake off water so that it stood, nakedly twisting in green and brown amid the concrete. Not just any tree root, *the* tree root. The root that is part of me. I tripped on it when I was thirteen, whacked myself, spun round, and managed to cut open my elbow. I bled all over it. There's a tiny bit of root still in there, small and dark beneath the skin. Scott asked about it once. I stopped to look at the root, and then I remembered where I was.

I looked to my left and there, just there, was the house I grew up in. I'd expected to feel, I don't know, something more than I did, but I found myself eyeing the place with a real estate agent's detachment. Paint was peeling from the ledges of the upper windows. One of the glass panes in the front door was cracked. It seemed quieter than the others, more alone and gaping. I thought that I was just projecting from what I knew, but then I realized what the difference was: all the curtains were open, the windows staring at the streets, hollow and vacant. I looked at the bunch of keys in my hand and I thought: right. Tonight's the night.

I pushed open the gate, grains of rust and paint coming away in my hand, and walked down the dank mildew-smelling passage at the side of the house to the back garden. I looked around the dark garden, making out the shapes by the trickle of light from the street. The lawn was overgrown and tangled—couldn't have been mown for a couple of months—but the apple trees were still where I remembered, and the hydrangea bush was still there, huge now against the fence. I did feel something then, just slightly. A prickle at the back of my mind, a locked-in hum. I looked at the bush, couchant. I could almost taste again the vegetable scent of hydrangeas in midsummer. I turned back to the house.

My hand found the kitchen light switch before I could remember that I might not know where it was. The light flickered on and the garden melted back into darkness, unseen and unknowable. The nakedness of the kitchen made me smile. The surfaces were bare, except for a scratched plastic vase of dead chrysanthemums and a lemon squeezer. A few bowls and utensils were visible on open shelves: blue for milk, red for meat, of course. To think I'd been dreading coming back to this place all this time. I breathed in and out and tried to work out if I was experiencing a profound revelation about my childhood. Didn't feel like it.

The dining room was no more help: a dining table and chairs, a silver cabinet (no candlesticks; I checked). The living room, too, seemed almost empty. The couch had been pulled out into a bed, which was made up with blankets and sheets. There was a small chest of drawers I didn't remember from my childhood, filled with my father's clothes neatly folded, and an oxygen tank with some plastic tubing and equipment in one corner of the room. He must have slept here once he became too weak to climb the stairs. Otherwise, there was only a bookshelf of what my father called "secular books"—no novels, of course, but atlases, dictionaries, some books about the natural world. I felt a vague sense of disappointment. No emotional breakthroughs, just a dull, empty house. If the whole house was as tidy as this, I could find the candlesticks tonight. Stay over Shabbat for the sake of politeness, get back to New York next week.

I crossed the hallway and pushed open the door opposite. I stopped and looked. I had forgotten this. I hadn't forgotten the kitchen or the dining room or the living room, but I had forgotten the books. They ran floor to ceiling, along all four walls, even covering over the window, though the dark red curtains were just visible, dangling half off their rails between the bookshelves. Rows of books, leather bound in black, bottle-green, brown, or dark blue, with their Hebrew titles tooled in gold on the spines, with patterns of fruit, leaves, crowns, and bells. I recognized most of the titles; the volumes were the commentaries on the Torah, and the comments on those commentaries, and the further notes on those comments and the debates regarding the notes, and the criticisms of the debates, and the discussions of the criticisms. And so on.

Disobedience

The rest of the room was disordered, more so than I remembered. Papers mingled with half-drunk mugs of coffee, pens, unanswered correspondence, plates and cutlery in teetering piles and collapsed mounds on the table and the floor. But the books were in perfect order. Each one had its place. They ran in flawless alphabetical order around the room, each tome muttering contentedly to its neighbor. Ah, I thought, and here we find the root to the weirdness of my life. I felt pleased with this evidence: no playroom in this house, no children's room, no family room, but a huge, knocked-through, double-length room for books. How many books were here? I estimated, by counting one shelf and multiplying by the number of shelves on the walls—5,922, give or take. I wondered if I'd read 5,922 books in total in my life. But you weren't supposed to read us, the quiet books murmured, you were supposed to get married and have children. You were to bring grandchildren to this house. Have you done so, wayward and rebellious daughter? Be quiet, I said, stop talking.

This is the problem with having been brought up in an Orthodox Jewish home, with those ancient stories in which Torah scrolls debate with one another, or letters of the alphabet have personality, or the sun and the moon have an argument. All that anthropomorphizing gets to you in the end. There's still a part of me that believes that books can talk. That isn't surprised when they start to do it. And, naturally, books in my father's house would be hypercritical. I could hear them, in that room, whispering to one another: no grandchildren, they said, not even a husband. The practices of Egyptian women. No Torah in her life, no goodness. I couldn't talk myself out of it. I felt ridiculous.

So I took the only route open to me. There was a radio in the kitchen. My father used it to listen to the news, carefully switching it on at precisely six p.m., then switching it off, unplugging it, and packing it away in its drawer at six-thirty. It took me till I got to New York to discover that many radio stations actually broadcast twenty-four hours a day and even, on occasion, include music in their programs. I knew exactly which drawer to find that radio in. I plugged it in, turned it on, and turned the dial until I found some pop music. I was looking for Britney, Madonna, Christina, Kylie; some woman singing indecent lyrics loudly. I turned it up as loud as it would go, counting on the thousands of books to soundproof the neighbors.

I went back to the study. The books were silent. I started work.

* * *

By seven-thirty that morning, I'd cleared off the entire central table and had heard every UK Top 20 song at least three times. There had been no candlesticks among the detritus, but at least order had begun to emerge. To be honest, the search for the candlesticks had become less important as I worked. I was enjoying myself, enjoying the sense of mastery over my past that this ordering gave me. Every item sorted or thrown away was another inch reclaimed from my father. The doorbell rang.

A religious woman, standing at the door in a big blond sheitel, with orangey-red lipstick and just a touch of mascara. She was wearing a stylish ensemble of purple and black blouse and long black skirt. Looking at her, I found myself thinking: Now, *that* is the outfit I should have worn.

She spoke quickly, as they all do, and I could hardly understand what she was saying: something about cleaning and Hartog was all I got.

I said, "Excuse me?"

She spoke more slowly. "It's great you've started so early. Has Dr. Hartog told you what needs to be cleaned and what we'll do ourselves?"

I said, "Umm. Not a cleaner."

She paused, puzzled.

I said, "I'm the Rav's daughter. Ronit."

She peered at me.

"Ronit? Ronit Krushka?"

I nodded.

"It's me! Hinda Rochel!"

I blinked. Surely not? I remembered a Hinda Rochel from school.

"Hinda Rochel Steinmetz?"

She beamed and waggled her left hand at me.

"It's Hinda Rochel Berditcher now. Do you know"—she was conspiratorial—"I didn't recognize you with those trousers on, and with such short hair!"

There was an edge to her voice, just a little. Perhaps an accusation, perhaps simply a question.

"Yes," I said. "I'm different now."

She waited. She was expecting more than that, I knew. But, oh well, she wasn't going to get it. After a moment, she beamed again.

"Anyway, it's so *wonderful* to see you."

She hugged me. A chaste hug, but a warm one, her palms flat against the center of my back. She stepped back and tilted her head to one side.

"I'm so sorry for your loss. I wish you a long life. "

I never know what to say to that. I remember it, from long ago, from when my mother died. I never knew what to say to it then, either.

"I've been sorting things out." I rolled my eyes. "The *junk* in this house is indescribable. It's going to take two or three days just to sort through the study. Still"—I put my hands on my hips—"I guess if I work straight through to evening today, I'll make good progress."

Hinda Rochel twisted her mouth, a lipstick convulsion.

"Not evening," she said. "Shabbat. It's Shabbat tonight. Unless . . . you don't . . . anymore?"

I could have said no, I don't anymore. I could have said Shabbat, what rubbish, what a strange way to allow God to bully you, limiting your behavior to the tiniest square of possibilities on one day in the week.

I ran my hand across my forehead. I grinned as though I were a little embarrassed.

I said, "Friday, of course. Sorry, jet lag. Forgotten what day it is, with all the travel. Shabbat tonight, of course."

Hinda Rochel smiled, but I felt an odd, hollow sensation inside, a sudden dissolution of all the pleasure I had taken in sorting through my father's study. I felt an urge to take back what I had just said to Hinda Rochel. But I didn't.

Chapter Five

Blessed are you, Hashem, our God, King of the universe,
who is wise in secrets.

A blessing spoken when one sees a great
multitude of Jews gathered together

There are those who believe all secrets to be guilty. If the truth is innocent, they declare, why can it not be revealed? The very existence of a secret indicates malice and wrongdoing. All should be open, all exposed.

But why, if this is so, is God not only the God of truth, but also the God of secrets? Why is it written of Him that He shall surely hide His face? This world is a mask, and the mask hides a face, and the face is a secret, for it is the visage of the Almighty Whom we shall only come to know on our day of judgment when He reveals Himself to us. It has been taught that if the Lord were to lift only a tiny corner of His veil, to show us but the slightest glimpse of His truth, we should be blinded by brightness, color, and pain.

From this we learn how facile it is to believe that all things should be known and revealed. We can observe this in our own lives. How often are we hurt by those who declare that they are "only speaking the truth"? Not all true thoughts must be spoken. How often do we witness others degrading themselves by revealing their emotions, experiences, and even the sacred places of their own bodies, when these things are not for all to gawk at? It is not necessary for all that exists to be seen.

The more powerful a force, the more holy a place, the more truth there is in wisdom, the more these things should be private, deep, accessible only to those who have worked to attain them. Thus it is that Kabbalistic texts must include mistakes, so that only those with sufficient knowledge may penetrate their mysteries. Thus it is that a woman conceals her visits to the mikvah even from her closest friend, that her inward times and tides may remain private. Thus it is that a sacred Torah scroll is robed in a velvet garment.

We should not rush to throw open doors, to allow light to shine on quiet places. For those who have seen the secret mysteries tell us not only of the beauty, but also of the pain. And certain things are better left unseen, and certain words unspoken.

"Naturally, we must now consider," said Hartog, "the hesped." He rested one arm on the wooden rail around the bimah, breathing heavily, and surveyed the empty synagogue. He took in the orderly rows of chairs, and neat bookshelves, ready for the Friday evening services later in the day.

Dovid closed his eyes, for the space of two or three heartbeats. He had awoken with a headache. He often experienced headaches—not always debilitating, but unaffected by any combination of tablets—which lent an indelible wash of color to his day. This headache was flaming blue. Tentacles of ice crept across his face from their nexus at his left temple. They stroked his cheek with an awful delicacy. One began to probe his ear, lovingly, the pain at first sharp, then gradually deeper and more blunt. He kept his features calm; to show discomfort would only encourage them.

Opening his eyes, he realized that Hartog was waiting for a response. He had spoken of . . . a hesped? A slight blue film cast across Dovid's left eye, striking a clear, high note. He made his mouth speak, noticing its rubbery elasticity.

"A hesped? Yes, of course. I hadn't thought . . ."

Hartog was right. The funeral had been a close thing, a quiet thing, as is proper. Bones and blood should return to the earth as soon as the spirit leaves them. But for a leader like the Rav, there should be a hesped, at the end of the thirty days of mourning. There should be a gathering of those who knew the man, of his peers and his flock, to praise and to extol his memory.

"Should I make the invitations?" Dovid asked. He glanced at the chairs behind the rail. He wanted to suggest that they sit down, but wondered if Hartog would consider that disrespectful to the memory of the Rav. The icy fingers were pressing more firmly now. His left eyeball was frozen solid; each blink sent a tremor across his face. It was difficult to concentrate on what Hartog was saying.

"Leave it with me, Dovid, leave it with me." Hartog smiled. "There is no need to bother yourself with the arrangements. There is one thing, though."

Hartog paused. The tip of a blue tentacle crossed Dovid's left pupil and tapped on his frozen eye, making a faint scratching sound as it did so. *Scritch. Scritch. Scritch.* The sound was quiet and nauseating. Hartog did not seem to notice.

"And, Dovid," he continued, "you should speak." Dovid was silent, so Hartog spoke again. "At the hesped, Dovid, you should speak."

Hartog stretched, rolling his head from side to side. Dovid, looking with his one good eye, seemed to see his features become tinged with ochre.

"I don't . . ." Dovid said. "I don't, I mean, I am not sufficiently senior. The honored guests will speak, surely?"

"That is certainly true. But nonetheless, as you know perfectly well, you must speak."

Dovid gripped the bimah rail. The cold probe knocked more insistently on his eye. Harder and harder. It would break through at any moment. The eye was brittle, ice-rimed. He spoke quickly.

"No. I don't think so. There will be so many others . . ."

"None of them knew him as you did, Dovid." Hartog smiled.

Dovid felt nauseous. He took two slow deep breaths and stared fixedly at the dark red carpet beneath his feet. This motion seemed to distract the pressure building in his eye, and he felt a little relief. He continued to look downward, as he said:

"I am no Rav. The people—"

Hartog spoke over him:

"The people want continuity." Hartog pursed his lips and took a half step toward Dovid. "I really do not understand why this simple request appears to pose a problem for you. The Rav, may his memory be blessed, is gone. For the congregation, this may come as a shock, but you and I know that it has been months in the waiting. You cannot, surely, be *surprised* now, that these duties are asked of you? It is time for you to accept the responsibilities that have been placed on your shoulders. We cannot be without a Rav."

Dovid looked up, jerking his neck as he did so. The frozen pain returned to his eye, his temple, his cheek and neck. He heard a loud crack, and the tentacle broke through. He felt his eye shatter. White lines crisscrossed his field of vision. A cobalt tendril was poking through his face, waving, softly, from side to side, slicing his muscles and nerves more and more finely with each pass.

Hartog's speech seemed to slow, his features suspended in odd contortions as he formed the words. Ah, Dovid thought, one of these. As he watched, glistening smears of yellow tweaked at Hartog's face, pulling it outward, the color becoming stronger and brighter, blending and confusing it until all that remained were the man's eyes, gleaming dark, amid a mass of throbbing poison-yellow. Dovid heard the yellow thrum in his ears, an insidious, electrical murmur.

Dovid had experienced such moments before. They began the year he was thirteen, his bar mitzvah year, when the headaches he had always felt lingering beneath the surface began to blossom, one by

one, across his skull, bringing with them orchestras of color, nauseating brightness.

The Rav had attended Dovid's bar mitzvah, in Manchester, had
spoken to him for an hour or so privately, asking him about his
studies and testing his understanding. And, in the summer after
school had ended, the Rav had suggested to Dovid's parents that
Dovid might come and spend a little time in London, learning with
his uncle. Dovid understood what this meant. The Rav had seven
other nephews, each of whose bar mitzvahs the Rav had attended,
but none of whom he had asked to come to London for the summer. The Rav had no son, only a daughter. He was a giant of
Torah; it was important that he should have a successor, someone
to whom he could pass on his teachings.

Dovid understood that he was being prepared, that this selection was a special honor and that every measure of talent brings
with it nine measures of work. He worked hard. In the mornings,
Dovid would spend four or five hours sitting at the long dark-
wood table in the Rav's study, as they learned Gemarah together,
the Rav explaining difficult words or constructions in a low, quiet
voice, the smell of cedarwood and old books tickling Dovid's nostrils. In the afternoons he prepared for the next day's lessons in his
bedroom, the volume propped up with a large, heavy can of plums
he'd found in the kitchen. He worried about using the can in this
way; was it too profane to touch the Gemarah? But surely it was
better to hold the book up with something than to let it stand un-
supported, and perhaps fall to the floor? He had a constant, nagging fear that the Rav might surprise him in his room and discover
the plum book stand. He would listen for the footfall on the landing. More often than not, it would not be the Rav, but Ronit.

She was then eight years old, with too much energy, too much
exuberance for the quiet of the Rav's house. The house was a place
for meditation, for thought, and, yes, for angry debate over words
of Torah as well. Ronit did not seem to understand that raised
voices and passionate argument should be reserved for Torah mat-

ters, that they were inappropriate in other interactions. She always seemed to be shouting out every thought that crossed her mind. "I'm hungry!" or "I'm tired!" or "I'm bored!" That last was the most common of all. She seemed unable to entertain herself, and once she had discovered that Dovid would participate in her games, she claimed that she could not possibly play without him. She created elaborate games of "let's pretend" in which she was always the hero, and Dovid the villain or the sidekick. She would set him to be Isaac, while she was Abraham, gleefully raising the set square that stood for the sacrificial knife, before the angel of the Lord stayed her hand. Or he would be Aharon, following behind her, while she—as Moses—hit rocks with a stick, then frowned at them because they did not produce water. Or he would be Goliath, roaring as she, the young shepherd-boy David, circled around, hefting pebbles in a handkerchief. In that instance, after a time, it seemed to her that Goliath might be as good a part, and she took both roles, first mocking the Israelites with her great strength, then becoming their fearless champion. All that afternoon, studying in his bedroom, Dovid heard her shouting:

"You will never defeat me, for I am a *giant*!"

And replying:

"No, Goliath, I will smite you and cut off your *head*!"

It was during one such game that Dovid experienced his first full attack. A headache had been buzzing around him since the morning, seeking to alight. He had warded it off with shade and quiet, lying very still on his bed, drinking slow glasses of water. But Ronit dragged him into the glaring afternoon. She was to be Gidon; he could be one of the disloyal soldiers who desert before the final battle. He stood awaiting her commands and felt the pain descend on his shoulders, before seeping up his neck, like ink into blotting paper, up into the bones of his face and his skull. His head grew warmer, brighter, concentrating all the heat of the day, of the sun, into a single, radiant, white-hot thumbprint above his left eye. His skull, soft and heavy, began to disintegrate. He looked about him as the grass, the apple trees, the hydrangeas became painfully vivid, the colors oversaturated and nauseating. He saw Ronit, suddenly, covered in a swarm of metallic-tasting purple sparks, flying like embers into a glittering sky. He gasped and fell.

They were worried for him. Ronit ran for help. The housekeeper put him to bed. The coolness of his pillow engulfed him in an ice cream calm; he wanted to lick or embrace it, but could not move.

The next morning, when he awoke, he found that the Rav was sitting by his bedside, perched uncomfortably on a stool in the little bedroom, his black coat bunched beneath him. Looking back, Dovid could understand that the Rav must have been afraid for his health. The fact that he had sat for so many hours waiting for him to wake betrayed a concern he had been unable to perceive at the time. As a child, Dovid had felt merely humiliated by the man's presence, ashamed of his own bodily weakness. His mind wandered erratically, even that morning. The can of plums had been placed to one side, the Gemarah closed. Dovid wondered who had done so, but could not hold on to his concern; his attention seemed distracted by small details. He noticed the incredible blueness of the veins in the Rav's hands and wrists as he gripped the book, a small semicircular spiderweb clouding the corner of the window, a white mark on the knee of the Rav's left trouser leg. They learned for only an hour that morning. The Rav proceeded more slowly than usual, asking gently if he had understood, waiting for his answers.

At the end of that hour, the Rav closed the book. Dovid thought he would leave the room, but he did not. He simply sat for several moments in silence. He removed his glasses and pressed finger and thumb to the bridge of his nose. At last, he said:

"Tell me what happened yesterday. Each detail, please, as exact as possible."

Dovid tried to explain: the headache, the heat, and the purple. The Rav leaned forward, tenting his fingers, and asked him to repeat, slowly, the description of what he had seen around Ronit. He should take his time. Did the color seem to emanate from the girl, or was it all-pervading? Did he hear anything, a voice, perhaps? What was the taste? How vivid? Was he certain he had not imagined it? Or dreamed it, perhaps?

Dovid saw the scene again in his mind: the violet swarm, the sharp metallic tang.

"No. I saw it. I didn't dream it." He paused, then said, "I was scared." He wondered if he had done something wrong. He asked for a glass of water. The Rav poured him one from the jug at his bedside and watched him gulp it down. Dovid felt some water drip onto his chin. He was ashamed to behave so crudely in front of the Rav. But when he looked up, he saw that the older man's eyes were closed.

Eventually, after a long pause, the Rav opened his eyes, pursed his pale lips, and spoke.

"Dovid," said the Rav, "this is a very subtle experience of the soul. But you should not be fearful. The Torah and our sages speak of experiences like this."

Dovid was very quiet.

"We learn that at Mount Sinai, when our forefathers received the Torah, God spoke to them directly, face-to-face." He smiled, suddenly, a great beaming smile across his face. "Can you imagine it! To be addressed by the Kodesh Boruch Hu Himself! The chachamim teach that the experience was overwhelming; it mingled one sense with another. The Children of Israel *saw* the words. They tasted them, they smelled them. They *heard* colors, and *saw* sounds. Confronted with this inhuman burden, they fainted.

"The Rambam also speaks of those people who can *see* the soul—the neshama. The neshama comes from God, it is part of His light and His glory. Thus, if it can be seen, it is a light, or a color, which are the same thing, truly. This may have been what you saw, Dovid."

Dovid found that he could hear his own breathing, soft and

rhythmic, in the stillness of the room. The Rav closed the book on his knee and kissed it. He traced the outline of the gold-embossed letters on the front with one flat, pale finger. Dovid watched the yellow, ridged nail move across the open houses of the two letter *beit*s, then around the broken *hei,* letter by letter over the surface of the book.

The Rav drew a long breath, and said quietly, "You should be careful whom you tell of these experiences, Dovid. They are not to be shouted in the playground.

"I will telephone your parents, and explain what has happened." He stood up, holding the book. "I think you should visit here more often, Dovid." He nodded. "Yes, I think that would be best."

Lying in his bed, finding himself too dizzy to stand up, Dovid considered himself in a new light. He could not feel these experiences as a gift or a blessing; the pain was too great. He thought of his four brothers at home, considering how long a thing like this could be kept secret from them. He imagined fainting in front of them, or at school, or in synagogue among the other boys. He had always been a quiet boy, not one of those who ran along corridors or fought, but this was something quite different. For the first time, Dovid felt afraid of seeing others, or being with them.

In a day or so, when he felt well enough to sit outside, Ronit asked him to tell her what had happened. He hesitated, but she was insistent, and he decided that there could be no harm in telling the Rav's own daughter. He described his headache, the pain and dizziness, the sudden explosion in his senses. He kept his description vague, concerned that Ronit might be frightened or upset. She looked at him with large eyes and he worried that she might begin to cry. After a few moments, though, she exclaimed:

"You're a wizard!" A grin peeled across her face. "And *I'm* purple!" She danced off across the scorched lawn.

When Dovid returned, the next holiday, and the holiday after that, Ronit would often pester him to tell her other people's colors. He had already learned to keep his secret better and better as the months went on, to notice the signs that he would faint, to make his excuses and leave the room. He had cultivated excuses, explanations, and denials. Nonetheless, Ronit, watching him closely, would sometimes be able to tell if he was seeing something. When the vision had passed, he would find her tugging his sleeve, asking:

"What do you see, Dovid? What do you see?"

Dovid blinked. He found he was leaning against the bimah rail. Hartog was looking at him, puzzled. The ice tentacles had gone. His eye was whole. The yellow hum had ceased. His head thumped, a dark roar of pounding blood, but there was nothing else.

"Are you all right, Dovid? You look pale." Hartog sounded accusatory.

Dovid remembered. Yes. Hartog had been angry about . . . something. He could not properly identify the memory. He had learned how to conceal this, however.

"Yes, yes, it's nothing. Just a slight headache."

Hartog's voice softened. "Of course, we don't need to finalize this today. Just think it over."

Dovid nodded. If he waited long enough, Hartog would lead him back into the conversation, repeating enough for him to follow once more.

"You needn't worry about taking a more active role in the community, you know," Hartog said. "The Rav thought a great deal of you. He wanted you to be central."

Ah, yes. It became clear now. The hesped. Hartog wanted him to speak. Because the Rav had wanted him to be "central." Dovid wondered how Hartog had formed this opinion. He was, despite himself, impressed by the man's certainty.

"By the way, you and Esti must come for dinner tonight. This is no time to be alone; you should be in easy company."

Dovid was amused by the phrase. Easy company.

"I don't think we can." He spoke quickly. "We have a guest."

"Oh, bring your guest!" Hartog smiled. "My wife always makes too much. You know how it is."

Dovid spoke slowly.

"I don't think it would be appropriate, Dr. Hartog. You see, the guest is . . . is a relative of the Rav's . . ."

Hartog's eyes brightened. He smiled more broadly. He clasped his hands together.

"In that case, you must certainly bring him! It will be an honor."

Dovid drew breath to speak, but a smoky yellow thought began to curl at the back of his mind. He said:

"All right. I'm sure we'd love to come."

As Dovid walked home, the residual pain telegraphing across his skull dissolved into simple bone-tiredness. He thought of Esti, who would be cooking, the ticking of the clock becoming louder in her head as the Sabbath approached. He thought of Ronit and of the absurd items in her carrier bags—the running shoes, the drawstring trousers, the mobile telephone and electronic diary. He thought how ridiculous it seemed for them to be together. And, in another way, not ridiculous at all.

He remembered how they used to talk and plan. In those years when the three of them were always making some plan. Ronit used to bind them together with words. She would say:

"Either we all go, or we all stay."

She would make them repeat it. There was a fierceness to the words, a certainty. "Either we all go, or we all stay."

And in the end, she had left, and accused them of betrayal.

In her father's house, sifting and resifting another heap of useless belongings, her dream of that morning already forgotten (although we are told that a dream is one-sixtieth of a prophecy), Ronit did not yet understand. But, Dovid saw, she would.

* * *

And it was evening, and it was morning, the sixth day. And when the sun set, it was Sabbath. I almost missed it completely. Dovid had to come around to my father's house to find me. I was in a happy frenzy of black rubbish bags and orderly piles slowly progressing across the room. Despite Hinda Rochel's reminder, I had forgotten, as the hours went past, the significance of sunset.

At the door, Dovid tapped his watch, smiled, pointed at the sun low on the horizon.

"It's time," he said. He looked different somehow. I was reminded of that game we used to play as children, where he would pretend that different people were also different colors. I almost had the urge to ask him what color I was.

As we walked home, he told me what he'd done and I found it barely surprised me. It seemed like something that had been waiting to be done. Something to do with rusted locks and wax-sealed caskets. Home again, home again, jiggety-jog and here were the Hartogs, just waiting to be startled. I relaxed into the sensation again; this was the person I could be here, the glamorous, unexpected guest, a bewildering presence.

I considered the Hartogs as I changed my clothes for Shabbat. I'd never liked them, even when I was quite small—he smelled funny and she wore real fur coats that made me sneeze. As I grew up, and saw what influence they had in the community, that dislike expanded into full-grown loathing. They're wealthy. That's not a crime, of course. But in the hothouse of humanity that is the northwest London Orthodox Jewish world, money can mean power. It can mean deciding the curriculum of a school, or choosing the Rabbi of a congregation, supporting one grocery shop by allowing it to undercut another, which goes broke. It can mean giving money only to education programs that, though they don't say so in the glossy brochures, do not allow women to study Gemarah. It can mean funding people like that guy on the street in New York, who hand out leaflets and persuade. All this, and more, Hartog had done.

For Mrs. Hartog—Fruma—I had a particular loathing, not so much institutional as personal. There was a period of my life when I used to spend every Sunday at their house. My father would be judging cases at the Beth Din until the evening, the housekeeper had her day off, and I would go to their house, to sit amid their opulence and do my homework. Fruma gave me lunch. She did not make good lunches; that wasn't her thing. Dry bread from the fridge and slices of cheese were about her limit. She wore clickety-click high heels all around the house, even when she was preparing food, and she was always telling me whether or not I looked pretty. Mostly not.

What I hated most of all, though, was the way she'd talk about my mother. For example, "Ronit, your mother wouldn't have liked you to eat like that," or "Ronit, your mother wouldn't have wanted you to shout so loudly." Even then, I didn't believe what she said, and even then I didn't feel guilty about it.

So, dinner with the Hartogs as an uninvited, unexpected guest. I chose a tight blue skirt with a long slit up one side and felt positively gleeful.

Sabbath, at Esti and Dovid's house, came in a welter of tiny, forgotten details, and sudden dashes to make sure that the stove was turned off, or the oven turned on, the urn plugged in, the hotplate properly ordered. I didn't participate; Esti and Dovid made it happen around me, reminding me strangely of children, playing at being adults while their parents are away. I was oddly charmed by the experience; it had been so long since I'd last seen anyone participate in this peculiar form of obsessive-compulsive disorder. Everything, everything must be ready before the Sabbath, nothing must be left undone. Esti had set up a pair of candles for me to light, next to her own. She offered me the matchbox shyly, looking down as she did so, and I thought what the hell and lit them. I thought of my mother's silver candlesticks, of the leaves and branches of them and the shining reflective surfaces. And I did feel it, a little bit. That feeling from long ago: Sabbath peace.

We walked to Hartog's house. I remembered which one it was perfectly: grand, set well back from the pavement behind a screen of trees, on a street of large houses. Everything about it was a little too big: the doors much taller than could be needed to accommodate anyone, the plant urns at each side of the doors oversized, the lion's-head door knocker twice the size of a fist.

I wondered what Hartog was trying to compensate for, which meant that I still had a smirk on my face when he came to the door, smiling, bustling, because she was still in the kitchen. He was wearing a dark suit with waistcoat, expensively tailored to hide the bulge over his waistband, a dark kippah, not quite concealing the increasing bald spot that was creeping out from under it. He smelled of a little too much very good quality aftershave.

Amazingly, he didn't seem to recognize me at first. He looked me hard in the face for a moment, as though he knew he ought to know me. Or perhaps to confirm his first, awful impression, that I was indeed a woman, and not some distinguished Rabbi. He said:

"Good Shabbos, Dovid, Rebbetzin Kuperman."

Dr. Feingold would probably say it was denial, shielding his mind from unpleasant truths.

So, I stuck out my hand and said:

"Dr. Hartog. Maybe you don't remember me. I'm Ronit, the Rav's daughter?"

As though we'd met at a cocktail party once. My God. I think if I'd gone through it all, the whole of the last thirty-two years, just to experience that moment, it would have been worth it. The man jumped. He literally jumped, as though a charge had jumped from my hand. I could almost hear a fizzing and popping in the air, could almost smell singed hair. His face turned a strange kind of yellow. He opened and closed his mouth a couple of times, his shaggy eyebrows moving as if they were trying to crawl off his forehead.

He said: "Ron ah, Ron ah, Miss ah, Miss Krushka. I don't, I don't, I didn't, I mean I wasn't, I mean, Dovid didn't, I mean . . ."

And he stopped. He looked at me, he looked at Dovid. And I swear, I swear, there was no sound from the kitchen, but he suddenly said:

"Coming, dear!"

And left us standing on the doorstep.

There was a very quiet moment. The three of us wandered into the vast arched space of the entrance hall and stood, our coats still on. We could hear some muffled conversation coming from the kitchen. Dovid was looking guilty as hell. Esti whispered:

"Do you think we should go?"

And I said:

"I think we're just getting started, don't you?"

And Esti and Dovid smiled, just a little, as they had when we were young. We took off our coats, leaving them on one of the velvet-covered benches next to a green marble side table, walked across the hall toward the main lounge, sat down, and waited. The place was just as I remembered it. The room was red: the carpet burgundy, the wallpaper scarlet with a repeated pattern in gold, the curtains dark crimson. I hadn't recalled the opulence, though, on the grandest, least tasteful scale. The huge mirrors on either side of a marble fireplace, decorated with gold curlicues, the vast crystal urns on the mantelpiece and the windowsills, the Versailles-style oil paintings, covering almost every spare inch of wall space—all of fruit and flowers, of course, rather than naked women, but nonetheless the style implied that Mrs. Hartog rather fancied herself a Marie Antoinette.

I sat back in one of the patterned velvet armchairs and waited. Eventually, Hartog and Fruma emerged from the kitchen to join us. Evidently they hadn't run screaming into the night, then. Hartog was smiling his what-big-teeth-I've-got smile, and Fruma had on a smaller, tighter-lipped version. She said:

"Ronit, how wonderful to see you again. We thought we never would."

Hoped you never would, I thought. I raised an eyebrow.

Hartog chimed in:

"Yes, it's a real mechaya to see you, Ronit. And a surprise."

They started a duet, each finishing the other's sentence.

"Dovid never mentioned you were back in London . . ."

"No, you never said, Dovid. We haven't heard anything from you . . ."

"And it's been so long, although of course we understand . . ."

"At a time like this you'd want to be home. With family . . ."

"And old friends. Which is good."

"Yes, it's wonderful, only we didn't know."

"Although of course we wouldn't have minded if we had known."

"But you see, we've got some people coming."

"We invited them before we knew . . ."

"We thought Dovid might like to see them."

"Seeing as they knew your father so well."

"Dayan and Rebbetzin Goldfarb."

Fruma stopped at that, but Hartog's voice was left, lonely and small. I almost felt sorry for the man. He said:

"And there won't be any trouble, will there?"

I said:

"Trouble, Hartog?" and attempted to look innocently puzzled.

There was a long pause, before Fruma smiled nervously and offered us drinks. Far away, I thought I could scent blood in the air. Or perhaps it was the smell of old, rusty iron.

The anxious waiting was positively delicious. Hartog lapsed into an uncharacteristic silence, while Fruma became ever more twittery and indecisive, roaming restlessly between hall, kitchen, and reception room. When the sound of knocking at the door finally came, they both leapt to answer it. We heard a whispered conversation in the hall, a protest from Hartog, a strangled yelp from Fruma.

I muttered to Dovid, "Do you see what's going on here?"

He frowned and shook his head.

"Succession, Dovid. Succession."

Esti and Dovid exchanged a glance.

Dovid said, "We don't think so. We talked about it this morning. I'm not eminent enough."

I rolled my eyes. "Look at what's happening here. Do you think it's a coincidence you were invited with the Goldfarbs?"

Dovid looked blank.

"Dayan Goldfarb was a good friend of your father. He supported the shul."

I sighed.

"Dovid, Dayan Goldfarb is one of the most influential Rabbis in Britain, and that's the reason he's here tonight. If Hartog wants you to become Rav, Dayan Goldfarb would be a perfect person to support you. With him behind you, the transfer of power would be smooth; no one would argue with the Dayan's backing. Just you wait and see. By the end of the evening Hartog will have impressed on him what a learned young man you are, how you've been too modest to step forward until now, what trust the community puts in you."

Dovid blinked. The door swung open and the Goldfarbs entered the room.

I was right. Naturally. Over dinner, Hartog attempted on several occasions to swing the conversation around to Dovid's achievements and merits. But, of course, Dayan and Rebbetzin Goldfarb were far more interested in hearing about what *I'd* been up to for the past few years. It wasn't anyone's fault, really. It was only to be expected; the Goldfarbs hadn't seen me for seven or eight years, weren't the kind of people to listen to malicious gossip, really were genuinely interested to find out about me, to listen to my little stories of New York life.

Fruma served her five courses with increasing irritation. They'd evidently had someone in to cook for them; the food was much too good for Fruma's mean-spirited catering. The gefilte fish arrived, each creamy disc crowned with a circle of carrot, as Dayan Goldfarb asked my opinion of Stern College, where I'd taken my undergraduate degree. The gefilte fish plates departed and the golden chicken soup arrived. We spoke about work prospects in the city; the Goldfarbs had a nephew working in the financial district. The soup bowls were gathered and two roast chickens were presented, dripping clear fat onto the roast potatoes beneath, accompanied by their vegetable entourage. Rebbetzin Goldfarb named and assessed her eight children and thirty-seven grandchildren, now living in London, Manchester, Leeds, Gateshead, New York, Chicago, Toronto, Jerusalem, Bnei Brak, Antwerp, Strasbourg, and two, she gasped, in Melbourne. Imagine. The plates were cleared and the desserts placed in the center: orange cake with oranges in thick, alcoholic syrup in the middle, circular meringues topped with strawberries. Hartog tried in vain to talk about Dovid's future; the Goldfarbs asked about my career prospects. We ate the cake. Rebbetzin Goldfarb took tiny bites and made appreciative noises.

She said, "This is *wonderful*, Fruma. *Wonderful*. You must give me the recipe."

Fruma's mouth drooped.

"Yes," she said. "Yes, but not on Shabbos, of course."

She was sallow. I smirked. I wanted to lean over and whisper, "You didn't make this at all, did you, Fruma?" but Rebbetzin Goldfarb was already posing another question, so sweetly it felt impossible not to respond.

She said, "So, Ronit, any young men in your life?"

She asked with that tender smile on her face, the one that older people always use when they want to let you know it's time to get married.

Now, here's the thing. I wanted to tell her what she wanted to hear. I really did. At that moment, after such a pleasant evening's conversation, I wanted to be able to say: Oh yes, a doctor. Is he Jewish? Why, certainly. We're getting married next year. We'll live in Manhattan. I could see how delightfully the conversation would proceed from that point, how we'd talk about wedding plans and about the future. I found myself longing for that conversation with all my heart.

I wanted to say that, and I saw myself wanting it and I hated the part of myself that wanted that to be true. I heard a screaming creak from far away and I found myself thinking of a lock and an old rusted key resting heavy in my palm. This is all the explanation I can offer because, honestly, which of us really understands why we do the things we do?

I said, "Actually, Rebbetzin Goldfarb, I'm a lesbian. I live with my partner in New York. Her name is Miriam. She's an architect."

It's not true. It's never been true. There was a Miriam, a long time ago, but we never lived together. And the architect was another woman entirely. And, let's face it, currently I'm sleeping with a married man, so I could have said *that* and shocked them just as much. Or maybe not.

I looked at Fruma. Her skin had a grayish cast. She was staring, not at me but at the Goldfarbs, unblinking and terrified. Onward, I thought. Onward and through is the only way.

"Yes, we're having a commitment ceremony next year. And then we're talking about kids, maybe a sperm bank, but a gay couple we know say they might want to be fathers but you know how it is." I leaned forward, conspiratorial. I noticed that no one else leaned with me. "They say they want children but they still want to be out every night. Still, four incomes are better than two and it'd save a lot of paperwork." I smiled, as though I were telling an amusing anecdote at a friend's party. "After all, the turkey baster only gets used at Thanksgiving anyway, right?"

I folded my hands in my lap and sat back to survey the damage.

The Hartogs were the best. Very satisfying to observe. Her mouth was hanging open and she was looking from Dayan Goldfarb to the Rebbetzin and back, glassily fish-eyed. He was staring down at the table, fingers at his temples, shaking his head slowly from side to side.

Dovid was smiling. He was looking up at the ceiling, with his hand half covering his mouth, silently smirking. Sitting next to me, Esti looked as though she might start crying, which made me want to shout at her because for God's sake did she expect me *not* to say what she already knew? Or did she expect to have been the only one for me, that I should have been as paralyzed as she's obviously been all these years?

And the Goldfarbs. I should have known. I could have known, but I didn't think of how they'd feel. Or maybe I did but I didn't care. Just a moment before I did care very much indeed. Dayan Goldfarb was looking at his hands, quiet, impassive. His lips were moving, but there was no sound. And the Rebbetzin. She wasn't looking away, or trying to gauge someone else's reaction. She was just looking at me, full of sadness.

I thought I had come to all sorts of decisions about what I believe. That it is better for things to be said than remain unsaid. That I have nothing to be ashamed about. That those who live narrow lives have only themselves to blame when they find themselves shocked. As it turns out, I don't seem to have got what Scott would call "total buy-in" from all levels of my brain on those principles. I thought I should phone Dr. Feingold, just to let her know that nothing had been resolved even after all this time.

Because I did feel it. Shame. They're not bad people. None of them are. Well, maybe the Hartogs. But the Goldfarbs aren't bad people. They're not cruel or unpleasant or malicious. They didn't deserve to have their peaceful Friday night dinner overturned. They didn't deserve me smashing my life straight into theirs. It can't have been right that I did. And if I hadn't? Yeah, that wouldn't have been right either.

Chapter Six

God instructed the moon to make itself new each month. It is a crown of splendor for those who are borne from the womb, because they are also destined to be renewed like her.
From the Kiddush Levana, recited every month after the third day of the lunar cycle and before the full moon

What is the shape of time?

On occasion, we may feel that time is circular. The seasons approach and retreat, the same every year. Night follows day follows night follows day. The festivals arrive in their time, cycling one after the other. And each month, the womb and the moon together grow fat and fertile, then bleed away, and begin to grow once more. It may seem that time leads us on a circling path, returning us to where we began.

In other moods, we may view time as a straight and infinite line, dizzying in its endlessness. We travel from birth to death, from past to future, and each second that ticks by is gone forever. We talk of managing time, but time manages us, hurrying us along where we might have wished to linger. We can no more halt time than the moon can halt her nightly journey across the sky.

As is so often the case, these two seemingly irreconcilable observations combine to form the truth. Time is spiral.

Our journey through time may be compared to an ascent around the outside of a round tower. We travel, it is true, and can never return to the places we have left. However, as each revolution brings us higher and farther, it also brings us around to encounter the same vistas we have seen before.

Every Shabbat is different from the Shabbat before; nonetheless every Shabbat is Shabbat. Each day brings evening and morning, yet no day will ever be repeated. The moon, waxing and waning in accordance with the wishes of her Creator, is our example: always changing, always the same.

We should remember this. Often it may seem that time has taken us very far from our origin. But if we take only a few more steps, we will round the corner and see a familiar place. And sometimes it may seem that in all our traveling we have returned to the place where we began. But although the view may be similar, it will never be identical; we should remember that there is no return.

Esti closed her eyes. Her breaths were soft and regular. She listened to the sounds of the synagogue around her. A low murmur of chatter, of pages being turned and children quieted, buzzed in the ladies' gallery. Below, in the men's section, a man was reading the Torah portion at an unhurried pace, speaking each word with its proper intonation and note. Dovid had shown her how each word in the Torah is written with ta'amim, small dots and lines that indicate whether its note should ascend or descend, which syllable should be stressed. The symbols, he had said, allow the reader to bring an individuality to his reading while ensuring a uniformity of tone. Because of this, a Torah reading is always the same, but always different. This reader's voice was rich and fluid. She allowed her mind to catch on one or two of the Hebrew words as they passed by, translating them, savoring them, and then releasing them. The subdued activity murmured on around her. Somewhere nearby in the ladies' gallery, someone was whispering, a child was speaking a little too loudly, a door was opened and allowed to swing shut. Let it go, let it all go.

Esti spread her mind wider and wider around the synagogue until she inhabited every space of it in her slow breathing. She was in the puckered ceiling plaster and the tired blue carpet, in the grilles that covered the windows, in the red plastic of the chairs, in the electric wires within the walls, and in the throat-pulse of every man and woman. She breathed and felt the synagogue inhale and exhale with her.

Dwelling within the congregation, she noted the familiar soup of thought and emotion. There were angers here, bitter hatreds, fear and boredom and resentment and guilt and sorrow. She saw herself from outside herself. Am I really? she thought. Can that be me, that person who appears so strange to all these others? She saw herself through a dozen pairs of eyes, each one registering her oddness with fear or disgust or confusion. She smiled at the people as she passed through them, saying, ah yes, you think I'm strange. But I know something you don't know.

She swept herself around the synagogue in a lazy arc from the men's section below, up, slowly, into the ladies' gallery, which is always, doubtless, reserved for ladies and not for women. She moved around the rims of the gallery, resting near the corners of the ceiling, where the three rows of chairs jostled together and the net curtain bunched and gathered, screening them from view. She investigated slowly. She knew what she was looking for. She allowed herself time to find it, among the sincere prayer and the insincere, among the worries and regrets and dedication and boredom and confusion and disapproval of the women. She imagined that she was surprised. Why, what is this? A new thought? A new mind? So unexpected. Who on earth could it be?

She took her time answering. She let the question hang, enjoying the suspense. She smiled. To herself, only to herself. It is Ronit, she said. I am sitting next to Ronit and her warm body is beside me as it always used to be. Time, which is a circle, which will always return us to our starting points, has returned her to me.

Esti thought, I am happy. This is happiness. I have remembered it.

* * *

When she was twelve or thirteen—young, but no longer a child—Esti once heard a snatch of conversation pass between two women standing outside the synagogue. She was good at remaining unobserved; people often failed to notice her, allowing her to hear things that were not meant for her. Her own parents sometimes passed by her in the synagogue hall, even while attempting to look for her; Esti considered this ability a gift.

"Did you see the Rav's daughter in shul today?" one of the women said.

The second woman nodded.

The first raised her eyebrows and inhaled loudly. "I didn't know where to look. Do you think the Rav knows she behaves like that?"

The second woman, older and kinder, said, "She'll settle down. She's only young and living in that motherless house, poor thing."

Esti would have heard more, but Ronit bounded over and it became impossible to remain unnoticed. The two women swiftly began to discuss an upcoming wedding.

For a while, Esti wondered whether to tell Ronit to behave better or differently. She wondered if Ronit would even know what the women had meant. Esti knew—she had an acute sense, always, of rectitude. She tried to imagine how Ronit might react to such a conversation and found it impossible. In her mind, she couldn't even get beyond the first line of discussion. She had already begun to love her. Not as she would do later, but in a fashion that made this conversation, the possibility of breach and separateness impossible. Loving Ronit seemed, already, to demand some denial of herself. Or perhaps, she reflected later, all love demands that.

In any case, she could not tell Ronit what she had heard. They continued as they had before. Sometimes, they would hang over the rail of the ladies' gallery together, desperate and comic, trying to attract Dovid's attention. They would wait until he turned in roughly their direction and Ronit would start to wave, or puff out her cheeks, or stick out her tongue. Esti, laughing and embarrassed, would hold back and then join in, so that Ronit wouldn't tug her arm or make a mocking face. And Dovid, who was sixteen or seventeen, would usually try to ignore them. His eyes would flick up to catch the unexpected motion, and when he saw the two gurning girls, they would flick down again. Generally his face would be grave, his eyes fixed on his prayer book. But sometimes he smiled. And sometimes he would look back up at them and, making sure he could not be observed, stick his tongue out, too. Those were the best moments, the ones they waited for, the ones for which Esti was willing to bear the risk that her mother would look up at the wrong moment and notice her behavior. Once or twice, Esti's mother noticed and, after synagogue, spoke to her quietly about behavior appropriate to a girl, about the quiet calm that she expected from her. At these times, Esti would listen and nod, but in her heart she knew she would disobey again.

Esti and Ronit would do other things, too. Before they were twelve, when they were still permitted to enter the men's section, Ronit once persuaded Esti to help her tie the ends of all the tallits together, in one long row, so that they became confused and tangled when the men stood up for prayer. Ronit would pull Esti out during boring parts of the service, to take part in complicated running, jumping, hopping, skipping games she used to invent in the corridor outside the main synagogue. They grew to have the reputation of "naughty girls," a matter that would occasionally cause Esti's parents some concern, some tutting and sighing. Ronit used to say: "We have to do *something*. Shul's so *boring*." She would roll her eyes.

Esti was always both shocked and impressed when Ronit spoke like this. A part of her wanted to remind Ronit of what they had learned together in school about God and prayer, about having the proper respect for synagogue and how wrong, how very wrong it was to call it boring. She wanted to mention to Ronit the words of her own father every week in synagogue, the reverence due to the prayers. But she found the words dried up and choked her before she could utter them.

She wondered, sometimes, how Ronit grew all these ideas, if perhaps they sprouted in the darkness of her head like mushrooms, fostered by the "motherless atmosphere," as certain plants need greenhouses and special soils. She wondered if she placed her head very close to Ronit's some of the spores of them might travel into her. She imagined Ronit's thoughts, light and downy, coming to rest in her brain, sending out first one exploratory root, then another, sinking themselves deep down into the spongy tissue, becoming matted and brain-logged. She would not know at first, as they grew, until the new thoughts began mushroom-popping inside her skull and she would find herself, without warning, different. She would belong to Ronit. Their ideas would be one. She did not know whether this idea pleased or frightened her.

Esti was surprised, sitting next to Ronit in the synagogue, to find that the place was still the same. She had thought, somehow, over these years, that the building itself, the fixtures and fittings, must have become different. But here, with Ronit here, she could see that was not the case. The place was just the same now as it had been ten years before—so that Esti was almost surprised to find that Ronit was not leaping, running, making faces. She was behaving with perfect propriety, hands folded, following the reading in the Chumash before her. Esti found that she could not behave so correctly. She missed the page, dropped her book, and had to pick it up from the floor and kiss it. She found herself still standing when everyone around her had already sat down. She could not concentrate. She was waiting for something.

She knew what was coming; she had realized it the previous day with finger-prickling delight. She thought perhaps Ronit might remember what the reading would be today, but had decided not. Esti did not remind her, did not say, "Do you know what day it is tomorrow?" She held the knowledge inside herself and waited for the moment.

The Torah portion was over. The measured intonations ended. Now there was only the Haftarah to be read, an extract from the writings of the prophets. A soft paper-rustling susurrus whispered in the shul as the congregation turned the pages of their books. The men shuffled. One left the bimah, returned to his seat at the other side of the synagogue. His neighbors shook his hand. Hartog looked up and around, gimlet-eyed.

"Tomorrow," he announced, "as we all know is Rosh Chodesh Cheshvan, the first day of the month of Cheshvan. So instead of our usual Haftarah, we will be reading the section for Rosh Chodesh eve." He announced the page number in the various editions of the Chumash.

Esti's smile reached all the way from her inside to her outside. She felt it tug at the corners of her lips. She promised herself she would not look at Ronit until the reading began, until they had gone, say, ten lines.

She waited. She wondered if Ronit was waiting, too, if she'd known all along. The reader began. A similar pattern of intonation, but not identical, to differentiate the words of the prophets from the words of Torah. The tones of the Haftarah, more melodic and more poignant than those of the Torah reading, speak so often of faithlessness and betrayal, of Israel's failures of love toward God. But not today. Esti followed the English with her eyes.

"Jonathan said to him: 'Tomorrow is the New Moon, and you will be missed because your seat will be empty . . .'"

That wasn't the best part. Esti's eyes skipped ahead, flicking through the familiar story. Jonathan was the son of King Saul. David was Jonathan's closest friend, and King Saul's favorite musician. King Saul was angry with David, but David had to be sure whether he really meant to harm him. So, together, Jonathan and David made a plan. David would hide in the countryside nearby. He would miss the feast to celebrate the start of the new month. Jonathan would wait to see what Saul did. If all was well, he would send word that David could return. But when Saul saw that

David was missing, he was enraged. Jonathan tried to calm his father, but Saul knew that he was trying to protect David. His anger flared and he said:

"Do you think I don't know that you have chosen this David, son of Jesse, to your shame and the shame of your mother's nakedness?"

The Haftarah reader was talented. Through the singsong notes he managed to produce King Saul's rough, anguished voice. Now. She had waited long enough. She touched Ronit very lightly on the arm.

"Do you remember?" she whispered.

Ronit looked at her and blinked.

"Sorry?"

"It's Machar Chodesh. Tomorrow is Rosh Chodesh, the new moon. Do you remember what you told me once about this day?"

Ronit frowned. Esti waited. The cadences of the reader's voice were low and melodious, recounting David and Jonathan's meeting in the fields outside the city, telling of a love that, the Rabbis record, was the greatest that has ever been known. The notes fluttered up and down the scales, falling like tears and rising like an arrow sprung from the bow.

"Machar Chodesh. When we read about David and Jonathan?" she whispered.

Ronit's face cleared.

"Oh! Right. Yes. Yes, it's today."

Esti smiled. She turned back to her book. It's today, she thought. It's today.

The reader came to the end of the portion. Jonathan went to David's hiding place and told him to run away, for King Saul meant to kill him.

"And the men kissed each other and wept with one another until David exceeded. And Jonathan said to David 'Go in peace. What we two have sworn in the name of God shall be forever.'"

* * *

At the end of the Sabbath, after they had eaten lunch, after Ronit had gone to and returned from her father's house, after the Sabbath detritus had been cleared away, Dovid set off for Manchester, where his mother had been sitting shiva, close to her other sons and kept company by them. He had been intending to go; he wanted to see his mother, to comfort her in the loss of her brother. It had all been arranged. The car was ready. He took Esti's hand, kissed her cheek, and he was gone. Esti and Ronit stood in the empty hallway. Ronit shuffled in place. She said:

"I think I'll . . ."

And Esti said, "Let's go out. Let's go for a walk. A coffee."

She said it so boldly that there was nothing for Ronit to say but yes.

Waiting for Ronit to change her clothes, Esti stepped out into the overgrown front garden. She looked up. The sky was blue and black and purple, uncertain as the skin of an aubergine. The moon was absent, a circle of darkness denoting the possibility of presence, the inevitability of return. Tomorrow is the new moon, she said to herself. Tomorrow the moon will return, as Ronit has returned to me. Esti breathed the cool night air, waiting.

They walked, side by side, along the quiet suburban streets, through one of the large, open parks of Hendon, heading toward Brent Street and Golders Green High Road. The path was heavily overgrown, with gangly tree arms sweeping this way and that from overhead. Although the evening was warm, a gusty breeze blew a few dry leaves across the face pathways and the tarmac playground with a skittering sound. The place was utterly deserted; Hendon rested contented and perhaps a little overfull from the Sabbath. Hendon might walk out later to buy bagels or for a cinema outing, but for now was satisfied to remain at home.

Esti took Ronit's arm as they walked. Ronit looked at Esti's arm, interlinked with her own, but did not try to move away.

"Do you remember," Esti said, "we used to come here after school? Over there"—she stretched her right arm across the dark expanse—"are the swings. Do you remember? We used to come here after school sometimes on Fridays in the winter. When they let us out early. It was a special place."

Ronit peered out into the darkness to the right of them. The movement brought her closer to Esti, pushing her into Esti's arm and side. She made a moue with her lips, a puzzlement.

"Was that here?" she said. "I can't see. Wasn't it nearer to the station? I think I remember some swings near the station."

Esti smiled.

"That was later. When we were older. Those were the swings we used to go to in the evenings. When we told our parents we were studying at each other's houses. You remember."

There was a pause. They walked on, more slowly now than they had been.

"Oh, *yes*," said Ronit. "I'd forgotten that. You do remember everything."

Yes, thought Esti, everything. She looked up at the stars. They were brighter here, away from the streetlights. The sky was almost cloudless, with only one long streak of thin cloud smudged across the blue-black. Beneath the heavens, she thought. This is where we are. Always, but especially here, with the heavens *looking*. She spoke to the stars silently. She said, "Can you still love me, after what I have done?" The stars were quiet, but they continued to shine. She took this as a positive indication. She said, "Your sister is gone." The stars thought for a moment. They said, "Our sister will return." Esti said, "As mine has?" The stars winked and smiled.

Ronit said, "Esti, what are you muttering about?"

Esti said, "Let's walk through the trees." She pulled on Ronit's arm, directing her gently toward the clump of trees by the side of the path. They stopped in the midst of the trees, where the leaves and branches obscured the heavens just a little.

Ronit said, "I don't think this is the way. Shouldn't we be going up the hill?"

Esti tugged on Ronit's arm.

Ronit said, "Esti, are you all right?"

Yes, Esti wanted to say. I am better than I have known myself to be. She did not speak for a moment. She took comfort from the stars and the whispering arms of the trees. A thought occurred to her. She said:

"Do you think that you are the stars, perhaps? And that I am the moon? I thought you were the moon. But I have been absent, too, you know. I think I have been absent all this time."

Ronit looked at her.

In the silence, a night bird called to others of its kind. Beneath the trees, under the heavens, Esti passed her hand across her face, tucking a strand of hair into the scarf wrapped respectably around her head. She wondered if she should have explained herself more clearly. She could not explain herself at all. There were no words, no permitted words, to explain anything that she wanted to say. All the words that could have communicated it had been banned, not only from her mouth but even from her mind. She was reduced to mere actions, which are both more and less than words.

Ronit took a step backward and said, "I really think it's up that way, Esti."

This was the time. If she was to do it, it would have to be done now.

"No," she said, "no, come here."

Ronit's eyes were very wide.

"Esti," she said, "you're behaving like a serial killer. Let's go and get a coffee, for goodness' sake."

Esti saw that she had begun this incorrectly, that she should have chosen other words, perhaps another place. It was too late now for such decisions. She looked up, through the branches of the tree, at the empty moon and the iron-cold sky. She pulled on Ronit's hand, smiling, and saw Ronit shake a little. She knew then that Ronit felt it, too. She pulled Ronit toward her. Ronit resisted a little and then surrendered. They were standing close, under the arms of the tree. She could smell the milky scent of Ronit's American soap and the slight tang of her sweat.

Ronit said, "Really, Esti, this is freaking me out."

Esti said, "Shhh," leaned forward, raised herself on the balls of her feet, and placed her lips, very softly, against those of her love.

Fuck.

Just when everything was going so well.

Fuck.

I should have seen it coming. Really. I should have seen it from the way she looked at me at the Hartogs. Or maybe earlier than that. Maybe when I knew she'd got married to Dovid. Or when she seemed so nervous to see me.

Perhaps I did see it coming, in a way. In synagogue she was so strange, going on about David and Jonathan as if they were in some way *significant*. As if they were more than a story in a book. And then at home, for lunch, when she asked about Miriam, my imaginary architect lover, with the strangest look on her face. Happiness and envy and disgust and disappointment and longing all mingled together. Or, being honest, maybe I'm making that up in retrospect. In any case, what I did then that perhaps with hindsight I shouldn't have done was to admit that there was no Miriam. That, for all the Hartogs' shock and the Goldfarbs' attempts at sensitivity the night before, I'd just made her up.

Dovid laughed. I was surprised. He laughed and said:

"So, are you single, then?"

And I said, "Yes."

Because I didn't want to say yes, although I've been seeing a married man who broke up with me a few weeks ago because he felt guilty about deceiving his wife, but we did sleep together last week, although only because I was feeling low. Honesty has its limits after all.

And Dovid said:

"You invented Miriam, to irritate the Hartogs?"

"Yes."

I expected him to give me a disapproving look, but instead he stared down at his plate with a tiny but discernible smile playing on his lips. I wondered what Dovid could possibly have against the Hartogs, the people who were offering him the glittering prize of being Rav of the synagogue. I didn't ask.

Esti didn't smile. Instead, she sort of looked at me. That's all she did. She *looked* at me and I started to get an uncomfortable prickly feeling somewhere in the back of my mind about that look, and the past and the future, so much so that after lunch I decided to walk back to my father's house. To look for the candlesticks again, although I didn't tell them that. I said, "There's all this stuff to be sorted out, better get on," remembering of course that sorting out of any description is another thing that's forbidden on the Sabbath day. Not to mention turning on the radio and dancing in the hallway to Shania Twain. But somehow I couldn't get out of the house fast enough. Somehow even the oppressiveness of my father's house, even the rows of disapproving books seemed preferable to staying with Esti and Dovid. So yeah, I guess in a way I must have known. Fuck.

But, in another way, I couldn't have known at all. Being here forbids it. It's this place, that's the problem. It's being back here with all those little couples sitting in their identical houses producing identical children. It was seeing them in synagogue, all those women in their smart Shabbat suits and their perfectly matched hats and each woman appropriately paired to a man, preferably with a child tugging at each arm. They just fit together, the whole set—like Orthodox Jew Barbie: comes complete with Orthodox Ken, two small children, the house, the car, and a selection of kosher foodstuffs. They make you believe it, until it seems obvious that people come in matched pairs and you don't think to look underneath and you give up wondering because it all seems just so neat.

And I *wanted* to believe it, too. That's the thing. In a part of my brain I really wanted to believe that even girls you used to sleep with can end up having the happily married Hendon dream as long as they just close their eyes and wish hard enough. I didn't think I still had that bit to my brain, thought I'd managed to excise it with therapy and anger. But no, there it was. I was convincing myself more and more strongly that everything was perfectly normal here and that Esti was probably completely happy right up until the moment when she kissed me.

I had forgotten how fragile she is. For the first moment, that was all I could think; that she was leaning into me, resting on my arms and chest, and she was so light I could hardly feel her. And I had forgotten her smell, little changed in all these years. She always smelled clean, something like lavender, soap, and maybe violets. I had forgotten how it had been between us. But I could see she hadn't forgotten. For just a moment, she made me remember it, too. For just that little piece of time, standing in a field in Hendon in the middle of the night, underneath the stars and the moonless sky, I remembered the taste of her. It was like a connection, a completed circuit linking the past to the present suddenly, unexpectedly, and for that instant I knew where I was but not when.

I pushed her away gently and said, "No."

She looked puzzled. She moved away and then moved toward me again.

I said, more firmly, "No."

She took a pace back. Her face half disappeared in shadow. The trees around us buzzed and hummed. She said:

"Do you not . . . with girls? Have you given up? Did you stop?"

How strange that this should be the first thing to cross her mind. As though that were the only thing she could think of. There was a sort of fearful hope in her eyes. Like she wanted to be taught how to quit.

"No, I haven't given up."

"And you're not, you're not seeing anyone?"

I wanted to laugh at that. I wanted to nudge her in the ribs and say no, I'm not seeing anyone, but that doesn't mean I want to see you, because it's been over for a long time, Esti. It's old. It was old a long time ago, wasn't it?

"No, look, it's just . . ." I passed a hand across my forehead. It wasn't *just* anything. It was a hundred things. A thousand. "It's just that you're married, Esti."

I heard her sigh in the darkness. She shifted her shoulders a little and moved toward me. She found my hand with hers and lifted it up, as if to inspect it, although it was too dark for that. With the tip of her finger, she traced a line across my palm. After a few seconds, she spoke slowly.

"Yes. I'm married. But that is a thing between me and Dovid, do you see? And whatever harm you might do to it has been done already. There is nothing more. And whatever pain I may give him, I have caused already. I know that. And whatever God may think of me, He thinks already."

Another long pause. The wind died down to nothing. Above us, an airplane blinked across the night, an artificial star in an empty sky.

She said, "Sometimes I think that God is punishing me. For what we did together. Sometimes I think that my life is a punishment for wanting. And the wanting is a punishment, too. But I think—if God wishes to punish me, so be it; that is His right. But it is my right to disobey."

She sounded more certain than Scott had ever been.

She said, "I've been waiting for you, all this time. I knew you couldn't stay, not then. But now, with your father gone, with everything that's happened. Now you can stay, can't you? Now we can be together like we always were."

This seemed impossible. Could she really think that I had been longing to come back to Hendon all this time, that I'd only been prevented because of some argument with my father? I took her arm and pulled her toward the path, where the sodium-orange streetlamps gave a little light.

I said, "Esti. What is it that you see happening here? I live in New York. I'm going back there in three weeks. I'm just here to sort out my father's stuff. This is not . . . Look, this was over a long time ago. You and me. It was a long time ago."

Esti smiled again and I started to see something in her, something I'd seen earlier but perhaps hadn't wanted to acknowledge was there, in her stillness in the house when she served us dinner, in her intensity in synagogue. I saw, at this moment, that she had been waiting for me all this time. Perhaps not for *me*, but for someone like me, for someone she thought I was. That while Esti and I had been over in my mind for a long time, it hadn't been that way for her at all. And I felt so intensely sad for a moment that I thought I might have to walk away from her without saying a word, to run across the park, out of Hendon, as far as I could run before I collapsed, but I didn't get the chance because as I was thinking all this she bloody well kissed me again.

I pushed her off me and held her at arm's length. I'm stronger than she is, always have been. It wasn't too difficult.

I said, "No! Look, Esti, you have to *stop that*. This is not, I mean, just stop that, okay?"

She frowned and twisted awkwardly, out of my grasp. She stood, feet apart, looking at me.

I said, more calmly, "It was a long time ago, Esti. I know we used to, but I don't want to anymore."

There was another long pause. I looked out across the park but it was too dark to see anything but the moving shapes of trees on the rise of the hill, stirring in the wind.

Esti spoke, and her voice was a little nearer to my left ear than I would really have liked. She said:

"But you were the only person . . ."

She broke off. I turned my head and saw that she was crying. Silent, streaming tears shining on her face like a medieval portrait of the Virgin Mary. What could I do? She didn't need me right now. She needed a whole bunch of friends who'd take her out for margaritas and tell her that I was a bitch. She needed my life in New York, just like I'd needed hers in Hendon the night my father died. There's no solution to these things. I took her hand and said:

"Look, it's going to be okay." This was a lie, of course. I think I was planning to follow it up with something like "plenty more fish in the sea" or "you'll get over it." Something pithy like that. But I didn't get the chance. Oh infinite joy of being in Hendon, out of the darkness spake a voice, and the voice said:

"Esti! Ronit! Shavua Tov! Did you have a good Shabbos?"

We turned to look. It was good old Hinda Rochel Berditcher, in wig, smart brown suit, and matching court shoes, on the arm of a tall, bearded man. Hinda Rochel was beaming.

"This is my husband, Lev," she said. "Lev, this is *Ronit*, the Rav's daughter, you remember I told you about her?"

I'll bet she did.

Lev nodded at me gravely and said:

"I'm sorry for your loss. I wish you a long life."

I thanked him, all the time thinking how much, how much did they see, walking through the darkness toward us, standing under a streetlamp? Not that it'd damage *my* life, but Esti's . . . well, it couldn't be *good*.

We exchanged a few words; it seemed impossible to get rid of them,

Hinda Rochel was so delighted to see us, did we want to come back with them for a drink? No? Maybe we'd be free a bit later? Or tomorrow? With Dovid? Oh, he was in Manchester, was he? Hinda Rochel and Lev exchanged a look. Maybe the following Shabbat? We'd give them a call, yes we would, we promised. Or rather, *I* promised. Esti was positively monosyllabic. And where were we going now? For coffee? Well, they really shouldn't keep us. Another look passed between them. They smiled. They moved off, out of the pool of light, leaving Esti and me standing underneath the streetlamp again, in silence.

I said, "Esti, let's just forget this happened, okay? It's the walk, the moonlight or, er, lack of moonlight. It's nothing. Let's have our coffee now."

But it was too late for salvage. She backed away from me, at first slowly, and then, turning, she started to run. She stumbled up the hill, back toward her house. I wondered if I should go after her. I turned away and walked up toward Golders Green.

Dr. Feingold would say that you can only free yourself. That we are all masters of our own destinies, and that the only person who can help you is you. She'd lean back in her white chair, in front of her white walls, and say, "Ronit, what makes you think that you can solve this situation? What makes that your responsibility?" And on one level she's right. You can't solve anyone else's life for them. But then, if you see someone struggling with a heavy load, isn't it forbidden to walk on without helping them?

I thought again about Esti's life. And I thought about what it is that I know, which isn't much but might be something. I thought about God. I hadn't thought about Him for quite a while but I remembered His voice then. I thought about how, whatever you do, once you've heard it, it continues to mutter in your ear, with its inexplicable certainties and unacceptable justifications.

I marched through Golders Green, passing by the rows of Jewish stores. The little world my people have built here. The kosher butcher shops frowned at me, asking why I hadn't tried their chopped liver, now only £2.25 a quarter. The recruitment agency smiled widely, inviting me to apply for a job with a Sabbath-observant company, half-day Fridays in the winter. Moishe's salon raised an eyebrow at my hairstyle and wondered if I wouldn't like something, maybe, a bit more like everyone else?

I thought about how God, belief in God, in this God, has done *violence* to these people. Has warped them and bent them so that they can't even acknowledge any longer that they *have* desires, let alone learn how to act on them.

I walked on, down the Golders Green Road, past the bagel shops where crowds of teenagers were shouting and laughing, past the grocery stores and the little kosher cafés that we used to visit so often we knew the menus by heart. Not much was still open, but as I came to Golders Green station, I saw a little patisserie that wouldn't be closing for a while. It wasn't kosher. It was mostly empty. I wondered if Esti had ever noticed that it was here: a piece of another life, a twenty-minute walk from her house.

I sat down and ordered a large slice of chocolate cake from a tired-looking waitress. When it came, I thought of all the nonkosher things that could be in it: gelatin holding the filling together, made of boiled pig bones, colorings made from dead insects, beef lard to grease the cake tin, shellfish extracts added to the flour to make it softer. I saw the plate full of dead, decaying, unclean things.

Things that the Rabbis tell us will harden our hearts and make us less able to hear the voice of God.

I took a bite. The cake was dry, the filling greasy. I ate it anyway. Bite after bite.

Chapter Seven

The Sages said: Anyone who converses excessively with a woman causes evil to himself, neglects Torah study, and will eventually inherit Gehinnom.

Pirkei Avot 1:5, studied on Sabbath afternoons
between Passover and New Year

Our sages warn us often against the perils of gossip: lashon hara, which means, literally, an evil tongue. Certainly, it is forbidden to spread false tales. Is this not bearing false witness—an action forbidden in the ten utterances from Mount Sinai? And as it is forbidden to speak false tales, so is it forbidden to listen to them, for he who speaks and he who listens both sin against the name of the Lord. And further, it is forbidden to tell, or to listen to, any stories, even if they are true, that might cause us to regard a person less favorably. In fact, it is generally held preferable to avoid speaking of others at all, even to spread good news.

Despite this, the temptations of lashon hara are difficult to resist. The Torah tells us that in the time when God's presence was not so hidden from the world, tzara'at, a virulent leprosy, was visited upon those who spoke lashon hara. No place was too high to be visited by tzara'at; when Miriam the sister of Moses spoke ill of his wife, she was afflicted with the disease. It is written that the destruction of the Temple in Jerusalem, for which we mourn with unceasing bitterness, was caused by the continual lashon hara of the people of Israel. Lashon hara is the most tempting of forbidden acts: easy, enjoyable, plentiful in supply. Yet we are enjoined to refrain from it.

One of our sages rebuked a woman who had spread gossip. He gave her a pillow and instructed her to take it to the top of the highest building in town and shake out its feathers to the four winds. The woman did so. Then the sage said to her, "Now go and gather up all of those feathers which you have scattered." The woman cried out that the task was impossible. "Ah," said the sage, "how much easier, though, than gathering up the tales you have spread." Easier to cause a mountain to skip like a lamb than to retrieve an evil story once it has passed the guard of our lips.

Hendon is a village. It exists within a city, certainly, one of the greatest in the world. It has links to this city, people travel to and fro between them. But it is a village. In Hendon, people know one another's business. In Hendon, a woman cannot walk from one end of the high street to the other without encountering an acquaintance, perhaps stopping for a chat visiting the butcher, baker, grocer. In Hendon, only frozen vegetables and washing powder are bought in supermarkets: all other goods are purchased at small shops, in which the shopkeepers know their customers by name, remember their favorite items and put them by. Though there is a wider world, in Hendon all that is needed has been provided: Torah-true schools and kosher shops and synagogues and mikvahs and businesses that are closed on the Sabbath and matchmakers and burial societies. We learned how to do this a long time ago, when there was no other way. We do it well. Like the turtle, we carry our home with us. We believe that we may soon have to depart for other shores. It is as well to be self-sufficient.

On Sunday, the first day of the month of Cheshvan, the moon revealed the tiniest glimpse of her pale flesh, and the week of mourning for Rav Krushka came to an end. Across northwest London, the event registered only a little. The *Jewish Chronicle* carried a half-page obituary, recording the events of the man's life. Its tone was slightly overenthusiastic, its detail a little hazy. The *Jewish Tribune*, a publication more certain in its convictions, printed a glowing and fulsome account of the Rav's achievements, accompanied by a large photograph taken in his late middle age. The Rav's death, they said, was like a hammer blow, crushing the heart of Anglo-Jewry. His loss left a void that could never be filled. The Rav had been a giant in his generation, the *Tribune* concluded, who was without doubt already supping at the table of the righteous in the world to come. It is not given to us, who dwell on earth and not in heaven, to know whether this statement was more accurate than the *Chronicle*'s more modest assertion that the Rav had left no children.

In Hendon, the end of the mourning week passed almost without note for members of other synagogues and congregations. The death had been felt a little among the congregants of the shtiebels, those small, hidden synagogues formed in hollowed-out houses or unused offices. The Ravs of these communities touched on the life and deeds of the dead man in their sermons. They had known him in boyhood or as a young man. He had been a leader, a teacher, a friend. Their congregations listened solemnly, but by the time they had eaten a good lunch, sung the Sabbath melodies, and slept a righteous sleep, their regret was largely forgotten. The worshipers at the larger synagogues, housed in suburban cul-de-sacs, cushioned by well-appointed detached properties and swaddled in the certainty that God prefers the comfortably off, read the *Chronicle* and shrugged or sighed or turned the page. And the young men and women of the "alternative" services held in drafty halls, bound together by earnest debate and accompanied by a monthly vegetarian dinner? It would be too far to say that they rejoiced. Let us say instead that, insofar as they were aware of the Rav, they felt only a slight sense of relief at the removal of an element that was neither liberal nor modern, and was therefore without merit.

But in the Rav's own community, the loss had cut more deeply. There had been, in those houses, over the mourning week, a troubling sense of distortion and inexplicability. The arrival of the first day of Cheshvan brought with it a certain easing of pressure. The mourning week was over. The Rav was dead. This fact contained not even a grain of mercy. But now a new thought occurred. He had, after all, been an old man. That he should pass was only natural. Once the people allowed this thought to dwell within their minds, they saw that they had always known it to be so. This occurrence was no tragedy. It was not even a surprise. And, a little freer, the members of Rav Krushka's congregation began to talk.

It began in Levene the butcher's, the morning of that first day of Cheshvan. The shop was crowded and a little too warm. Mr. Levene, son of old Mr. Levene, was serving behind the counter, portioning out minced meat and chopped liver, shouting for his son, young Levene, to bring through more chicken thighs. Mrs. Levene sat behind the till, writing receipts into a carbon book with a firm pencil hand. It was in Levene's that Mrs. Bloom spotted Mrs. Kohn bending over the refrigerator to retrieve a package of sliced tongue. Mrs. Bloom and Mrs. Kohn had been customers of Levene's since the days when old Mr. Levene still sold cheap not-yet-koshered chickens that had to be salted and drained at home. Now his son had introduced lamb chops marinated in sticky orange fluid "for the barbecue," and the chicken schnitzels were called low-fat skinless chicken breasts. Nonetheless, the calf's-foot jelly remained garlicky and good, the meatball gravy paste-thick. To speak with each other in Levene the butcher's was easy, a simple thing that could do no harm.

The two women's conversation proceeded smoothly from enquiries about family and friends to the Rav, and from there to his poor family, who must now be suffering so terribly, and from there, of course, to the matter of the woman who had sat next to Esti in synagogue the previous morning. There they stopped for a moment, neither wanting to voice her thought. But, emboldened by the shop's noise, they continued. Could it possibly have been her? Neither of them had liked to approach and ask because she seemed so different, and with the Rav's death, but can it have been her? She'd cut her hair, of course, and was thinner and somehow harder-looking, but it could scarcely be anyone else, really. What had she been doing all this time? Perhaps she'd been living in Manchester with her family? No. There had been that slit in her skirt. Unless standards in Manchester had fallen dramatically—and the women did not entirely discount this possibility—it seemed unlikely. So had it been her? The Rav's daughter, the one who . . . Well, there had been rumors at the time. Of some rift with her father, of some improper behavior on her part. It was impossible to know. The conversation drifted into silence and, left thus, without relief, the women went on their way.

They had, however, been overheard by Mrs. Stone, wife of Stone the orthodontist, who had been unintentionally concealed behind the large poultry freezers. Mr. and Mrs. Stone-the-orthodontist had attended the Rav's synagogue for only three years. Newcomer as she was, Mrs. Stone had not recognized the surprisingly modern young woman seated next to Esti Kuperman in shul. However, as it happened, that Shabbat had been her turn to assist Fruma Hartog in setting out kiddush: the biscuits, crisps, fish balls, chopped herring, pickles, and small glasses of sweet red wine provided after the service. Mrs. Stone had noted that Fruma, never the most amiable of cocaterers, had been positively monosyllabic. Mrs. Stone, a woman who took pleasure in allowing her mouth to open, if only to reveal her flawless, even teeth, was not to be dissuaded. As they arranged the crackers in concentric circles on doily-covered plates and ensured that each gefilte-fish ball was pierced by a single cocktail stick, she made another attempt.

"So, Fruma, did you have guests last night?"

Fruma's hand shook, the tray of tiny wine cups clattering nervously. She thinned her lips and replied:

"Esti and Dovid Kuperman. Not that it's any of your business."

Mrs. Stone had closed her lips over her teeth, reflecting that perhaps Fruma might be more inclined to smile if her crooked right canine were straightened. Now, however, standing before the poultry freezer, she began to wonder whether Fruma's mood had been entirely related to orthodontic concerns.

Mrs. Stone communicated her suspicions to her friends Mrs. Abramson and Mrs. Berditcher, when she happened to encounter them later that morning in the bakery, purchasing soft, warm onion platzels and aromatic granary loaves. The clean smell of bread engulfed them as they stood to one side, allowing others to elbow their way toward the counter. Mrs. Stone tried to keep her voice low, but among the demands for "two loaves of rye, sliced thin!" or "two dozen bridge rolls—the large ones, not the small!" she was forced to declare her troubling thoughts loudly. The women nodded as she spoke. The return of the Rav's daughter, the mysterious anger of Fruma Hartog, her failure to mention Ronit as one of the guests at her Shabbat table. It all seemed to have some significance. But what?

Mrs. Berditcher drew breath. She might know something. Just a little piece of news. The bread slicer clattered, its comb-blades flickering up and down as the women drew closer. What? What did Mrs. Berditcher know? Mrs. Berditcher shook her head. It would not be right to speak of such things. She and Mr. Berditcher thought they had seen something on their walk home after Shabbat the previous evening. But they could not be sure. It had been dark. They had been far away. Their eyes might have deceived them. Although, seeing Ronit so different, her hair so short, her demeanor so assertive and still unmarried at thirty-two, well, there seemed a kind of sense to it. But what? What had been seen? The bread slicer roared into life again, a limp-haired assistant by its side feeding it four large, square white loaves. Mrs. Berditcher demurred. It would certainly be lashon hara to speak the words, and lashon hara is a thing of evil, as they had learned many years before. Mrs.

Stone and Mrs. Abramson heard, as though from far away, a faint and calming voice telling them to desist. Move on, it said, go on with your shopping. Buy bagels and kichels and rugelach. But nearer at hand they felt a quickening pulse at their temples. Go on, they pressed, go on. Mrs. Berditcher hesitated and, in a low voice, went on.

The shameful suspicion unrolled, binding them together silently and firmly. Each looked at the other two to ensure that they had fully understood the significance of the remarks. They looked around. The clamor of the customers demanding half pounds of cheesecake and savory rolls continued unabated. None of the three wanted to speak first and perhaps reveal herself ignorant or naive.

"It can't be true, surely," said Mrs. Abramson at last.

Mrs. Berditcher, despite the nagging of that quiet voice reminding her patiently that she could *not* be sure, declared that she was. Absolutely. Ronit had always been wayward, even as a girl. There had been half-stated rumors about improper behavior even then, Mrs. Abramson could surely confirm. Mrs. Abramson nodded thoughtfully.

"What is the halachic status of that, actually?" she asked.

There was a moment of silence.

"It must be forbidden, surely," said Mrs. Berditcher.

The women nodded.

"It's not in the Torah," Mrs. Abramson said. "It only says about men lying with other men."

"I think it was forbidden by the Rabbis," said Mrs. Stone. "It's called the 'practices of Egyptian women.' I think it's in the Gemarah."

Then Mrs. Abramson, who perhaps of the three had heard the small and tranquil voice most clearly, said:

"What if it is forbidden? Hinda Rochel, your brother-in-law's children eat treif meat and don't keep Shabbos. You still invite them to visit you. How is it different?"

Mrs. Berditcher looked at first ashamed, and then angry. She opened her mouth, then closed it, then, decisive, opened it.

"This is a completely different thing. You know it is. Especially *forcing yourself* on someone like that."

"And you're sure that's what you saw?" asked Mrs. Abramson. There was another momentary pause. The bread-slicing machine hummed.

"Yes," said Mrs. Berditcher. "I told you. Ronit was *holding* her. She had to struggle to break free. She had been crying. I could tell."

She adjusted her hat, to ensure that no stray locks had fallen into view.

The shop assistant, feeding the last of three black bread loaves into the bread slicer, felt its teeth brush her fingers and pulled back, stung and frightened. A red bead welled from the tip of her middle finger.

Mrs. Abramson spoke. "If this is true, we must act. Esti may be in danger. We must do something."

The three women blinked simultaneously. This story, which only moments ago had seemed so full of innocent interest, had now become filled with difficulty. Action was called for, but what? In another time, one of them might have consulted the Rav with this dilemma. But to whom were they now to turn?

"One of us should speak to Dovid," said Mrs. Berditcher.

There was another silence.

"Or to Esti?" asked Mrs. Stone.

The other two women shook their heads. It was understood that Esti Kuperman could not be spoken to in such a way or about such matters.

"Perhaps," said Mrs. Abramson, "perhaps I could ask Pinchas his opinion? That would not be lashon hara, surely. To ask my husband for his view?"

The women nodded and smiled. A marvelous solution. Pinchas Abramson had completed two years' study at a men's seminary and learned Torah five times a week. He would know the answer.

* * *

Given that this conversation had concluded in such a righteous and honorable manner, it can scarcely be considered the fault of these three women if, by the time Mrs. Abramson managed to speak to her husband, seeds of their suspicions had already been swept up by the winds and had begun to fall to earth across Hendon. For a baker's shop on a Sunday morning is scarcely the place to conduct a discussion that one wishes to remain private. It must be conceded that, as various half-thoughts and barely expressed changes in attitude started to seep from one person to another, several men and women did indeed turn their faces away, saying, "No, this is lashon hara." And such people deserve our admiration and our respect, for to obey the words of the Lord when every desire within us urges a different course is difficult beyond measure. The rewards due to such souls are surely bountiful indeed.

But most of the people of Hendon did not possess such strength within their souls. Like Miriam, the sister of Moses, they bore tales, or like Aharon, the brother of Moses, they listened to them. And it is not given to us to know, in the days when the tzara'at leprosy, like all forms of prophecy, has passed from the earth, what punishment the Lord has ordained for them. Whatever it might be, they nonetheless ensured that by the time Pinchas Abramson had discussed the matter with his friends Horovitz and Mench (for, despite the opinions of some of our sages, the dangers of lashon hara are not confined to women), the matter had already become known, or at least suspected, in several houses around Hendon. And by the time Mench, who learned Gemarah with Dovid, had decided to telephone the house in Manchester, the tongues had done their work. And this work, as we have seen, can never be undone.

For no particularly obvious reason, there are *seagulls* in Hendon. I mean, there's no particular reason there shouldn't be, either—it's near enough to the coast. And yet it's incongruous, walking down Brent Street past the kosher shops and the Talmud Trove bookshop to see seagulls whirling in the sky overhead, swooping down to pick up a piece of discarded bagel, their wings so wide, gray and white, and their beaks so unexpectedly large and vicious. I was surprised to find, on my walk through Hendon on Saturday night, that they were still about even after midnight, swooping and circling.

I didn't go back to Esti's house until very late that Saturday night. She was already in bed, the house was dark, and that seemed all for the best. I sat in my bedroom and considered my options. I could go home now, get the hell out of this increasingly creepy, claustrophobic environment, utterly fail to interact with the difficulties of my old friend and lover Esti and her ineffectual husband. And, let's state it for the record, that option certainly had some attraction. But it also seemed kind of an overreaction. I could talk to Dovid, talk to Esti, sit down and have the three of us "work through it." I am, after all, to some extent an American now. That's the good old American, therapeutic way. Does it make me a coward that I felt I couldn't possibly? That I didn't *want* to have that conversation with either of them?

So where did that leave me? Oh, yes, when in Britain, do as the British do. Stiff upper lip. Repression. Muttering quietly under my breath and carrying on. Sticking it out. In other words, ignoring the issue. I set my alarm for six a.m. and went to sleep. That night I dreamed of the seagulls of Hendon, of the extreme sharpness of their beaks and the flexing of their claws. Of the way they set their heads on one side and *look* at you with one unfathomable beady eye. It was a Tippi Hedren sort of dream, of running away from flocks of seagulls, except that these birds weren't *doing* anything, not attacking or coming down the chimney or cracking glass. They were just *looking*.

I woke up promptly, pulled on my clothes, and without stopping to talk to Esti or even see if she was awake, I walked straight over to my father's house. I had a mission. If I could complete it, I could be on my way and feel that it hadn't been a completely wasted trip. I pulled open the front door; the house held no fear for me now, not since I'd learned the trick with the radio. I surveyed my work so far. The table in the center of the study was clear, as was the floor. I'd thrown out five black plastic bags full of rubbish and stacked any papers that looked useful along one of the side tables. I spent another couple of hours going through the cupboards. Magazines, thirty years' worth of back issues of various Jewish papers. A couple of things that made me feel I was on the right track: in a little velvet-lined box I found a small silver kiddush cup I remember using when I was a child. Crammed into the corner of a shelf, trapped behind a pile of Yiddish books, was a glass bowl my mother used to serve pickles in on Friday nights. It was triangular, spiky on the outside but somehow curved inside, with a pattern of red and yellow flowers decaled on the side. It was so redolent of that time in my life that, holding it, tracing my fingers over the smooth inner surface, I could almost *smell* the vinegary-dill scent, taste the clean-sharp combination of pickled cucumbers and roast chicken.

Thinking this made me angry. What *right* had my father to hide my childhood from me in this way? This mess, this confusion, felt as though it had been contrived on purpose to keep me from finding what I wanted. I stood up and surveyed the room. The candlesticks weren't here. I had been through every cupboard and every shelf. I supposed I could check behind the bookcases but that felt ridiculous. No. In my mind, I felt them in my hands, felt the slight roughness on one of the leaves of the candlestick that always sat on the right. I remembered how he had shown me how to light them, when I was seven and my mother was gone, my hand holding the match, his blue-veined hand clasped over mine to keep it steady. I was a biddable child then, a long time ago. He would not have given them away. No one else in the family had a claim to them. They must be here somewhere. He would have put them somewhere safe. Not on display. They were precious, family things. They belonged . . . upstairs.

I walked upstairs. I had done so earlier, had glanced through the bedrooms and had found nothing of interest. I hadn't been able to enter my old bedroom, the door had been stuck shut and I'd been a little unwilling to force it. But if force was required, force it would be. Perhaps there was a key, though? I would have to look through the other bedrooms.

In my father's bedroom, large cardboard boxes filled with, at a cursory glance, manuscripts and old newspaper cuttings, were piled on the bed and the floor. A few yellowed pages had fallen to the floor; articles dating from the 1960s on kosher food labeling and the endless debate over the *eruv*. The wardrobe had been plundered at some point: the doors were standing open, and some of the clothes were gone, probably moved to the neat drawers I'd seen downstairs. The chest of drawers was also partly open, a tie hanging over the edge of one of the drawers like a lolling blue tongue. It looked as if this room had been ransacked for clothes in a hurry—perhaps when my father was first taken to hospital—and never straightened out. It felt slightly uncanny to stand in this room without him. As if he might still be here, somewhere just out of my field of vision. As if we might be about to have one of those old arguments about the inappropriate shortness of my midcalf-length skirt, or the report he had received about how I had spoken back to one of the Rabbis at school. He did not materialize. I left the room without looking too hard.

The spare room was far more ordered; I guessed Dovid must have slept here, as he did when he was young, if my father needed him in the night. The single bed was made, spread with a blue knitted quilt I recognized: made by my father's mother years before. Three or four books were neatly stacked on the desk. I pulled open the top drawer and found two pads of A4 paper and several pencils, all sharpened, all pointing the same way. Dovid. The second drawer, for some reason, contained nothing but a large can of plums, the label old and peeling. Out of the window, I could see the hydrangea bush by the fence, but I didn't look at it. I sat on the bed, stroking the soft woollen cover and thinking. It occurred to me that I could spend the night here, if I liked. It was my childhood home, after all. The house still belonged to the synagogue, but the furnishings and so on were surely mine if I wanted them, and they could hardly begrudge me a few nights' stay in my father's house. Yes, that might solve the Esti and Dovid problem very nicely. I could even stay in my old room. I walked across the hall and pushed open the door.

I suppose I was, in a small part of my mind, hoping that my old bedroom would have been kept as a shrine to me, everything exactly as it was the day I left. There might have been evidence of some private grieving ritual: a hockey stick clearly polished lovingly once a week, a large photograph decked at both sides with vases of dying roses. Of course, there was none of this, but some aspects of the room had remained the same. My school photograph was still on the wall, my netball medal—dating from the brief period after I was made team captain but before I was demoted for making one of the other girls cry by criticizing her performance on the field—pinned up slightly askew beneath it. But these things were only barely visible above the boxes, suitcases, and black dustbin bags piled in a great disorderly mound across the room. The accumulation reached to just above my waist and stretched across the entire floor space; a very small area just inside the doorway was clear, to allow the door to open, but other than that there was no space large enough for a person to enter. I reached into one of the nearest bags and came up with a pair of men's shoes, one of the soles flapping open at the toe, and a light blue mug, missing its handle. The shoes smelled slightly. After a while, I began to wonder whether the smell was coming from somewhere else in the room. Perhaps, underneath all the bags and boxes and cases and holdalls, there was a mouse or rat's nest. Listening, I thought I could hear a faint rustling. I can't say how long I stood looking. I wondered what Dr. Feingold would make of it. Something irritatingly accurate, no doubt. A way to forget I ever existed, perhaps? An expression of anger? An attempt to fill the void of loss? A pathological determination never to throw anything away? Only my father could have told me, and, well, he's not around to be asked anymore.

Looking at that room, two things became quite clear to me. The first was that I couldn't stay the night in this house. Not in Dovid's room, not at all. And the second was that I was going to cry. Real, proper, huge, gut-wrenching, cheek-rolling, superfluous, unanswerable tears. I half ran to the bathroom, as though I were going to vomit, not cry, sat on the closed lid of the toilet, and cried and cried without being in any way able to explain to myself why. I looked up at my reflection in the bathroom mirror, tearstained and red-eyed, and remembered something, just something, a moment like this, a time like this. Looking at myself in this mirror. Crying. I knew what I was remembering.

And the doorbell rang.

I sat quite still. Perhaps they'd go away. The bell rang again, twice in quick succession. Then, through the letterbox came a woman's voice:

"Helloo . . . Ronit . . . are you there? It's me, Hinda Rochel . . ."

Another brisk push on the doorbell.

And, hiccupping, I walked down the stairs to answer the door.

Hinda Rochel Berditcher was, indeed, standing on the doorstep, with two other women I vaguely seemed to recognize, one blond and tall, the other shorter and darker.

Hinda Rochel beamed. She said:

"You remember Devora? And Nechama Tova?"

I frowned.

"Devora . . . Lipsitz?"

The blond woman smiled.

"And . . . Nechama Tova . . ." I squinted. "I'm sorry, I just can't . . ."

The shorter woman smiled, too.

"Nechama Tova Weinberg. I used to be Nechama Tova Benstock. I was in the year below you."

Three matrons of the town, paying a call. Women who had all, naturally, changed their names.

"We saw the lights on," Hinda Rochel said. "We thought we'd come and say hello."

And I thought: saw the *lights on*? All three of you? Wandering down the road together early on a Sunday evening just to see whose lights were on? I couldn't quite piece it together. It was stupid of me, really. I thought: how odd. How strange. How I have forgotten that Hendon really is a village. Instead of thinking what I should have thought, that someone had been watching the house and knew when I was there and when I wasn't.

They came in, the three wise women of Hendon. Came in, sat in the lounge, made themselves cups of tea. They knew better than I did where the teabags were kept and which were the milky teacups. Hinda Rochel explained that they'd often been here to help the Rav, may he rest in peace, through his illness. I told her that was very kind of her and she smiled and told me they were only performing a mitzvah. They were impressed by the job I'd done in tidying the house. I explained I was looking for one or two family things to take home with me and they nodded sympathetically.

After the tea was made, the room descended into silence. I looked at them. They beamed at me. I never could leave a silence alone.

I said, "So, what are you all doing nowadays?"

Nechama Tova told me about her husband and her four children. And Devora told me about her husband and their *five* children: I detected a note of quiet pride in her voice at this. Hinda Rochel works a couple of mornings a week as Dr. Hartog's assistant and only has two children, but she didn't seem downhearted. She smiled at me, her lipstick-mouth peeling back to leave a slight film of red on her teeth, and said:

"What about you, Ronit? Are you married?"

She said it as though she already knew the answer.

I looked back at her and said, "No. No, I'm not."

There was a pause as the three women took that fact in. Nechama Tova let out a little sigh. There was no doubt that in the eyes of these women it was late, far far too late for me now. It was not simply that I would never marry, but that through never marrying I would never become an adult, would never grow into myself, would remain like the aged grape on the vine, withered without ever having been plucked. Marriage, in this community, isn't just a religious act or a legal binding, it isn't even a thing you do because you like someone and want to be with them; it's a rite of passage from childhood to adulthood. Those who never do it never grow up. To say that I had never married was tantamount to saying that I had never become a full human being.

Nechama Tova wrinkled her brow and said, "Oh! I'm sorry."

Devora smiled sympathetically.

For all the world as if *this* and not the loss of my father were the real bereavement.

And I looked at her, sweet, quiet Devora who had always been so good at math and had even—good Lord—taken *A levels*. Well, one A level at least. And I said:

"What do you do, Devora?"

She blinked at me. She said:

"Just what I told you; Tzvi and I have five children . . ."

I said, "You mean you don't work? But you were always so good in school, so academic! What happened?"

This was a nasty thing to do. She didn't really deserve it. Except insofar as they all do, for their collusion in the silence, for simply accepting that things must be thus and so, for never stopping to consider that this little protective world can damage as much as it cushions.

She began to stumble over her words. "Well, I always intended, th-that is Tzvi and I have always said that maybe when the children are grown . . ."

Hinda Rochel broke in. "Why? What do *you* do, Ronit?"

She did not, I have to say, sound convinced that any answer I could provide would be satisfactory.

Still, I told them what I did. It gave me a certain satisfaction. I live in New York. I own my apartment. I'm a financial analyst. Devora gave a little start when I mentioned the name of my firm. Her husband's company does a lot of business with them, it transpired. I explained some of the enormous transactions I had worked on, household names even in Orthodox Jewish households. Their eyes went wide.

They were silent when I had finished.

At last, Hinda Rochel cocked her head to one side and said, with all the appearance of concern, "But does it make you *happy*, Ronit? Does it make you *fulfilled*?"

In the evening, I waited in the house as the day grew dark outside. I kept the radio on, did the crossword in the paper, wondered how long it would be until Esti went to bed. I knew I couldn't do this forever. But maybe just today and tomorrow. Maybe just that would be enough. And then, because I was lonely, I think, or just tired or far away from people I knew, I went into the hall and picked up the phone, the same phone we'd always had, cream Bakelite with a rotary dial. I put the phone to my ear and listened to the buzz of the dial tone. And before I'd really considered why, I was dialing a number.

Far away, very very far away, I made a sleek black telephone on a pale wood desk ring.

"Hello?"

"Scott? Is that you?"

"Ronit?" There was warmth in his voice, as though he were genuinely pleased to hear from me. "How are things in jolly old England?"

Oh, yes, this again. It's a thing that ceases to rankle after you spend much time in the States but can suddenly begin to irritate again.

"Old but not jolly," I said.

"Aha?" he said, and I thought I could hear the sound of pages turning in the background. "And how's the family?"

"Ummm . . . weird. Listen, Scott, can I talk to you seriously for a second?"

He paused.

He said, "Yeah, sure, just a moment."

The sound, from 3,500 miles away, of him putting the phone down on his desk, crossing the office, closing the door, and walking back. I felt as though I could hear the distance in the wires, the sound of Scott walking in New York echoing across all those thousands of miles of thin electrical cable. Ridiculous.

"Okay, I am all yours."

There was a smile in his voice, the kind he used to have when he'd call me from his cell phone outside my apartment to ask if I had time for "a brief social call."

"Do you remember I told you about Esti? That girl I was at school with?"

Another smile in the voice. "Sure do. You guys were an item at school, huh? And then you both went your separate ways?"

"Yeah, except . . . well, it looks like she didn't go anywhere. She's still here. She got married. To my cousin."

Scott laughed. I hadn't been expecting that; I hadn't realized it was funny.

"Married? Hey, well I guess that happens. Maybe you put her off girls, my dear. Good thing there are a few of us still around who aren't immune to your charms."

"No," I said. "It turns out I didn't put her off girls at all. Last night she made a pass at me."

Scott laughed again and I wanted to say no, don't laugh, it's not funny at all, there's *nothing* about this that is funny.

"You gonna take her up on it?"

"No," I said. "That's not what I—"

"Hey, well, up to you, I guess."

And I thought of saying a whole bunch of things. About this place, about how the thin sticky strands of it get all over you, encircle and engulf. About the horror and the desperation of living a narrow little life here. Of how I could feel that life start to close around my neck again. But instead I just told him I had to go but I'd call soon and not to forget that the McKinnon analysis still had to be completed. He told me sure, and that he was looking forward to seeing me when I got back, and for a moment, I felt warm. But when I put the phone down, the room was still cold. I sat in the empty house, and waited.

Chapter Eight

Rejoice and make joyful this precious couple, as You brought joy to Your creations in the Garden of Eden before the beginning.

From the Sheva Brachot, sung at a wedding banquet

The more we examine marriage, the more absurd it seems. Marriage is only permitted between those who have little in common. One may not marry a close relative. One may not marry a person of the same sex. God, Who created the heavens and the earth, might easily have ordained that a brother and sister could marry, that two women together could produce offspring. He could have so ordered the world that those who were the closest were able to mate. And thus He might have given His creations more comfort. Why, therefore, did He not do so?

To answer this question, we must first understand that this world exists to teach us. It is to be enjoyed, true, but also to be studied and pored over, as is the Torah, which is also the world. Just as every tiny stroke that goes to form a letter in the Torah contains an infinity of meaning, just so does every aspect of creation. Nothing is arbitrary, nothing has been left to chance. All has been foreseen and all has been intended.

What, then, does marriage teach us? It teaches us to strive for closeness. That intimacy cannot be attained or retained without effort. And what is the spiritual analog of this earthly manifestation? It is the burning of the spirit for its Source, and His burning for us. Those who believe that marriage is an end in itself, that it is a guarantee of contentment, are fools. Marriage is difficult. It is painful. And it was meant to be so. For in trying to approach more closely to a human being who is so different to us, we begin to understand the task before us in approaching the Almighty. This is our work upon the earth, and the work of marriage prepares us for it. And although marriage may, in slow and unexpected ways, bring us much joy and satisfaction, nothing of the sort has been promised.

We may abandon this truth, but if so we shall have to abandon everything. We may declare that marriage stands for nothing but the desire in the hearts and the minds and the loins of two people. We may insist that our Creator could not have intended us to live in discomfort. We may, if we desire, stand atop a low mound of earth and declare ourselves lords of creation. But we should not then be surprised if we cease to burn with desire for the Source of the world, and if we cease to feel the warmth of His yearning for us.

Dovid spent six nights and five days in Manchester. At the end of those days he returned home to pass the Sabbath with his wife. And in the midst of the days he passed in Manchester there was a telephone call.

It was not an easy visit. His mother was more distressed by her brother's death than Dovid had anticipated from their measured telephone conversations. She was restless, tearful, and agitated over small details: a rescheduled appointment, an unexpected caller. His father, uncertain of how to respond to his wife, retreated frequently to his dental surgery, claiming an urgent need to deal with paperwork. On Monday night, they ate dinner with Dovid's brother Binyomin and his new wife. Pnina was already pregnant and looked tired and gray, despite declaring that she felt wonderful. They both seemed oddly deferential toward Dovid, with fixed smiles and enquiries after his health. Dovid wondered if they still thought that he might be the next Rav of the community.

That night, Dovid and his mother sat alone in the living room. She began to cry after Binyomin and Pnina left. Dr. Kuperman left the room immediately, muttering about his backlog of work, the likelihood of several emergency appointments in the morning. Dovid sat with his mother, watching her cry, wishing that he had felt able to retreat, like his father. He passed her tissues and she patted his hand, thanking him and apologizing. He wished she would not apologize. After a few minutes, her tears ceased, she dabbed at her eyes with a fresh tissue, and drank a few sips of water. She gave a flat-lipped smile.

"They seem happy, Binyomin and Pnina."

Dovid nodded.

"I wouldn't have thought it at one time; it took them long enough to decide on each other, but now they seem so happy."

Dovid nodded once more.

"They've been married only a year, and already a baby on the way."

These are simple little statements, thought Dovid, surely they are only gentle words, to bring comfort to the lips.

"I don't suppose . . .?" His mother broke off.

Not here, not here. Let her not speak these words, not now. Let there be silence.

She leaned forward and said to him:

"Dovid, are you happy?"

"What?"

"With Esti. Are you and Esti happy?"

"Yes," he said. "I'm sorry, I'm very tired now. I really would like to go to bed."

Dovid knew that some people in the community considered him stupid. Even though he had completed his time at Yeshiva and become a Rabbi, he was not the spiritual heir who could have eased this rough and unsettling time for them. Even while studying at Yeshiva, he had not been a brilliant Torah scholar. He did not have the quickness of mind of the great ones, the easy grasp of new material, or the ability to hold each step of a complex argument in a separate vessel of his mind, combining and reordering them at will. The knowledge that he gained had been hewn each day from solid rock and would crumble into sand and stones if not constantly revisited and reshaped. The Rav used to remind him of the story of Rabbi Akiva, famously a slow scholar and yet one whose Torah knowledge was beyond compare. The community did not appreciate this possibility. His mind was not quick, and there was a slowness to his manner that sometimes gave the impression that he had not fully followed a line of conversation or understood what was being asked.

And it was for another reason, too, that the people considered him foolish, a reason not connected to his lack of rabbinical stature. Dovid was aware, bitterly so, that there were those who had noted his public demeanor with Esti, and hers with him. They had taken notice of her uncanny stillness, of the strength of her silence. Esti was not well liked among the women of the community; she did not participate in their lives of chatter and busyness. He knew that one or two members of the synagogue had gone so far as to ask the Rav, quietly but insistently, if it might not be best if Esti were to leave. They had questioned whether she was a suitable wife for one as near to being the Rav's successor as Dovid.

The Rav, who had understood that not every relationship is easy, and that ease is not necessarily to be prized above all, had told him of these opinions, so that he might be prepared. Dovid had not passed this news to Esti. He had not attempted to change his behavior, or to influence her to alter hers. His demeanor with her had remained as it had always been and he had borne the glances, the knowing looks, and whispered comments, in the synagogue or on the street.

It is a terrible, wretched thing to love someone whom you know cannot love you. There are things that are more dreadful. There are many human pains more grievous. And yet it remains both terrible and wretched. Like so many things, it is insoluble.

The remainder of the visit passed a little more easily. His mother appeared to regain a certain amount of calm. On Wednesday, Dovid's elder brother, Reuven, brought two of his children to visit—the two-year-old boy and four-year-old girl. Dovid's mother drew them into the kitchen and showed them how to make chocolate-drop faces on the tops of fairy cakes.

"Do you remember," she said, as she brought in the tray, "do you remember how you two used to enjoy this? Dovid, do you remember how you used to eat the cakes from the bottom, so you could save the faces for last?"

His mother's face became anxious, as though she were concerned that he might have mislaid something of vital importance, or perhaps concerned that she had only invented this thought, that he would challenge her over its authenticity. Dovid remembered; they passed a happy afternoon.

On Thursday, Dr. Hartog telephoned from London. To update Dovid on the plans, he said. The plans? For the hesped, naturally. Hartog was proud of the progress of his plans. Several learned and widely respected Rabbis would be attending the memorial service. Also some significant figures in Jewish life in Britain—not those who were the best known, the well-recognized faces, but those, like Hartog himself, who provided the money, who purchased the influence, whose backing was all-important. Hartog had reserved a place of honor in the schedule of speakers for Dovid.

"You will speak, Dovid?" he said.

Dovid was silent.

"It will please the community," Hartog continued, "for you to speak some personal words about the Rav. To discuss him as he was. As a man. He was a father to us all, but to you above any."

Dovid remained silent.

"I have prepared some thoughts for you, Dovid. For you to look over when you return. Just some suggestions."

"I will consider the matter," said Dovid.

When Dovid was eighteen, he began his rabbinical studies in Israel. The week before his departure, the Rav had requested that he visit him in London. Dovid thought the Rav was going to give him a blessing for his trip, or for his study. Every word of blessing spoken has power, but the Almighty hearkens in particular to the blessings of the wise and holy. He imagined that the Rav would place his hands upon his head and ask the Lord to make his study deep and fruitful. It was only right; the Rav, the community, hoped that they would one day benefit from Dovid's learning. And, indeed, the Rav had certain words of blessing for Dovid. But once they were seated, alone and quiet in his study, the books around them softly inhaling and exhaling musty, mildewed breaths, the Rav spoke of another matter.

"We should speak," he said, "of your marriage."

Dovid blinked and tried not to smirk. This conversation was surely a little early? Girls could be married at seventeen, but a boy should wait at least until he was twenty. Why were they discussing this now?

The Rav paused to observe Dovid's reaction and continued in a dry and measured tone:

"It will be more difficult to find a wife for you, Dovid, than it is for most. It is not enough that your wife be kind, modest, and observant, although these things are important. She must be . . . mmmm . . . sympathetic. We must find you someone who will understand your gift, who will allow you to have time and quiet. No one too noisy, not one of these chatterers. Someone"—the Rav sighed a little—"someone who sees to the heart of things, someone who hears the voice of Hashem in the world. Someone capable of silence." He removed his glasses and rubbed the bridge of his nose, then looked up at Dovid.

"Dovid, you need not worry. It is not time yet. I simply wanted you to know that your parents and I have discussed the matter, that they are happy for me to locate a suitable girl. Perhaps we will have one or two for you to meet when you come home for Pesach, perhaps not. It may take a little time, but we shall know her when we find her."

The Rav clasped one of Dovid's hands between his and squeezed it.

Dovid had left this interview feeling both reassured and unsettled. He had the sensation that currents of air were moving far above his head. Now they merely ruffled his hair and kissed his forehead, but one day they would sweep him up and bear him lightly but firmly to a new and mysterious shore. He wondered who the Rav would introduce him to and on what basis he would make his choice. Although the Rav had said that they would know her, how would he, Dovid, know?

On Friday morning, early, in his parents' house in Manchester, Dovid received a telephone call from Mench, with whom he learned Gemarah on Tuesdays and Thursdays.

At first, Mench spoke hesitantly, then, as though gaining confidence from the utterances of his own lips, he proceeded with greater speed and ease. Dovid listened in silence. Once or twice, Mench grew concerned at the quiet and said, "Hello?" panic rising in his voice. Dovid said, "I'm here," and continued to listen, saying nothing. Mench spoke of the things he had heard, the things that had been told to him. "The people," he said, "the people are saying," and Dovid thought: our words will swallow us. We have spat them out, but in the end they will drown us.

As Mench continued explaining what might be said in the future, what could be said of him if he did not speak, the fluency he had developed became verbosity. Dovid, listening, had the sense that Mench was no longer in control of his words. He began to feel that it would be a positive service to the man to call a halt.

Without waiting for Mench to finish a sentence or pause, Dovid said, "Thank you."

Mench stopped speaking altogether. Dovid could see that he had been correct; the words had taken Mench over and he was clearly glad to be rid of them.

"Thank you," Dovid said again. "It was good of you to call."

"But don't you want to . . ."

Evidently the words had not utterly loosened their grip.

"I understand why you called," said Dovid. "Thank you for your kind intentions."

"Well, I . . ."

"I must go now, I'm afraid. Good-bye, Ya'akov."

Dovid replaced the handset. He sat down on the small upholstered bench in the hallway of his parents' house. He stood up again. He ran his hand down the spine of the telephone handset, almost picking it up before withdrawing his hand completely. He stood, hands in pockets, and examined the pictures on the walls, the same ones that had hung there when he and his brothers were boys: a photograph of the Western Wall in Jerusalem, a painting of a man blowing the shofar, his parents' ketubah, decorated with pomegranates, wheat sheaves, and fat-bodied bees. The pictures, he noted, were covered in a fine film of dust. He supposed that his mother no longer had the energy, or possibly the inclination, to dust pictures.

It was time to leave. He had promised his wife he would return to London for Shabbat, and Friday does not tarry for any man. His mother prepared him several packages of sandwiches, pieces of fruit in paper bags, little cardboard boxes of juice. His father clasped Dovid's shoulder and thanked him for coming, as though, Dovid thought, he had been a doctor paying a house call, or an unexpected and distinguished visitor. He felt a sudden sadness, hanging like a stone pendant within his throat, the cold, smooth mass preventing him from speaking. He swallowed two or three times, kissed his mother, wished his parents a good Shabbat, and left.

As it fell out, he had known, just as the Rav had said. It had been in one of his holidays from Yeshiva. After Ronit had left, just after. During that time that Esti had seemed most vulnerable and most alone. It was at the end of a week he had spent bathed in a constant film of light, rose-colored headache, sharp points of iridescence at the corners. Esti had attended the house as though she expected Ronit to return at any moment, as though if she waited she might find her still in her old bedroom. As though Ronit had not explained to them, with all excitement, that she would not return, that she never would. Esti had been waiting. She had the look of someone who might wait forever.

And Dovid had simply looked at her one day and known. It had not been utterly simple, for no true knowledge is ever reached without pain. At the instant of knowledge, his rose-colored headache had put forth a bloom from his mouth, and he had run, retching, to the toilet basin. But in that moment of viscous certainty, he had known, as the Rav had told him he would. Unwilling to trust, he had sent her away. But when she returned the next day, he still knew, more strongly, even, than he had the previous day. And the knowledge brought with it its own sadnesses and burdens, but it was not to be denied. And when his parents and the Rav had told him that it was not yet time, that he must return to Yeshiva, he had held the knowledge within him, a pool of deep water, its surface untroubled by the tempests that raged without.

As Dovid pondered these things, he felt an ache in his heart for his wife, an eagerness to see her. It was like a sudden craving for a food he had not eaten since he was a child, a flicker of taste in his mouth, reminding him of a sensation he had long forgotten. He felt, with brief clarity, that she was there beside him, and the next moment could not bear that she was not. He turned the nose of his car toward London and began his journey.

* * *

Over the years, I've had a lot of conversations with Dr. Feingold about silence. Generally, they'll go something like this. She'll say that I'm concealing something, that I should be honest with myself, and there's something I'm not saying. And I'll say, well, I'm English, it's difficult for me to talk about anything except the weather. And she'll say I don't buy that. And I'll say maybe I'm just repressed. And she'll say yes you are; the way to become less repressed is to talk to me. And I'll say but silence. You see, silence. When in doubt, silence. To most things, silence is the answer. And she'll say no, it's not. Silence is not power. It's not strength. Silence is the means by which the weak remain weak and the strong remain strong. Silence is a method of oppression.

Well, I guess she has to say that. She'd be out of a job if everyone in New York suddenly decided that silence was the answer.

In New York, life, my life, is full of noise. If I open the window, I can hear the chatter of the people, the growl of traffic below. Wherever I go, shopping in Gristedes or Duane Reade, riding the subway, even standing in an elevator, there'll be music or someone trying to sell me something. I like to leave the TV babbling to itself while I'm eating or getting dressed or reading. I'm just not used to silence anymore. Which is perhaps why I found the few days Dovid was away so weird.

I went back to Esti and Dovid's house. I slept there every night; it had become clear to me when I saw my old bedroom filled with piles of detritus that there was no room for me there. In Esti and Dovid's house there was, at least, space to breathe. And, after the first night, I plucked up courage to go back when I thought Esti might still be awake. But she wouldn't talk to me. More than that, she wouldn't be in the same room as me or, for preference, on the same floor. If I came downstairs, she'd wait until I'd gone into the living room or the kitchen and then scurry upstairs to hide in her bedroom. If I went upstairs, she'd race back down again. Once, I trapped her in the entrance hall. I waited in the living room until I heard her emerge from the kitchen and the creaky floorboard in the hall squeaked, and then I sprang out. I said, "Esti, don't you think we should . . ."

She stared at me for maybe a couple of seconds, and I thought, hey, we're going to manage a conversation. And she ran into the little bathroom just off the hall. She stayed there for forty-eight minutes. I timed it. When she finally did reemerge, she made straight for the kitchen and locked herself in. I thought of walking up to the door and shouting, "You know, Esti, this is neither a healthy nor a mature way of dealing with rejection." But I didn't.

I spent the next week at my father's house, arriving early in the mornings and not returning until the evenings. I couldn't go into my old bedroom, I just couldn't make myself, but I went through the things in my father's bedroom, and the boxes in Dovid's room. I wasn't sure what to do with my discoveries. Was there an organization out there that might be interested in a huge archive of Judaism-related newspaper articles dating from the 1940s to the late nineties? How about the old clothes, the paperbacks, the kitchenware so old it might actually now be retro-chic? I accumulated another small pile of items I might want: a few books, some more photographs, but I still hadn't found the candlesticks.

When I returned in the evenings, Esti had left food for me in the kitchen; I thought of asking her not to do so, telling her I could fend for myself, but I knew that leaving such a note would upset her, and actually discussing the matter was clearly impossible. In any case, the food was good and I was grateful. So, every evening, I helped myself to a bowl of whatever had been left out in the kitchen, glad at least to be in a place where the indications of life continued, however faintly.

And on Thursday night, the night before Dovid arrived back from Manchester, we had a visitor. As usual, Esti had eaten before I arrived back and was in her bedroom. I'd taken a plate of spaghetti Bolognese to the living room and was eating it while flicking through the newspaper, mourning the lack of television to make solitary meals less oppressive. I could hear the sound of the newspaper turning, my fork picking up the food, my chewing and swallowing. On the mantelpiece, a large and ornate clock ticked loudly (a gift from the Sara Rifka Hartog Memorial Day School to Miss Bloomfield on the occasion of her marriage, the plaque read). Each tick seemed like a word uttered into the quiet of the house, a spoken thing created and then dropped to fall back into the ocean of silence. I wondered, looking at the clock, whether all this silence might not be having a bad effect on me.

The doorbell rang, shrill and shocking. I stayed where I was; it wasn't my house, after all. A few seconds passed and I couldn't hear any movement from upstairs. Maybe Esti was afraid that I'd try to get it, and she'd also try to get it, and we might actually encounter each other and have to speak. The bell rang again. I felt suddenly irritated with Esti. Clearly *I* wasn't going to be having visitors, particularly unexpected ones at nine p.m. on a Thursday. So either it was some friend of hers or Dovid's, or a man visiting every house with a mezuzah to collect for some Jewish charity. Regardless, it was really her responsibility. There were three sharp taps on the door, as though the caller were unconvinced by the bell. Still no noise from upstairs. I put down my paper and went to answer the door.

Hartog was standing on the doorstep. He was smartly dressed, navy blue pinstripe, burgundy tie, a black leather folder in his hand. He looked as though he were about to attend a board meeting. He said:

"Good evening, Miss Krushka, I hope this isn't too late to call?"

I realized that I was standing at the door in a pair of jogging bottoms, and a T-shirt reading LOUD WOMAN with a tomato sauce stain down the front. I said:

"No, no, it's fine, come in."

He nodded, walked into the living room, surveyed the different seating options, chose the least frayed armchair, and sat down, crossing one well-tailored trouser leg over the other. He placed the black leather folder on the coffee table next to him and allowed his hand to rest on it, relaxed. As though he owned the place, I thought, as though it belonged to him.

He paused. I waited. We looked at each other for a strained, silent moment.

"Is there something I can do for you, Hartog?"

Hartog leaned back into the armchair and stretched his neck, swiveling his head from side to side. He took his time. He said:

"We were surprised to see you last week, you know." He raised his eyebrows a little. "I hope we didn't make you feel unwelcome. Dovid hadn't mentioned to us that you were here, although of course, Dovid . . ."

He left the sentence unfinished, making a sweeping gesture with his arm as he did so, as if inviting me to take in all that I saw around me and understand that this went to answer the question of Dovid.

I sat down, folding my arms. Damned if I was going to stand around like his secretary. I said:

"No, Hartog, you can rest assured that I enjoyed myself very much. I can't remember, in fact, having enjoyed a Friday night dinner quite so much as that."

Hartog narrowed his eyes slightly and pursed his lips. He seemed about to say something, and then thought better of it. He gripped the black folder. He said:

"Well, then, to business."

"Business?"

He reached over, placed the folder on his knee, and opened it. Inside, the contents were meticulously ordered, documents in clear plastic folders with labeled tabs identifying each one. It was a slim file, perhaps only thirty or forty pieces of paper in it. I tried to read the top one upside down, but he tipped it away from me so that all I saw was DEED.

"There are a number of purely administrative matters that we ought to clear up, pursuant to your father's death," he said, flicking through the folder. "I hope it's not too distressing for you to discuss at this time?"

I shook my head.

"Well, then." Hartog gently pulled out the first in his collection of documents and handed it to me. It was the deed to my father's house. "If you will direct your attention to page five," he said, his tone measured, professional, "you will notice that the registered owner of the house is the synagogue board."

I nodded. Hartog looked at me, as though expecting more of a reaction. Perhaps he'd thought this news would come as a shock. I wasn't shocked. My father had explained it to me years ago; the synagogue owns the house, the Rav lives in it. Perfectly normal practice. What were they going to do, accuse me of trespassing on their property? I studied the deed for a few moments and handed it back to Hartog.

"Presumably you'll be removing the house contents before the new Rav is chosen, then?" I said.

Hartog looked at me.

"You needn't worry," I continued, "there are only a few things I want. I'll be finished soon."

Hartog smiled.

"I'm glad you raised that matter, Miss Krushka." He replaced the deed in his folder and began flipping again as he spoke. "The contents of the house, of course, belonged to the Rav. His collection of Talmudic books, largely donated by friends from across the world, was particularly fine. But you know this."

I nodded.

Hartog smiled again and removed a second sheet from his file, placing it on the table in front of me with the air of a poker player revealing a winning hand.

"This is the Rav's will, properly signed and witnessed. As you can see, he leaves the contents of the house, all the contents, to the synagogue."

He looked at me.

"Now, Miss Krushka, I understand that you have been visiting your late father's house and are intending to remove some items."

I thought of Hinda Rochel Berditcher, who works for Hartog and whose lipstick always seems to stain her teeth red. I thought of the friendly visit on Sunday.

"I must tell you," Hartog continued, still smiling faintly, "that as a representative of the synagogue, not to mention"—he looked down—"a great admirer of your late father, I would consider it a dereliction of my duty were I to allow you to remove synagogal property from his residence. I'm afraid that I cannot permit it."

He looked at me. The clock kindly presented by the Sara Rifka Hartog Memorial Day School ticked. The silence between us grew and resounded until I could almost hear it, a slow and steady heartbeat of silence.

"What do you want, Hartog?"

He wrinkled his brow.

"What do I want, Miss Krushka? Nothing more than to do my duty as an elected officer of the synagogue."

Bullshit, I wanted to say, bull-fucking-shit. I dug my nails into the arm of the chair. I waited. He'd have to come out with it, whatever it was.

Hartog rearranged one or two pages in his folder. His hands were steady. I thought about what a wealthy man Hartog was. Does wealth do this for you?

Disobedience

Does being wealthy give a person this capability, to say anything to another human being, never to feel even slightly concerned that you might one day need their assistance? Hartog, apparently satisfied with the order of his documents, looked back up at me.

"There is one other matter we should discuss, though," he said. "As you know, we are arranging a hesped for the end of the month of mourning—two weeks away, in fact. Many distinguished rabbonim will be joining us from across the world. Your father was a well-respected, much-loved man."

I nodded. I'd already heard some of the plans from Dovid.

"We, that is the synagogue board and I, very much want this hesped to be a fitting memorial to your father, to his religious and spiritual legacy. We want to avoid unnecessary difficulties, do you see? We would like the event to run smoothly."

He looked at me levelly, as though trying to assess whether I had followed him so far. I looked back. I had an idea of what was coming next; I wasn't going to say it for him.

"We would prefer it, the synagogue board would prefer it, if you did not attend the hesped." He paused. "In exchange, we are prepared to allow you to remove whatever personal items, reminders of your father and so on, you wish from the house."

Hartog looked back up at me. His face was calm, showing no hint of worry or agitation. I wondered how long he'd been planning this speech.

"So, let me just be sure I've understood you," I said. "You don't want me to go to my own father's memorial service, and you're bribing me not to by offering to give me some things that are mine by right anyway?"

"I wouldn't like to use the word 'bribe,' Miss Krushka. I think we can both agree that for the good of the community . . ."

I was angry now.

"What? What is supposed to happen to the community if I attend the hesped?"

"Well," he said, spreading his arms wide again, smiling that faint, supercilious smile, "we don't need to go into that, do we? There have been certain rumors, Miss Krushka, certain pieces of information that you yourself do not deny. Of course, the synagogue board does not listen to lashon hara, but as you have admitted the matter yourself . . . well, it would simply be inappropriate. Surely you can see that?"

"Inappropriate because I told you I was gay?"

Hartog's smile disappeared.

"No, Miss Krushka, inappropriate because, in the past four days, seven other people have told me so. You are becoming somewhat . . . notorious. We wish the hesped to be a quiet and joyful celebration of the Rav's life, not"—he paused—"a circus of freaks."

I became very calm at that. I began to think what a profoundly punchable face Hartog has, how his nose sits in the middle, so round, so like a target.

I almost laughed.

I said, "You know, you can't make this go away by making *me* go away. I'll be gone in a few weeks, anyway, but it's not me, Hartog, *I'm* not your problem."

"Really?" said Hartog. "It is strange, then, that this problem seems to have arrived just as you did. I would call that a coincidence. Would you not, Miss Krushka?"

We looked at each other. I thought of telling him everything then, to explain to him how his perfect little world could never *be* perfect. That they weren't going to be able to make unsettling things go away by closing their eyes and *believing* they weren't there. I thought of telling him that it had never been perfect here at all, not even a little bit, and I had the evidence to prove it. But honestly, he wouldn't have understood. He wouldn't and Hinda Rochel wouldn't, and the members of the synagogue board wouldn't. Like Dr. Feingold says, you can only save yourself.

I said, "And you don't think it's 'inappropriate' to hold a memorial service without the Rav's family?"

Hartog waved an arm. "Dovid will be there, of course, and the Rav's sister, possibly his brother will fly over from Jerusalem. The family will be represented, you need not concern yourself with that."

My right hand involuntarily curled into a fist.

"So what is it, exactly, that you want me to do?"

Hartog leaned back in his chair. He stretched his neck again, moving his head slowly from side to side.

"We would like you to leave quietly just before the hesped. There's no need to make it dramatic. You could simply say that some matters have come up at work requiring your attention. You will have to rearrange your travel plans, of course. We understand that this may incur some expenses, which we are quite willing to reimburse, as well as compensating you for your trouble."

He turned to the back of his folder and produced a check, which he held between thumb and forefinger.

"As you'll see, we feel we're being more than generous."

He passed me the check. I looked at it. £20,000. About $33,000. More than enough to cover twenty return flights to New York. I noticed that although Hartog had spoken as "we," the check didn't come from the synagogue account; it was from his own personal account, signed in broad, firm strokes, Dr. Hartog. Clearly, Hartog was bankrolling this little scheme himself, however much he wanted to present it as being the will of the community.

I turned the check over in my hands.

"And you wouldn't like to use the word 'bribe,' Hartog?"

Hartog thinned his lips. His face, I noticed, had become more white. "I don't think that would be appropriate, no."

"So what if I refuse? What if I decide to attend the hesped?"

Hartog breathed in sharply.

"Don't you understand?" he said. "You would be bringing shame on everyone, and for no purpose. No one *wants* you here. Most of the people barely remember you, and for those who do you are nothing but an embarrassment. Can you imagine how difficult it is for Esti and Dovid to have you here? To be spoken of in this way? Can't you see? They are much-respected members of the community. They have a place here, and you"—he paused— "you I'm sure have a place somewhere else."

He looked down at his hands, then back up at me.

"Miss Krushka," he said. "Ronit, I believe that we, the synagogue board and I, have made you a very generous offer. We are simply protecting our community, your father's legacy. I don't understand, I really don't understand, why you want to come here after all this time and attack us. Surely you have made a life for yourself in New York? It seems a more, a more appropriate place for you. We simply want to live in our accustomed way, as, I'm sure, you do."

My first instinct, of course, was to tell Hartog that both he and his check could go to hell. I wasn't going to be dictated to, or told where I could and couldn't go, where I was and wasn't wanted. But as I looked at him, with his punchable face, and his smug, supercilious smile, I found myself thinking: no. This is not my fight. Hartog's right about that, at least, I left here a long time ago precisely because of this kind of bullshit. Instead of fighting, I could pretend that Hartog and I are both civilized people, I could take the things that I wanted from the house, get on a plane, and go. I could just leave. After all, I've done it before. And instead of punching Hartog, I found myself saying:

"Can you give me a little time to think it over?"

Hartog nodded, as though this were the outcome he had anticipated, and closed his folder.

I followed Hartog to the door and let him out. He walked briskly away, calm and assured, swinging his black leather folder in one hand. I stood at the door, watching him until he was out of sight. I turned back into the house and, as I did so, caught a glimpse of movement and heard a sound on the stairs. I looked up and saw Esti, sitting toward the top of the staircase, arms hugged around her knees, watching and listening. Her face was pale and her eyes were endless black.

Chapter Nine

*Between Me and the Children of Israel, it is a sign for ever
that in six days the Lord made the heavens and the earth,
and on the seventh day He rested.*

Exodus 31:17, recited on Friday night,
at the commencement of the Sabbath

It is ridiculous, of course, to speak of the Lord resting. Are we to
believe that the Ein Sof—He who is without end—became tired
from His labors? That His muscles were exhausted? We are not
children, to believe such nonsense. What, then, does the Torah
mean when it tells us that God rested on the seventh day? Our
sages explain that it is not that the Lord rested on the seventh day,
it is rather that on the seventh day he invented rest.

It must be understood that we are not speaking here of sleep or
food or time for tired muscles to knit. These are only forms of
work. They exist to service work. We sleep, we eat, we relax our
limbs and our minds in order that we may be nourished and fit for
further work. And if all that we are is work, what are we? We
work in order to gain food to swallow or a pillow to press our
head into. And we eat and sleep in order to work. We are ma-
chines, doing nothing more than reproducing ourselves endlessly.

But Shabbat shows us that this is not so. Shabbat is not a day of

Naomi Alderman

recreation, of pastimes, it is a day of abstention from creativity. It is a day of treading lightly upon the world. We do not use wheeled or motorized transport, we do not spend money, we do not speak on the telephone or use any electrical item. We do not carry outside our houses, even an object as small as a handkerchief, even in a pocket. We do not cook, we do not dig, we do not write, we do not weave, we do not sew, we do not draw. As far as possible, the world is not altered by our sojourn in it over Shabbat. Instead, we eat food we have already prepared, we talk, we sleep, we pray, we walk—simple, human things. And by these actions we resist our impulse to be constantly meddling with the world, altering it, making it conform more closely to our desires, as though our desires were all that mattered. Shabbat is simply to take our hands from the wheel and let it spin.

And here we reach the heart of the matter. For if we cannot be distracted by our actions, our creation, we must, at last, come to ourselves. Man-and-woman were created at the moment before sunset on the sixth day. We should recall that each Friday, at sunset, is the anniversary of our birth. Shabbat draws us back to ourselves. Shabbat presents us with all we have achieved, but nothing more. Shabbat asks, quietly but insistently, who we are. And Shabbat will not relieve us if we should have no answer.

Friday, Esti thought, hums like a frightened insect. It buzzes. Trapped inside the head, it flits from one side to the other, striking the skull, making a noise like a clock ticking. With each tick, it declares: these are the minutes until Shabbat. And now these. And now these.

This hum, this ticking, is a light thing, a simple thing, but as demanding and as impossible to disobey as the rhythm of one's own need for breath, or of the times and days of the menstrual cycle. Friday will not go unanswered. Friday may not be postponed. If that which is needful is not accomplished on Friday, no mercy will be shown. For the Sabbath cannot be delayed by even half a minute from its appointed time, and all who think to halt its arrival commit thereby a grave transgression.

Esti rose at just after six a.m. The dawn had not yet whispered its morning words into the sky, but, as she looked out the window, she could see a few touches of a lighter and more tremulous blue beginning to caress it in the east. She washed her face briskly at the basin and stared out for a few moments at the insidious fingers of light creeping into the sky. It was Friday, and Friday would not wait. It was Friday, and at every minute from now until sunset, she would know what time it was. She checked the printed calendar on the wall. Sabbath would begin at 6:18 p.m. She dressed quickly, gathering up her hair into a loose bun, pulled on a beret, and tucked in the loose strands. She had things to do. Like Friday, she could not be detained.

She ran through her mental list. There were clothes to be washed and ironed, the food to buy and cook, the rooms should be cleaned and ordered, the table laid, the time switches set, the urn filled, the hotplate prepared, and, and, was there anything else? Of course. The special errand. How long would it take? It was hard to know. The other things should be completed first. Then she could think further.

For the next eight hours, she worked. It was the same work as every week, the same dishes to be prepared, the same food to be bought. There was an order to it, a calming pattern. She found that while she worked she did not worry. At the baker's shop, she picked out three large plaited challot, glossy and warm. At the greengrocer's, she chose fresh fruit and vegetables. She passed by a chemist's shop, paused fractionally outside it, contemplating. Mrs. Salman, from synagogue, passed by on the far side of the street laden with butcher's bags. Mrs. Salman noticed Esti, smiled, and, with some difficulty, raised a hand. Well. It could not be done here, then, the special errand. Not in Hendon. Esti walked on from the chemist's.

At the butcher's, she selected some raw chicken livers. At home, she koshered them over an open flame, the blood dripping down, the smell distinctive as of singed hair or nails. She made soup, boiling the water in her large stockpot. Drops of condensation formed on the outside of the pot. She held the three chicken carcasses up to the light, admiring their tracery of veins and rosy muscle filaments. Their bones moved beneath the clinging remnants of flesh, in a fine articulated motion. She turned them over, considering their elements of life, and, suddenly decisive, dropped them, one by one, into the boiling water. They rose to the surface, the meat blinking from living pink to white, a sudden sharp aroma of soup causing her to swallow. And so it goes, she said to the chickens, and so it goes. From muscle and bone to soup. So it goes. And what are you, after all, but chickens? A life of feathers and squawking, what is that? She looked at the clock. 10:07 a.m.

Toward the end of the morning, Dovid telephoned to say that he was leaving Manchester, that he expected to be home in four and a half hours. At some point, too, Esti became aware that Ronit was no longer in the house. Earlier in the week, she might have wondered where she'd gone or paused to reflect on her presence. On another day, she might have felt the same stomach-dropping despair, the same caught-breath fear as ever. But today was Friday.

At last, early in the afternoon, Esti finished. The clothing was clean, the Shabbat outfits ironed, the house in order. In the oven, the chickens were almost roasted, though not quite brown enough. On the stove, the soup was merry, bubbling, and wakeful. The tzimmes, the liver, the kugels, the cakes, the gefilte, the potatoes, the vegetables were all as complete as they could be without spoiling. A few small things remained to be done, but they could be completed on her return. Her body spoke to her in a quiet, unrelenting voice. Today. It should be done today. She turned off the oven and the stove, took up her bag, and left for the station.

The day was unseasonably warm and as she walked she began to sweat, a thin, unpleasant dampness sticking her skin to her clothes. The prickling sensations in her arms and legs were the thousand eyes of the people of Hendon. "Isn't that Esti Kuperman?" "Where could she be going in such a hurry?" "And on a Friday afternoon!" There could only be one possible answer to the riddle. Where would a married woman be going at great speed only hours before Shabbat? They would know, they would all know. These were not friendly eyes, she realized that now. She could not trust them to keep her secrets, she could not trust them not to think. Esti tried to breathe slowly, speaking softly to the muscles of her thighs and calves, telling them to be easy, for there could be any number of reasons, no one, she murmured, would ever guess. Her legs would not listen to her. They sped on, faster and faster.

At the station, she was confronted with the fact, bold and unanswerable, that she did not know where to go. It should be somewhere she would not meet anyone, somewhere no one would look at her and note: Esti Kuperman. But where in London could she be certain of that? She looked at her watch—3:20 p.m. Dovid would be home very soon. Shabbat was at 6:18 p.m. She did not have time for this uncertainty. The buzzing in her head was louder and more insistent, the knocking sound on the inside of her skull stating more firmly: ticktock, ticktock. She ran her eye along the map of the Northern Line. Where could she be certain? Which of these little unfolding buds? There. A point of intersection. Camden Town. She purchased her ticket from the impersonal machine, grateful for its simple questions: Where are you going? How many zones? Not: Why are you going? Not: For what?

She counted again as she traveled. The rhythm of the journey was good for counting. She counted first these days, then those, then the extra ones. She counted again and again, and the total was always the same, and always wrong. She leaned her head against the cool glass partition, feeling tired, and a little faint. She closed her eyes and listened to the click-clack of the train, so like the ticktock in her own head. It was only as the doors were about to close that she noticed she had reached Camden Town. She leapt up and bolted through the door.

Camden sweated. It was loud. It smelled. Esti stood outside the station simply looking, her bag clutched tight against her body. A thin young man, whose chest read SCREW THE PEOPLE, was leaning against the railing, eating a baked potato from a plastic container. He jabbed up every mouthful with his fork as though hoping to cause the potato pain. Without warning, he twisted his mouth, glared at his food, and threw it onto the floor. He walked away. The melted butter trickled onto the pavement, its scent rising. A small dog, dragged past by a woman teetering in pink sandals, stopped to lick the paving stones two or three times. The world spun. Esti wondered if she was about to faint. The shops and people began to merge into a distorted inner-ear judder. Everything became suddenly upside down, inside out. Bingle-mingle.

Camden would not cease at 6:18 p.m., the streets would not become quiet, the people still. These people had not prepared for the Sabbath, they did not hear the sound of Friday in their skulls. The thought made her weak, a dizzying ache, a breath of compassion. She held on to the railing, breathing deeply. This would not do, she thought. She must restore order. She must continue to breathe. She looked at her watch—3:53 p.m. Two hours and twenty-five minutes left before Shabbat. The thought quieted her a little. Still gripping the railing, she looked about her. She glanced at the faces walking past, each one absorbed in its own confusion. Never to hear Friday, never to know it. It was as though they had never known love: both terrible and wonderful. She had considered them before, the people who did not know Friday. She wondered now if this was how Ronit felt in New York, without lines and demarcations, without order and sense, without anchor. A thing both to be feared and desired.

She lifted her head and looked a little farther, searching for the right kind of shop, a chemist's shop. Her heart pounded in her chest. She tried not to breathe too rapidly. There was one, on the opposite side of the road. She hurled herself toward it, racing between the angry cars. Things were cooler in the chemist's shop, clearer. The people moved more slowly, spoke more quietly. Although she was surrounded by aisles of products, they remained in their lines and orders, there were small labels by which they could be identified. She felt calmed by the sense that all this had been intended. She began to search.

She walked along each aisle, turning her head to the right and to the left. As she walked, she counted. She had been counting for two days now, adding and subtracting, figuring and refiguring. But perhaps she had been mistaken? How foolish she would feel, how absurd, if all this time she had simply counted incorrectly. She counted again. The numbers remained the same, mute and unanswerable. She walked on, past shampoos and conditioners, creams to remove hair and sprays to replace it, deodorants and perfumes, vitamins and minerals. She found the thing she was seeking just past the array of contraceptive products, the two sitting next to each other like an exhibit demonstrating the law of cause and effect.

She turned the packet over in her hand. "**Fastest**, most **accurate** results" it proclaimed. "**Recommended** by **doctors**" and "Use from the **first day** your period is due." She counted the days again. The days of bleeding, and the days of counting after bleeding, the day of mikvah, the days between mikvah and when Ronit arrived, the days since then. Twenty-nine days. And tomorrow it would be thirty. She had felt none of the signs, had experienced no pain. She knew it would not begin tomorrow. She held the thing in her hand and looked up and down the aisle to see if she was being watched, to see if anyone had noted her interest in this most private and holy of all areas.

An elderly man with yellowed eyes was examining the toothbrushes, holding them to the light in turns, squinting as if to detect some esoteric flaw. Nearer to her, a young black woman, her hair braided into cornrows dotted at the ends with colored beads, was standing before the moisturizers. Both her arms were red and scaly, wrist to elbow. It looked painful. Esti felt another wave of fatigue break over her, veined-pink and roiling. Her eyes defocused and for a moment there were two women in front of her, not one, each of their cornrows swaying slightly. Esti leaned heavily against a shelf and dislodged two or three boxes, which clattered to the floor. The young woman looked at her and moved away. Esti clutched the thing in her hand, looked at it again. "Results in **one** minute," it said. She looked at her watch—4:25 p.m. Friday muttered and growled. Less than two hours to go. Ticktock, ticktock, no time for this nonsense.

There was a short queue at the checkout. The elderly man in front of her had laid out seven toothbrushes and was asking for the price of each one before he made his final selection. Behind her, an Indian woman, plump midriff deliciously exposed, rummaged through her handbag, clucking and sighing. She smiled at Esti. Esti smiled back. The elderly man decided not to purchase any toothbrush at all and moved away. Esti handed her item to the cashier. The Indian woman, peering over Esti's shoulder, said, "Oh!"

Esti turned. The woman was beaming. She placed a soft hand on Esti's arm.

"It is a blessing from God. You understand? A blessing from God." She pointed upward, lifting her eyes to emphasize. Esti nodded. In her confusion, she gave too much money to the cashier, three five-pound notes. Some had to be handed back. She tried to move away, but the woman plucked at her sleeve.

"Remember," she said. "From God."

The time of the commencement of the Sabbath is known to the Almighty more precisely than any clock can declare it. In His infinite mind (if we may be permitted to speak of the contents of His mind) the sixth day becomes the seventh without fuss, without effort, the border between one and the next perfectly clear. The minds of man, however, do not admit of such ecstasies of understanding. For the Sabbath was created by the Lord; it is an object of the Divine, but a man is simply a man. And thus our sages, whose interest was ever in translating the Divine to a human tongue, instituted the eighteen minutes. For although the Sabbath begins precisely at the moment of sunset, the printed Sabbath times in calendars or newspapers in fact allow a margin of eighteen minutes before the setting of the sun. This knowledge is not to be used lightly. It is infinitely preferable and meritorious to commence the Sabbath at the printed time, and thus to avoid all doubt. But if one finds oneself without resource, that margin still remains. Eighteen minutes of grace before the start of the holy day.

By the time Esti arrived home, only thirty-four minutes remained before the start of Shabbat. The small package in her handbag spoke of its **reliable** results available in only **one** minute. But the soup muttered coldly, with round syllables of fat on its surface. And the chickens, knowing their own incompleteness, ruffled nonexistent feathers, demanding a perfect brown to replace them. Dovid and Ronit had both returned, but Esti could not consider that now. She worked, warming the soup, roasting the chickens, glazing the potatoes, seasoning the cholent, icing the cake. Friday marked off the moments more and more clearly: ticktock, ticktock, ticktock. Slow and steady, neither aggrieved nor impatient, but inexorable as the tide. Ticktock. Ticktock.

At three minutes before the printed time of Shabbat, the final items had been prepared. She switched off the oven and the hob, tucked a strand of hair back into her hat, and looked about her with satisfaction. Two full meals were cooked, chickens and potatoes, glistening rice, cholent deliciously bubbling in its slow cooker, vegetables steamed, cakes baked and decorated, soup magnificently rich, fish clad in carrot scales. Dovid had left for synagogue; she heard the door slam behind him. Her candles were set out in the dining room. It was time to light. Was there anything she had forgotten? She swept her eyes across the kitchen, the dining room, the hallway. In the hall, in her handbag, a small voice squeaked. "Test at **any** time of day. Accuracy **guaranteed**." Tick, said Friday, tock. It was time to light her candles. Shabbat was coming.

Tick

Esti ran upstairs to the bathroom, the package concealed in her sleeve. She looked at her watch. The eighteen minutes had begun. Locking the door, she examined the packaging again. **One** minute for a reliable result. There was time. She pulled open the packet.

Tock

The instructions were more confusing than she had anticipated. It took several minutes to read and comprehend them fully. The tip of the plastic stick should be immersed for five seconds only. She must time it, counting off the seconds, allowing no errors. She tore at the inner plastic wrapping.

Tick

She waited for the color to change. This, surely this, was the necessary emergency, the thing that cannot be postponed until after the Sabbath day. She looked at her watch. Thirteen minutes slid over to fourteen. She must leave time to light her candles. The moisture crept up, fiber by fiber, taking its own time. Was it even permissible to look at the thing after the Sabbath had begun? Surely it must be forbidden even to touch it, a device that changes color, an object with no purpose on the Sabbath. How long could she wait?

Tock

She looked out the bathroom window. A certain ripeness had fallen over the blue of the sky. The leaves of the apple trees, the red-tiled roofs, the parked cars, the roads all exhaled, saying, we are done, for this week our work is completed. They settled into the earth, allowing themselves to sag. Esti looked at her watch. Sixteen minutes. She looked at the sky. The blue was even more profound. The Sabbath was beginning. She looked back at the window in the plastic wand. And she found a blue line held in that small space. And that line was a boundary between one state and another. And that blue spoke to her of other beginnings, and changes of an even more perfect order.

* * *

Disobedience

Dr. Feingold says: the subconscious knows no past or future. For the subconscious, everything is happening right now. Trauma that happened when you were four still feels exactly as threatening now as it did then. Trauma that happened when I was four, I say, like the death of my mother? Yes, she says, for example. Do you want to talk about that?

I tell her that her ideas about the subconscious remind me of God. She says, "God?" In the Torah, Moses asks God to tell him His name. And God gives him a word: YHVH. No vowels, so it can't be pronounced, even if you wanted to. It's an impossible conjugation, three separate tenses of the verb "to be" smashed together in one word. It means having been, going on being, and going to be in the future, all together. From this, we learn the timeless nature of God. The past, the present, and the future are all the same to Him.

Dr. Feingold listens to this silently. When I'm finished, she leaves a space of another few seconds. She says, "There's a difference, though. The subconscious is wrong about the past and future. Things that were threatening in the past aren't so scary anymore. That's different than your idea about God, isn't it?"

I say, "Yes. If 'my idea' about God is correct, then the subconscious is quite right. The past hasn't gone anywhere. It's right here."

On Sunday, I went back to my father's house, just to check. The locks had been changed. I tried one key, then another, then another, jiggling each one, pulling the door toward me, pushing it away. I stood holding the whole useless bunch, flicking at the peeling red paint by the hinges with the toe of my shoe, as though that's what I'd intended to do all along.

I walked to the side of the house, pushed open the rotten gate, and walked through into the garden. The overgrown lawn had yellowed in the heat. One of the apple trees was bent double, its branches scraping along the weed-ridden flower beds. And by the fence was the hydrangea bush. I picked my way along the path and bent over to examine it. A few flowers were still hanging on, petals beginning to curl up and brown. I crushed one between finger and thumb and inhaled the succulent scent.

I remember only in fragments. The bare legs, the hydrangeas, the taste of her mouth. There was a place, between the hydrangea bush and the fence, where two girls could crawl, if they were little enough, and not afraid to scratch their knees. It was one of those places that seems obvious to children, hidden to adults. A secret place. In winter it was nothing; the bush was bare. But every summer the little room bloomed again.

Now there was nothing; the bush had become overgrown, the ground was too wet to crawl on. I couldn't have sat underneath there, even if I'd wanted to. Plus, I was much bigger than I'd been back then. I knelt for a long time, though, my palms resting on the damp earth, my fingernails sinking into it. When I got up, finally, and started the walk back to Esti and Dovid's house, I tried to scrape the lines of dirt out from under my nails. The harder I scraped, the deeper I pushed them in, black ingrained against red.

We'd known about the hydrangea bush for years. Once we were inside, we were unseen, screened from the house, from the eyes around and above. It smelled, I remember. The thick, sweet smell of rotting hydrangeas, and damp old earth. Even now, the vegetable scent of hydrangeas holds power. In springtime, passing by hydrangea-filled buckets at Grand Central Station will flicker into a sudden, sharp memory of dirt underneath my fingernails and too-warm, maroon-colored sweaters and the bare whiteness of the tops of her legs when she'd taken off her tights.

It was a school rule: we had to wear thick, dark, opaque tights, so that no man could see our legs and become aroused. Because, of course, in the minds of the teachers at the Sara Rifka Hartog Memorial Day School, no man would *ever* become aroused by a schoolgirl in tights. After school, Esti would come back to my house to do homework. So I suppose that's where it started. With the heat of summer, with Esti and me racing to my bedroom, wrestling our tights off and standing bare-legged and triumphant.

To begin with, we just enjoyed sitting where no one could see us. No one being my father, who wouldn't have been looking, and Bella, the housekeeper, who'd generally gone home by then anyway. To begin with we just sat, talking or reading or staring up at the sky through the geometric flowers. But it was there that things started. Like the thing with the blood.

We'd learned it in school, studying ancient customs in geography. Miss

Cohen explained it, sniffing and curling her lip to make us understand that this was something primitive and disgusting. But I listened, and I didn't think it was disgusting. It felt like I was remembering something I'd always known, or heard long ago.

Esti had cut her knee, that was the next thing. She was always cutting something; she could barely make it through a games lesson or a walk across the playground without tripping. The heels of her hands and her knees were constantly dotted with little scabs: fresh, half healed, and old. This cut on her knee was more than the usual skid-scrape. She'd fallen on broken glass left at the corner of the sports field and had needed five stitches. All the girls talked about it afterward, mentioning the "five stitches" with glee, imagining the needle passing in and out of flesh for each one. The wound was long and curved, with puckered stitches. It looked like her knee was smiling, with crooked teeth. Even after the stitches, if you pulled at the edges, you could still make it bleed: fresh, new blood, running in red viscous lines down her shin.

Anyway, that's how it happened. We were sitting behind the hydrangea bush, Esti with her knees pulled up tightly to her chest, me sprawled on my back, staring at the leaf-roof above us, panting in the heat. Our shirts were rolled up above our elbows, tights off, skirts pushed back. Such careless exposure of flesh. If we'd dressed that way at school, we would have been punished for immodest behavior. Esti craned her neck to examine the smiling scar on her knee. I had a little scab on the palm of my hand, about the size of a halfpence piece. I peeled the brown cover off my hand and watched with satisfaction as a bead of red rose to the surface.

I said, "We should become blood sisters."

She looked at me.

"You remember, from geography? We mingle our blood, and then we're sisters forever."

She shifted uncomfortably, bringing her knees tightly into her chest.

"Will it hurt?"

"Only a little bit, we just have to open your cut. See, I'm bleeding on my hand. We have to let them mix. Come on."

She stretched her leg toward me. I pulled on the cut at the edge until it seeped water, and then blood. Her legs were cool, despite the warmth of the day. When I looked at her face, I saw that she was biting her lower lip, eyes ready to overflow.

"Don't cry," I said. "You're such a baby."

I squeezed the graze on my hand, scratching it with my nail until the blood was flowing more freely. I looked carefully to see where the hole was, then clasped my hand to her knee, matching up the places, blood to blood. I looked at Esti. She looked at me. An insect thrummed in my ear. A small breeze disturbed the leaves above us. Somewhere a few gardens along, someone was mowing the lawn. I realized that I was sweating, just at my hairline. On Esti's leg, a crust of blood, like watery jam, had congealed around the edges of my palm.

I said, "There. Now we're sisters." I took my hand away.

Esti looked at her knee, still bleeding, and my palm, rosy with her blood. She took my hand, examined it for a moment, and put it back in place on her knee, blood to blood. She held my hand firmly there on her leg, her palm cold against my knuckles.

What you have to understand, I say to Dr. Feingold, is that it was *our* place. We found it. We sat there from the leaf-buddings of spring until the autumn destroyed it again. We never mentioned it to anyone else, or invited anyone else in.

She says, "So you felt betrayed?"

Did I? It's plausible. But that's not how I remember it. I remember feeling angry.

On Monday, I made the telephone call. I told myself it meant absolutely nothing. I checked with them that, yes, the ticket could be canceled up to twenty-four hours in advance. One hundred percent refund, yes. And as I gave them my credit card details I concentrated on the thought that it was just a precaution; I'd never use it. But I chose the times of the flight with care, as though I were thinking of getting on that plane.

That evening, at supper, Esti's hand crept over to Dovid's. Her fingers touched his knuckles lightly. He looked as surprised as I was, both of us flicking our eyes down and then up again. But her hand stayed where it was, her head bent down, concentrating on her plate.

What really annoys me about Esti is not how inarticulate she is, or how sensitive, or how really, at bottom, conventional. It's the fact that she just can't admit who she is, can't look herself in the face. Neither one way nor the other. Even then, she couldn't see what I could see. She didn't know. Maybe she still doesn't bloody know. But I knew.

It was the summer we were thirteen. The summer of becoming blood sisters. Dovid had headache after headache that summer. He was supposed to go to Yeshiva the next year, but he spent days just lying in bed. In the afternoons, when a headache had left him weak, I used to sit by his bed talking to him. And that was how it happened. I introduced them.

They'd met before, of course, but never really talked until that summer. I brought Esti up to sit with him, and he told me later that he liked her, because she was so quiet and peaceful. I was proud that I'd found him something he liked, as though I'd brought him a toy or a book he'd enjoyed. So we three used to sit, talking, in his room, most afternoons. If I'm honest, I did most of the talking. I used to think that if I hadn't been there, they probably would have just sat together in silence. So at least I rescued them from that.

Dovid got a little better, and a little better. After three weeks, he only had a headache every four days, and he went back to studying with my father in the mornings, and by himself in the afternoons. But somehow, he still found time to play or talk with me most afternoons. Whenever Esti was around. I didn't really notice that, then. Not until the very end of the holidays.

The last day of summer holidays always contains a certain fluttery fear— of the return to school, of returning to the person you *are* at school. My father didn't notice. He kept me busy, running errands for him all afternoon, returning a book to someone, picking up spare tallits for the shul from someone else. So much so that I was late. Esti was supposed to be coming over to say good-bye to Dovid. He was going back to Manchester, we were going back to school, and we wouldn't see each other until the winter holidays. I remember thinking as I ran home how awful it'd be for the two of them to be there together without me. They wouldn't have anything to say.

I ran faster, gym shoes pounding on the pavement, skirt swaying against my calves and ankles in the way that always made me wish I could just rip it off and run without. When I arrived back they weren't in the lounge. Maybe in Dovid's room? I dashed upstairs. Nothing. I looked out the window. The garden was still, but a little movement stirred the hydrangea bush. I walked downstairs, through the kitchen, and into the garden.

I heard laughter coming from the place and a rustling of leaves. I ducked my head under and crawled through. Dovid and Esti were sitting in the hydrangea nest together, laughing. His legs were stretched out, trousers covered in dust, and he was smiling, a thin laugh escaping from the side of his mouth. She was tightless, legs drawn up, skirt tented over her knees, choking on little high-pitched laughs. As I entered, they both turned toward me, then looked at each other, then smiled back at me, and Esti said:

"Oh, Ronit, Dovid just said something so funny . . ."

And she stopped, looked back at Dovid, and started to laugh again.

It wasn't really as though I wanted either of them. I just expected them to be there when I needed them. I just expected that they'd stay where I put them, wouldn't cause trouble. They were both so obedient.

I ran out, back through the kitchen, into the hallway, out of the house, running and running, and not really looking where I was going because I just needed to keep on moving and moving, which in retrospect was dangerous and I was quite lucky that I didn't run into the road but instead just into a tree. I whacked it with my elbow. The force was strong enough to make me cry out, and when I turned my arm I saw that I'd ripped a gash in my upper arm. Blood was splashing onto the ground. And then there was pain.

Esti and Dovid followed me up to the bathroom, hovering on the threshold. Esti said, "Can I do anything? Does it hurt?" Dovid said, "We must call your father, Ronit. This could be serious."

I closed the door and locked it, shutting them out. I remember the blood dripping into the basin, startling crimson drops, the swirl of red and pink when I turned on the tap. I remember crying, just a bit. Being surprised to find myself crying. Looking at myself in the mirror above the basin, seeing my own face crying and not knowing my own reflection.

I didn't have stitches. I washed it and put plasters on, gathering it together, and hid it under my sleeve. By the time I came out of the bathroom,

Disobedience

Esti was gone. And the next day, so was Dovid. The wound healed unevenly, leaving a piece of tree bark lodged in my elbow.

I didn't do anything the first day of school. Or the second, or the third. I don't know why. It wasn't as though Esti would have known what I was thinking. Maybe I remembered that God was watching me, and I thought I could put Him off the scent by leaving a few days between cause and effect. So I left it till the fourth day after Dovid left. I waited until we were sitting after school, warm and drowsy, in our secret place, bare-legged and open-necked.

"Esti," I said, "I have a new game."

She blinked at me.

"You have to lie very still, and I have to try to make you laugh, okay?"

She rolled away from me, lying on one side. I lay down next to her, not quite touching her, but feeling the heat from her body on my skin. Softly, I stroked the curve of her neck, from ear to shoulder—a ticklish place. She didn't move, or speak. I ran my hand along her arm, brushing the delicate hairs gently. So far, this was charted territory. She remained perfectly still. I moved in a little closer, my stomach against the small of her back, my knees tucking into hers. I slipped my hand under her shirt, circling my thumb around her navel, and still she lay, inert. I began to wonder if I had misunderstood. Was she about to leap to her feet, accuse me of terrible things? I shifted a little, to look at her face. Her eyes were closed, her lips curved in a smile. Her breath was long and shallow, a flush on her cheeks. She moved a little and opened her eyes, as blue as water. And her skin, on her belly and her thigh, was so soft, like the skin of a child. As delicious as wine. And as she stirred against me, her lips parted and she uttered a breath, like a sigh. And she turned and placed her lips against mine.

The tree of unhappiness, they say, grows from a seed of bitterness and brings forth the fruit of despair. What would have happened if I had never touched her? Might she have gone to Dovid as freely as a bird, knowing no different? If I had not existed, might she have found peace, or would she simply have sown her discontentment elsewhere? If I had not existed, how would she have found Dovid at all? No one can answer these questions, not even she or I.

We didn't know what to do, really, that first time. We leaned on each other's hair, fumbled and blushed. But there, behind the hydrangea bush, slowly, we learned. We went from one thing to another as we wished, as we understood. After the moment when her lips touched mine, when we knew we had transgressed, there was no road to travel back. Everything was already done. I remember the sensation of her cool fingers passing over the tip of my breast, hardening, wrinkling the skin like a whisper of wind. I remember the shock of it, the unmistakable heat. I remember her shiver of delight. I remember learning in school later that human beings are electric animals, flowing with current, and thinking, I know, I have already learned this fact of electricity within the skin. I remember only in moments.

On Tuesday night I had a dream, one that I hadn't dreamed for a long time, although it was as familiar as my own skin. I dreamed that I was getting ready for Shabbat, but I was late, much too late. We all have this dream—perhaps I could suggest it to Dr. Feingold as a subject for a book: *The Anxiety Dreams of Orthodox Jews, Ex–Orthodox Jews, and Heretics.*

I was in an unfamiliar place trying to get home, but I didn't know how and the sun was setting. I was racing through unfamiliar, dirty streets, looking for a subway or for a taxi. But all the taxis were full, and there was no station. I had to watch the sun dip lower and lower until it finally disappeared over the horizon. And after that, what, really, is there to lose? I noticed my office and decided to go in. But when I went through the door it wasn't my office at all. It was Esti and Dovid's house and they were perched on a kitchen work-top, hand in hand, kissing like schoolgirls.

On Wednesday, I went to see Hartog. I showed him my ticket and he smiled everywhere except for his eyes, and told me what a wise decision I'd made. We went to my father's house that night and he watched with a supercilious air as I gathered together a clutch of items I'd found: the pictures, the kiddush cup, the spice box, the Seder plate. Under the sink in the kitchen, I found a plastic bag and swept them all in, shielding them from him. As we were leaving the house, I tried to take the bag, but he shook his head, as though speaking to a small child, and said:

"No, no, Ronit. I will accompany you to the airport. I will watch you check in your luggage. I will see you go through passport control. And as you do, I will give you this bag. Not before."

He shook his head again, chuckling slightly.

The urge to punch him in the face welled up in me again. I could see it. His nose bent crooked, blood gushing down his chin, dribbling onto his yellow silk tie. I held on to that image, pure and clear, as he locked the front door behind us, jangling his bunch of keys in my face when he was finished.

Dovid and Esti conspired over the washing-up that night, as if I had already gone, laughing little, meaningful laughs, flicking foam at each other. I sat in the other room, trying to read my newspaper. And I thought: I am taking something home with me. I'm not leaving with nothing.

So the next morning, Thursday, I did an evil thing. Dovid left early for a meeting of the synagogue board. I remember those meetings: my father used to attend them. Four hours at least of old men expressing the same point several times very slowly. I had time. Esti had school in the afternoon but not the morning. She and I were alone in the house, but there was no fear in her. She had been more relaxed, more whole, since Dovid's return. That was best; it would make everything easier.

I walked to the shops. I understood my own intentions. I looked for exactly the right item. No near misses would do. I felt the guilt strike my face with heat when I asked for what I wanted and a voice in my head said she is not for you, this one.

And I said I thought I told you to shut up. I *thought* I killed you with chocolate cake and prawn sandwiches.

And the voice said no.

And I said fine, talk all you like. *I'm* not listening.

You are doing wrong, said nothing and no one.

Oh, what do you know? She's gay, any fool can see it. She fancies *women*. If you're so bothered by that, why didn't *you* make her straight?

There are more kinds of belonging than you know, Ronit, my joy. The world is not so easily categorized as you might prefer. And you are trying to steal that which you do not even desire.

Oh, what do you know about *desire*? That, at least, is our area, not yours. And what do you mean, steal? *I* found her first.

Childish games, my dear one. You are more than this.

And I said I will stoop to whatever I like, because I don't have to listen to you anymore. I have learned to disobey.

And the voice said other things, but my heart was hardened to them.

I crept into the house. I listened. Deep, penetrating silence. I could almost hear the motes of dust in the hallway softly settling on the dried flower arrangement, the pile of letters, the scuffed shoes lined up against the wall. Where would she be? A noise from the kitchen, a glass being put down. Of course. I turned the door handle. There she was, at the sink, staring into the garden, one arm wrapped around her waist, her hair in a collapsing bun, soft tendrils at her neck. I watched her for a moment. It's funny, but I'd forgotten that she was beautiful. There was a sensuousness to her, a grace in the angle of her jaw and the curve of her breast. I felt it then. I wanted what I had decided. Well, that's always been my way.

I walked over to her. She was absorbed in the view, twisting her hair around her fingers, thinking. I looked at the garden for a few seconds. The day was damp, mist curling through the trees, droplets clinging to the leaves. Esti was warm and slow-breathing next to me. I wanted, suddenly, to embrace her, to circle her waist with my arm, to gather the folds of her dress in my hands, to explore her again, as I used to. I ran my thumb slowly down her spine, from the nape of her neck to the curve of her buttocks. She turned around, not startled or surprised, but smiling. I let my hand rest on her waist and, with the other, offered her my gift.

"Here. For you. Hydrangeas."

Chapter Ten

It is a vitally important commandment always to be happy.
                                                    Chasidic saying

How is it possible always to be happy? Does not King Solomon tell us that there is a time for weeping and a time for laughter? Should we attend at a house of mourning, show our beaming faces to the bereaved, and declare, "Be happy"? Such behavior should be far from us. What, then, is the meaning of the commandment to be always happy?

To answer this question, it is necessary first to understand the nature of human happiness. Happiness is not the same as comfort; it is not necessarily to be found in ease, in luxury and plenty. Ease, luxury, and plenty are not shameful, but they are not happiness. Too much comfort can, in fact, cause weakening of the body, depression of the spirit, and despair of the soul. We human beings, like the Lord Almighty Who created us, yearn to build. Our happiness, in this world at least, is to be found in creation.

And when we are creating, any fleeting pain becomes not only irrelevant, but actually joyful. An example. One who walks by mistake into a birthing room might think, at first glance, that he has entered a torture chamber. The room is covered with blood. At the center, a woman is screaming in agony while attendants look on.

The scene is medieval in its cruelty. And yet. Were we to ask this woman, in the instant at which the pain is most extreme, whether she is *unhappy*, we would be met with incomprehension. She may be worried, exhausted, experiencing physical agony, but *unhappy*? Absurd. This is the happiest day of her life. Because that which she has built, that which she has created in her inmost self, is about to burst forth.

Happiness is not a sensation of ease and comfort. Happiness is the deeper satisfaction we find when we create: when we construct a physical object, or compose a work of art, or raise a child. We experience happiness when we have touched the world and left it different, according to our will. We experience the *greatest* happiness when we have touched the world and left it *better*, according to the Will of the Almighty.

And though the work itself may be on occasion enjoyable, certain works can only be accomplished through struggle. Thus it is that happiness often resides where we find pain. And the greatest agony often presages the greatest triumph.

Red. It had begun as a film of red, a passage of circles surrounding and rebounding. The red was in the circles of his eyes, in the roundness of his head, singing through his ears like a train, around and around, its curve allowing no purchase. It was a vector of destruction, a soft and unfortunate muffling, concealing its true identity.

When he woke, it was barely anything. A less experienced man might have disregarded it. He imagined himself as a guide, taking tourists around his head. "You see this," he said, indicating the swirling circles of gentle red gathering on the horizon. "Doesn't look like much, does it? But in an hour or two, mark my words, there'll be a raging storm here." The tourists gasped, bewilderment mixing with skepticism, gazed fearfully at the far-off clouds, and walked to shelter. Far away, red gathered.

Dovid wondered sometimes if the headaches were always there, at the edges. If, like weather, they never really went away, only became subtler, less demanding. Even while feeling quite well, if he took his thoughts around his head he could find the shadow of one cooling its heels in his temples or the bridge of his nose. Sometimes, when a headache had shrunk him so that he could only gaze fixedly at a single tiny object—a smooth stone, or the rubber on the end of a pencil—he wondered what it was doing with all the room it had made, whether some secret process was taking place in the fractured other segments of himself. Perhaps it was he himself who did these things. Often, at the times of greatest agony, Dovid had the disconcerting feeling that some element of his mind was observing his discomfort, noting it down and commenting, "Yes, this is interesting."

"Dovid, what are you doing?" asked Kirschbaum, the secretary, sharply. Kirschbaum *was* sharp, from the point of his nose to the crisp corners of his shirts and the glinting buttons of his jacket. Dovid's eyes hurt to look at him, but he supposed he could not go on indefinitely staring at the rubber end of his pencil, absorbing its comforting and insightful roundness. He raised his head, allowing a few circles of red to slide down into his neck. The boardroom was paneled in wood and furnished in leather. He rested his gaze on the blond panels just above Kirschbaum's head and strove to make a remark. He said:

"Hmmm?"

"On the morning of the hesped, Dovid, what are you doing?"

Dovid wondered if it was time to lower his head yet. The red circles invaded his eyes, tiny and clustering. They chattered there, among themselves, and every time he tried to look at them, they moved away, remaining forever at the edge of his vision. He knew this was a very bad sign indeed. He explained the matter to his imaginary brain-tourists, gratified by their cowering and shivering. He wondered whether he himself ought to be cowering somewhere. Home. Bed. Sleep. Yes. No. He could not return home. It was vital to be here, to listen to all that was being said, to understand it all. It was vital because something was happening. Something he did not want, something out of his control. Red beads rolled and tumbled inside the dome of his skull, cutting off lines of enquiry.

"Now, now, Kirschbaum," said Hartog. "Dovid doesn't need to do anything. Just arrive like any other guest, Dovid. That's best."

Hartog sounded concerned. The red circles, jostling one another, began to tumble out of Dovid's ears onto the table. He wondered why the other board members couldn't see them, then realized that, of course, they vanished once they left his body.

It had all begun so much better than this.

The morning had been clear, insightful, and sharp. It was often that way on red days. The beginning of red, a transparent, crystalline pink, manufactured the world in perfect order. The air saluted. A slight hum behind his eyes assured him that all was well. He knew better than to believe it.

In bed, before rising, he made his calculations. His wife was curled alongside him, the two beds pushed together to make one, although he was sure—certain, in fact—that the time for this had passed. Her nightgown was rucked up, swirled between her thighs. He buried his face in her shoulder, inhaling her biscuity fragrance. She stirred, sighed, and settled back into sleep. He put his arm around her waist. Nothing more, the decisive pink made apparent. Nothing more than this was possible, but this, itself, was something.

The beds had been pushed together when he returned from Manchester, a large sheet spread over them, making them one again. He had stood, staring at the beds for several minutes, wondering if he ought to comment or if it would be better to say nothing. He could not remember when they had last slept together in one bed; perhaps their first year of marriage? Yes, it might have been then. He decided to say nothing. She also said nothing. It was, Dovid reflected, best. Words would only have complicated this simple thing.

Nonetheless, he found a perilous joy in those next few days. There was a sweetness in allowing his hand to brush against her back or shoulder while they lay in bed. On the pink morning, he found that she had rolled near to him in her sleep, that she was curled like a mouse facing him, that her hair touched his arm. She was close enough that he could feel the warmth of her body in the nest they had made. He looked into her face and smelled her breath. Its scent was warm bread. It had been a long time.

He remembered an incident from their wedding day. He recalled almost nothing of the day itself, only moments: the terrible lurch when he was lifted up on his chair during the dancing, the way his hand had trembled as he placed the ring on her forefinger, and the vast crowds of smiling faces. He remembered her, cool beside him. And he remembered the half hour they had spent alone together, in the midst of all the confusion. It is the law. After the wedding ceremony, the bride and groom must spend a little time together, alone in a room, witnessed as they enter, witnessed as they leave.

The room set aside for this purpose at the Rav's synagogue was a small windowless antechamber, a storage place for the festival prayer books. They were stacked in cardboard boxes against the walls. A space had been cleared in the center of the room and a folding table and two chairs set up. Someone had thought to leave some small sandwiches and plastic cups of fruit juice. Dovid remembered that Esti had walked across the threshold of the room first and that, as he walked in behind her, one of the guardians of the gatepost, an uncle of Esti's in his late fifties with a small mustache, had winked and smiled at him. As though they shared some knowledge, although, he reflected, they shared the very opposite of that. The purpose of this yichud room is privacy. It is the first creation of that space which lives forever between a husband and a wife, and which only they inhabit. What he shared with Esti's uncle, Dovid supposed, what all married men shared, was the knowledge that that secret space existed, the understanding that each possessed a room whose contents would remain forever hidden.

Esti's dress seemed to fill three quarters of the room. It billowed around the table leg and nudged up against the boxes. Within it, she seemed small and inconsequential, an ornament for the dress. Dovid almost wished she would take it off. He experienced a sharp pang, somewhere between joy and pain, when he realized that later in the day she would take off her dress. That he would be present. That even this was no longer forbidden. She sat down. He sat down. She looked at him.

Dovid had studied for three months the laws pertaining to marriage, those governing the contract between husband and wife and those dealing with more intimate relations. But his knowledge was nothing in the face of this slender woman and the life pulsing through the blue veins in her wrists. Dovid had never before done so much as hold the hand of a woman. He wondered how he should proceed. It had all seemed so obvious when he had decided on marriage, so simple when she had agreed. But now, what was to be done?

Esti cast her eyes downward at his hand resting on the table. Her own pale hands were in her lap. With the lightest of touches, she ran a single finger along the back of his hand. It was the first time they had touched. He had not anticipated how soft the pads of her fingers would be. He had never before considered the pads of the fingers of any other human being. He could find no words that seemed appropriate to express this.

She took his hand in hers and brought it, gently, to her face. She held it there, his palm cupping her chin and jaw. He could feel the fine hairs of her cheek, her fingerprints burning into the back of his hand. They sat together like that for a long while.

Dovid knew nothing, he realized, of the contents of Esti's mind. He could not hope to discover, let alone understand, what thoughts moved her as she sat holding his hand to her cheek. He was alone, in the smallness of the room, in the space within him. And yet they were both together, alone. He understood, as if the knowledge had been waiting for him in this windowless chamber. That was, at bottom, what it amounted to. To be alone, together.

That thought returned to him as he lay in bed, crystalline pink, watching her sleep. Alone. Together.

There were six members of the synagogue board. They would have been seven with the Rav. A divine number, as the Rav used to point out, the days of creation. A useful number, as Hartog had it, an odd number with no possibility of a stalemate in voting. In any case, a good number. But now they were six, and decisions would still have to be reached.

They passed easily over the first few items of business: agreeing to repoint the synagogue's brickwork before the winter, raising the membership fee by fifty pounds. The debate over the hesped began sedately: quick agreement on how the tables in the hall should be arranged, a brief discussion about which caterer to appoint. No expense should be spared, this was certain, particularly because so many eminent figures would be attending from around the world.

The pink slowly deepened into red. As the color accumulated drop by drop, Dovid found that the words of the board members began to lose meaning. It was something like listening to a conversation while falling asleep. Some sentences would be perfectly comprehensible, but then he would find that the words had vanished, that he had missed some important point. The discussion gradually began to lose coherence. They were discussing how the honored guests should best be treated. Or was it . . . no, now they seemed to be discussing where the wives should sit? Or, no? The order of the speakers, how long each should speak for. There. Something there. He had heard his name. He struggled, concentrated, and pushed back the tide of red, splitting it to make a dry path.

"Yes?" he said.

"Dovid, at what point in the service would you like to speak?" Rigler asked. He was holding a pencil, running it down a list on a sheaf of papers. "We think, perhaps, the end would be best. A *grand finale!*" Rigler smiled a little too eagerly.

Dovid blinked.

"Now, now," said Hartog, "let's not frighten Dovid. There's no need for it to be seen as a grand finale. Simply a fitting end to the service."

Around the table, the men nodded.

"But I don't," said Dovid, "I don't *want* to speak. It's not, I mean, I'm not. Someone else, surely?"

"No, no," said Kirschbaum, "we are quite convinced. We've discussed the matter at some length. It will be quite right for you to speak. And, perhaps"—he paused, looked at Hartog, who nodded—"also to take over one or two of the Rav's other duties. To give the sermon on Shabbat, for example. After the hesped is over, naturally. We wouldn't want to rush things."

Dovid looked around the table. Red pulsed at the corners of his eyes, a drumbeat, a military march. There was pain now. It increased steadily, beat by beat. He summoned his strength and stared at the red, congealing it into a single point of blood above his left eye. He held it there, throbbing and complaining. He was making it worse by refusing. There was no refusing, in the end. Concentrate, concentrate.

"You mean," he said, aware that his speech was a little slurred, "you mean until we appoint a new Rav?"

The men around the table leaned back and smiled.

"Perhaps," said Hartog.

And Dovid knew. He grasped, all at once, Hartog's intentions, those of the board. But the red precluded full understanding. Its force gathered. It was creeping out again, soaking through the interior of his skull fiber by fiber, invading him.

"No," he said. "No, I can't, I'm not." He looked at the men. A swarm of red encircled them.

Hartog leaned back in his chair. He spread his arms, broad and expansive. He said, "It is time for this coyness to be over, Dovid."

The table turned their heads to Hartog, swift as birds. Red pounded in Dovid's head.

Hartog smiled again. "We need you," he said. "The community

needs you. You were at the Rav's right hand. You will not, obviously, *be* the Rav. But the community needs order, continuity. You will provide it for us. We have, after all, provided your education for this purpose, Dovid."

Red had reached its zenith. It was strong, a mighty power, a sea of red, held back only by his will. Soon, very soon, it would break through all defenses, sweeping over him like a tide of scalding water, defeating him.

He saw the whole thing as if it had already occurred. He saw how it would happen, so simply, so smoothly. Inch by inch, he would be given the Rav's place. It had already been connived at. He would speak from the Rav's book and from his notes. He would speak *of* the Rav. He would give an illusion of unchanging continuity. He would desiccate, like an elderly book. He had, as Hartog said, been prepared for this role. He could tolerate it. But Esti.

"But my wife," was all he managed to say.

"Yes," said Hartog, "we have considered that. We know that you have held back. Your wife, it is difficult. She is not, perhaps, ideally *suited* to this role. This place may not be right for her. But we would be happy"—Hartog beamed, a demonstration of happiness—"to enable her to spend much of her time elsewhere. She has family in Israel, yes? It would, perhaps, be appropriate for her to spend more time there, away from the demands of the synagogue."

Red circled and recircled a thought in Dovid's mind. He thought, I will lose her. If you make me do this thing I will lose her. She will not return, whether you send her away or not. He thought, I may already have lost her. He thought, perhaps that is best. He thought, this place kills women, it bleeds them dry. Red took up that thought. It enjoyed it, rolling it back and forth in the tide of his mind.

"There is no need, of course, for this to be decided now. We have time. All that is needed today is to arrange the hesped. This, at least, is simple. You will speak, Dovid."

Dovid strained to think. This was, he realized later, a mistake. There should be no struggle on a red day, not when the strings were so tight, so precise. As he worried at his mind he felt something strain, then snap. Red broke through, small circles marching in the corners of his eyes, chattering. Not now, not now. Oh, yes, said red. Now.

"You will speak," said Hartog. It was not a question.

Red overcame him. There could be no more arguing now.

"Yes," whispered Dovid.

Red surged and pounded. It began to trickle out from its bright spot, out, out across his skull, more powerful than he had known. He found that he was breathing more deeply, more quickly. Red thrummed to the rhythm of his pulse. It was coming and the only thing left was surrender, to let it be over quickly, smoothly, without fuss. Since childhood, Dovid had kept a certain phrase for moments like this, unbearable moments. He considered it now, turned it over and over. He thought of nothing else, as red boiled in his skull, bubbling and spitting, preparing to burst forth, raw-hot from his ears, his mouth, his nose, his eyes. This is only pain, he thought, all that this is, all that it can possibly be, is pain. It cannot do anything more. Just pain. Only pain. Like a diver casting off into the ocean, he took a breath and went down into red.

Hartog drove Dovid home. The interior of the car smelled of leather and paint, a stench that reached inside him, revolved in his stomach, conspired with red in flashes of color. Hartog tried to speak to him when they reached the house, but Dovid could not remain. He needed to be inside. Bed. Cool. Complete. All that had transpired could be considered soon, when sleep had drained the red from his skull. He aimed his key at the lock precisely, well done, well done, and opened the door. The house was quiet. Solitary. Very well. Better than noise, better than confusion and concern. Feet must go on stairs. One by one. Each step forced some red back into his head, bubbling and puncturing the center of his ears, but the steps were only thirteen, he had counted them before. And then it would be over, and then there would be a cool blank space of rest. He paused at the top of the stairs, panting. A sound of great rushing was in his ears, and all the objects around him seemed streaked with light: the bookcase, the laundry basket, a bunch of pink and blue flowers lying incongruously on it. How odd, thought a part of his mind separate from the rest. Flowers.

Nonetheless, the house was quiet and his bed was near, promising white space and blankness. All this, all this, could be considered later. He closed his eyes, resting his hand on the small table next to the stairs. He need not open them again. He had walked these steps many times before with his eyes closed to keep the brightness in. From here it was four steps to the bedroom door, five steps to the bed, and then nothing, nothing more was necessary. He took a step. Red danced behind his eyelids. Another step, quiet, quiet, not to disturb any element of his skull. But the house was not quiet. It seemed to laugh and rustle. Was it the house? The bedroom? The red within him? Very hard to know. Another step. He was almost sure that the sigh, the light sound of movement was not part of the red, but to ascertain this would mean the opening of eyes and all he could possibly achieve was bed. He took the final step and opened the door.

The brightness at first. Such that he imagined the sun must be standing at the window, opening its mouth at the room. He wanted to open his eyes. He wanted to close them more, double or triple close them because once was not enough to keep this out. He could hear the light in his ears and it sounded like sharp, painful music. Beautiful and terrible all together.

He opened his eyes. Bad move, said red, stupid, idiotic move. Yes, he said, I know. But I have to see. The instant elongated. Red was breaking through, surging upward, crashing over his head and down his body, boiling him alive. It was fine. He saw what he needed to see.

In the bed, there was not perfect blankness and whiteness.

There was his wife and there was her lover. Esti had wrapped a sheet around herself, but imperfectly, one tender pink nipple was bare, and her hair was let down around her shoulders. Ronit had a face of fear and he wanted to say it's all right, it's all right, but he had only two or three words at best and he wanted to keep them, emergency rations. Because he could see Esti: not one, but two.

He thought, and the thought amused him: then I have lost her already. But still, all this can be is pain.

She said, "Dovid."

"Yes," he said, "I know."

It's funny, some element of Dovid chattered, how this headache is not ending at all. I thought that it was spent, that it had produced all the fire it could, but it has simply become more cunning, better concealed. I shall have to remember. The knowledge will be useful for the future. The flames spread quickly across his face, down his neck, into his chest, his arms, the small of his back. When his hips and the backs of his legs began to burn, he dropped to his knees and knew nothing more.

Scott's wife, Cheryl, is a doctor. I never really thought much about her, it must be said, but I picked up that much from the odd snippets he'd drop into conversation. It's funny, before Scott I always imagined that the wives of men who have affairs would be mousy little things, stay-at-home mums, who the guys stay with for the sake of the kids or because they can't bear to hurt something so defenseless. But no, Scott's wife is an epidemiologist. While he's at the office, slaying another corporate dragon, she's off researching vaccination patterns or delivering a paper on, I don't know, why it's important to cover your mouth when you cough or something. They're a power couple. They look it in the framed picture on his desk, he in a casual open-necked shirt exposing a tuft of chest hair, she in a cream blouse and a necklace of small blue flowers; their white-blond children, a boy and a girl, stand in front of them, tidy and smiling. I don't know, he can be so dirty, so vulgar and crude and funny when we're together, but there he is, looking like the American dream.

He said to me once, "Marriage is an enigma, Ronnie. You barely understand it when you're in it, and no one on earth can understand it from the outside."

He was pretty drunk.

I said, "What about us? Aren't we an enigma, too?"

"Sure, sure. But you, you make me happy. Y'know? We have fun. But she is my *wife*. That's a sacred thing. Do you see what I'm saying?"

I kind of did see what he was saying. Of course, I was pretty drunk, too.

Scott always said that if Cheryl found out about us, it'd be over. In fact, it was over sooner than that. She asked a couple of awkward questions, didn't take his usual answers. She started demanding to know where he'd been, with whom. Just that.

He was so apologetic, I remember. That was what annoyed me. He held my hand and kept apologizing and apologizing as though he'd killed my cat or something. As he kept on, I got more and more angry. I just wanted him to be quiet. He'd never promised me anything, I'd never promised him anything. There was no need to apologize.

That night, I did a thing I'd never done before. It was about seven o'clock. I knew he'd still be in the office, but Cheryl would be home with the kids. I called his house. She answered the phone after a few rings. She said, "Hello? Hello?" I sat in silence for a few seconds. There was a kind of potential in those seconds, like when you're doing ninety down the fast lane of a motorway, really smooth and easy, flying past all the traffic, and it suddenly occurs to you that if you just flicked your wrist a couple of inches to the right you'd die. Just like that. I listened to the silence like I was watching the speedometer push upward: ninety-three, ninety-four, ninety-five, and then I put the phone down.

I wanted Esti to call an ambulance. As soon as Dovid collapsed, I reached for the bedroom phone. She pulled it out of my hands, wrapping her arms around it and clasping it to her chest. She spoke softly.

"No. No. This has happened before. Sometimes, when it's really bad . . ." She petered out, then looked directly at me. "It's happened before. We just wait. It'll pass. He wouldn't want us to make any fuss."

I looked down at Dovid, crumpled awkwardly on the bedroom floor, one leg painfully folded underneath him. His face was blue-white. His lips were gray. From the bed, I couldn't even see if he was breathing. I looked back at Esti, clasping the telephone.

"What are you talking about?"

"It's happened before. It's a private thing. No need for doctors."

Her eyes were large, her hair straggly around her shoulders. The skin of her stomach was rippled, folded over itself. My eyes were opened and I saw that we were naked.

I said, "We should put some clothes on. I'll help you get him into bed."

We dressed in silence, not looking at each other. I couldn't find my tights, but I didn't feel like scouting around under the bed for them. We lifted Dovid into bed. He looked more peaceful there. He *was* breathing after all, and looked a little less gray-faced.

I suppose it was for the best we didn't go to a hospital, really. How would I have explained my presence? Are you his sister? Well, no, I'm his wife's lover. Do you think if I stick around long enough I can finish him off?

Esti said, "He'll be like this for hours. He might wake up in the evening. Maybe tomorrow morning."

She looked at me. I looked at her.

She looked down at her watch.

She said, "I have to go to school. They're expecting me."

And she left.

I sat in the living room. I wanted to go to my father's house, to make another attack on it, to find my mother's candlesticks and leave. But I couldn't. The clock on the mantelpiece ticked. I wanted to go and sit in Dr. Feingold's nice safe office and tell her all about everything that'd happened over the past few weeks. I looked around the room. There was nothing to look at except the photograph of Esti and Dovid on their wedding day. I thought about Scott and Cheryl and about how it always seems to work out this way with me. I wanted to take back everything that I'd ever done, to start again from the moment of birth and see if I could make a better job of it next time. I couldn't do that either. I fidgeted. I was supposed to go back to New York soon. Maybe I could change my ticket? Go this afternoon? Tomorrow morning? The thought seemed utterly marvelous to me. Even the idea of how happy it'd make Hartog didn't unduly distress me. Wonderful. This time tomorrow I could be back in my own apartment, in my own life. All I had to do was let Esti know what I was doing.

I pulled on my running shoes and marched over to the Sara Rifka Hartog Memorial Day School.

The school wasn't exactly as I remembered it. It had crept from the two large houses it used to occupy into a third, another complicated network of staircases linking the new building in. The entrance was in a slightly different location. They'd done some building work at the back. Still, it was pretty much the same. I buzzed the intercom, told them I was there to see Esti Kuperman, and they let me in. Oh, yes, security as excellent as ever.

I looked around the hallway. Strange architecture—two front doors next to each other separated only by a stub of wall, two arching hallways mirroring each other, two staircases heading away from each other—the insides of two suburban houses, twisted and made strange. Displays of work on the history of Israel, a math project, some pieces of art. All mounted on colored craft paper, curling at the edges. The place still smelled the same, too, chalk and sweat and Copydex and old gym shoes. I couldn't very well go and see Esti in her classroom. God only knew what all those schoolgirls would make of me just turning up. But she'd probably come back to the staff room between classes. I wondered if everything was still where it used to be. Staff room. Basement, in the left-hand house. I headed down the left-hand stairs.

I actually paused in front of the staff-room door before knocking. I raised my hand to knock, and then just held it there, in midair. Looking at the notice that said, "Girls must not knock during break time except for the last ten minutes." Feeling intimidated by it. I held there for a few seconds, looking, thinking. And I knocked.

The door was opened by a rather pretty redheaded girl in her early twenties. Were the teachers at the school always this young? She looked suspicious, glancing down at my definitely nonregulation skirt and still-bare legs, but her face cleared when I mentioned Esti's name. Of course, I must come in and wait. She held the door wide for me, smiling. The staff room was empty;

a few battered armchairs, some lockers, and three desks held all the mystique that was to be found here. I sat down and put my feet up on the small table in the center of the room.

She offered me a coffee and I accepted gratefully. As she puttered with mugs, kettle, and teaspoons, she said:

"I'm Tali, by the way, Tali Schnitzler. I teach geography. And you?"

"I'm Ronit," I said. "Ronit Krushka. I'm, well, I guess, Esti's cousin-in-law."

There wasn't exactly a crash of broken mugs or a sudden gasp. But there was a definite pause in the proceedings. This Schnitzler turned her head around to look at me.

"Ronit Krushka? Are you the Rav's daughter?"

I nodded. She wished me a long life. I thanked her. She continued to look at me for a little too long, then turned back to the coffee making.

She attempted a smile as she handed me my mug.

"Esti will be back soon, I'm sure. I . . . I have to go now."

Schnitzler gathered her books and made her escape. I didn't wonder very long over what she was afraid of. It was pretty obvious by now. There could no longer be any concealment of anything, not even from myself.

I wonder, now, if everyone knew when we were in school. In a way, I can't see how they could have missed it. And in a way, I can't imagine that they would have suspected and done nothing. But we lit each other up, those few school-hydrangea years. We spent our breaks together in the playground, chasing each other or talking or climbing things, we studied together after school, we were at each other's houses for Shabbat and on Sundays. I suppose a lot of schoolgirls have friendships like that.

It was good, I can't deny it. At the time, it was good. We had a plan for a while, the three of us. Esti and I would go to seminary in Manchester, and Dovid would be there soon as well, back from Yeshiva in Israel. And then the three of us would be together. And then? I don't think we'd quite decided. Being together in the same city, away from my home seemed enough. I suppose even then I was swallowing something down, denying something. There was still a piece of tree bark in the skin under my elbow, after all.

All the other girls were surprised, I remember, when in the end Esti and I didn't even go to the same sem. My father had made me an offer I couldn't refuse. He sent me to Stern College in New York, a seminary and university combined. He said he thought it would suit me better, something more "modern." I did not question his decision; the mere idea of leaving seemed too wonderful to be real.

It happened quite simply after that. I avoided the other English girls—who tended to huddle together in any case, sharing hot water bottles and tea. I hung out with the American girls, then with the cool American girls who had TVs in their rooms, then with their cooler friends at NYU. And then I was off. It wasn't easy, but I made it happen, as though I'd made the decision without realizing in some deep, automatic part of my brain. I got a job, using my student visa, saved every dollar I could. I started cutting classes at sem, switched to more secular studies, more useful subjects. One of the NYU girls had an opening in her apartment.

I remember the feeling of putting down the deposit on that cramped little bedroom and moving my things in. It was a great, glorious open feeling, like I'd just unsealed my lungs for the first time and realized that there was air to breathe.

You can only save yourself, says Dr. Feingold, but at least you can do that.

Esti and I went walking. We couldn't go far. Esti was due back in lessons shortly, so we ended up taking several turns around the school playground. Although it was still warm, the sky was iron-gray, that gray that English skies take on for days at a time, constantly threatening to rain but never quite working up the enthusiasm. Autumn was coming. Two large black birds were wrestling with a half-eaten burger the wind must have blown into the playground. They were holding it down with their feet, tearing chunks off, gulping it down, beaks to the sky.

I said:

"I came to tell you that I'm going to leave. This isn't my place. I can't stay here anymore. I'll move my plane ticket. I'll leave tomorrow or the next day."

She sighed, bit her lower lip, stared at the birds some more. One of them was trying to fly off with half a bun in its mouth, but couldn't quite achieve takeoff. I wondered if Esti had even heard me.

She took a deep breath in and said:

"Leaving again, Ronit? Why is it, do you think, that you're always leaving or planning to leave?"

I wasn't shocked. Not really. It wasn't a shocking sort of conversation. We were just staring at these two huge black birds and talking like we were discussing why it is that I like apples but not apple pie. Her speech was quite casual, just like that. I thought, okay then, if that's how it is. Fine. I said:

"Why is it that you never ask me to stay?"

She smiled and looked down at her hands, and then back up. She didn't look at me, just at the birds, cawing and parading.

"I think because I couldn't bear to hear you say no. Better not to ask."

We looked some more, at the birds and the pieces of cardboard wrapping blowing around the playground. She hugged her arms to her ribs. She said:

"I knew before you did, I think, that you were going to leave. I saw you slipping away and when they sent you to America I thought you would never come back. And you didn't."

I should have let it lie.

"I did come back, Esti. A couple of times when I was at college, in the vacations."

She smiled again, a mournful half-smile.

"You came back to tell me you were leaving. Don't you remember, you told me your plan?"

I didn't remember.

"You told me you'd got a job in a bank. It was after your first year at Stern. We sat on your bed. We were staring at the ceiling and holding hands. And you said, 'I've got a job.'"

"What did you say?"

"I asked you what it was. Right then, before you went into details, talking about apartments and passports, I knew you'd never come back. You were scarcely there, even that visit."

I did remember, maybe a little. Maybe a tiny bit. Maybe just the feeling of holding her hand in mine.

What is the truth? How is it possible to reach out to that person I was and ask the question? If these words, and these, and these, had been spoken, would I have stayed? Sometimes I think that she was nothing to me, nothing at all, that I shrugged her off and never looked back. But it's more complicated than you think, how you feel about a person. Sometimes I think that if she'd asked me, even once, to stay, I would have stayed forever. The Rabbis teach that we each hold worlds within us. Maybe both these things are true. But she never asked. And so I had to leave.

I said, "Esti, why did you marry him?"

She said, "You were gone."

"I was gone, so you, what, jumped on the nearest available body?"

She passed a hand across her brow.

"That's not. It's not. You know that Dovid and I don't . . ."

Her voice trailed off into empty air. I thought, now, right now. This is, as it turns out, the moment I came to London for. I said:

"Esti, you fancy girls, don't you?"

She nodded.

"And you don't fancy men, do you?"

She shook her head.

"And you're married to a man, aren't you?"

She nodded again.

I spread my hands wide.

"Well, now, Esti, doesn't there seem to be something wrong with this picture to you?"

She sighed. I waited. Her skin was even whiter than usual, I noticed, and creased under the eyes, at the corners of her mouth. At last, she said:

"Do you remember 'tomorrow is the new moon'? The story of David and Jonathan?"

I nodded.

"And do you remember how much David loved Jonathan? He loved him with 'a love surpassing the love of women.' Do you remember?"

"Yes, I remember. David loved Jonathan. Jonathan died in battle. David was miserable. The end."

"No, not the end. The beginning. David had to go on living. He had no choice. Do you remember who he married?"

I had to think about that one. It'd been a good few years since I last learned Torah. I sifted around the facts in my brain and eventually came up with it.

"He married Michal. They weren't very happy. Didn't she insult him in public, or something?"

"And who was Michal?"

It clicked. I understood. Michal was Jonathan's sister. The man he loved with all his heart died, and he married his sister. I thought about that for a moment, taking it in. I wondered whether Michal and Jonathan had looked anything like each other. I thought about King David and his grief, his need for someone like Jonathan, near to Jonathan. I was quite moved, until I realized that this idea was insane.

I said, "Esti you have got to be kidding. You married Dovid because you think you're David, King of the Jews?"

She sighed and ran her hand through her hair.

"Oh, Ronit, why do you always . . ." She paused and shook her head. "Why must you always make a joke out of serious things?"

Ah, I thought, why is the sky blue? Why does love never last?

"But, Esti, it's bonkers! I wasn't dead. You weren't the King. There's a whole world out there to live in. Go and have a look!"

Esti sighed again.

The two black birds had finished with their burger. They were stalking across the tarmac away from us, pecking at any speck or shiny thing that caught their eye.

"Dovid was always there, Ronit. He cared for me and, in a way, I cared for him. He seemed so, I don't know, so peaceful. I thought, at least this way I'll have some peace."

The wind blew, cold and shrill. It penetrated the thinness of my shirt, swirled the pieces of rubbish around the playground, lifting them up.

I said, "And did you find it? Did you find peace?"

"Yes, I think that I did."

"And did you find happiness?"

"In a way, Ronit." She looked at me. "Perhaps you can't understand this, but in a way I found happiness, too."

"And is it still enough for you?"

Disobedience

She reached her arms around me, resting her head on my chest. I stroked her back and kissed her forehead. Away, across the playground, I could see the rows of schoolgirls and teachers in their classes. Some were looking at their blackboards and their books, and some were looking at us, at me and Esti standing in the playground together. I said nothing. I pulled Esti more tightly toward me and held her, like that, in my arms.

Chapter Eleven

And God said, let us make man, in our likeness, in our image.
Genesis 1:26

I n the beginning of God's creating the world, He made three types of creatures: the angels, the beasts, and the human beings.

Angels, He created from His pure word. The angels have no will to do evil, they go about the world simply performing their Creator's commands. Angels cannot rebel. They cannot deviate for one moment from His purpose; all that they are is His will. They know nothing else.

Beasts, in a similar fashion, have only their instinct to guide them. Does a lion do wrong when he devours the shivering lamb? By no means. He, too, is following the commands of his Maker, which he knows in the form of his own desires.

The Torah tells us that God spent almost all of the six days of creation fashioning these creatures and their dwelling-places. But just before sunset on the sixth day, He took a small quantity of earth and from it He fashioned man-and-woman. An afterthought? The crowning achievement? The matter is not clear. And the sun set, the day was over, and creation was complete.

What is this thing, man-and-woman? It is a being with the power to disobey. Alone among all the creatures proceeding from the mouth of the Lord, human beings have freedom of will. We do not hear simply the pure voice of the Almighty as the angels do. We are not ruled by blind instinct like the beasts. Uniquely, we can listen to the commands of God, can understand them, yet can choose disobedience. It is this, and only this, which gives our obedience its value.

This is the glory of mankind, and this is its tragedy. God has veiled Himself from us, that we may see a part of His light, but not the whole of it. We hang suspended between two certainties: the clarity of the angels and the desires of the beasts. Thus, we remain forever uncertain. Our lives present us with choices, further choices and more choices, each multiplying, our ability to find our way forever in doubt. Unhappy creatures! Luckiest of all beings! Our triumph is our downfall, our opportunity for condemnation is also our chance for greatness. And all we have, in the end, are the choices we make.

It was raining in the freezer. A soft rain, splashing down, gathering, pouring onto the floor. The rain had carved glassy pathways of ice and meltwater. There were stalactites and areas of snow, wastelands and hidden, cold places behind the pipes. From time to time a great crack resounded as a piece of ice broke off.

On the kitchen floor, the rainwater had gathered into a small, ice-cold lake, a tiny perfection of winter. Esti dabbled her fingers in the pool of water, thrilling to the cold wetness. There was a release of the scents that had been frozen solid, a slightly chemical, stale odor. There was a rhythmic drip, drip, drip. She found herself imagining the moment when the job would be complete, when the freezer would regain its creamy professionalism. It made her a little sad. But she had only just begun: the thaw would be hours yet.

Esti had woken at dawn. It was Friday, there were things to be done. She ought to begin work. And yet. She remained lying next to Dovid, whose profound sleep still continued from the previous day. There was a twist in her stomach. She thought of the work that was to be done, the food that must be prepared. She felt increasingly nauseous. She wondered if she had eaten bad food, or whether she had caught some seed of illness from one of the pupils. The nausea became urgent, thick like the scent of burning meat in her nostrils or a catch at the back of her throat. She ran to the bathroom, remembering that of course there was a reason. She hadn't expected it so soon. Things were progressing; nothing remained the same. Drip, drip, drip.

She cleaned herself and dressed. She was already behind schedule. Very well, she thought, and the thought was all calmness, all order. Very well. This Friday will be different. The kitchen felt her difference when she entered it. "Where are the chickens?" it seemed to say. "Where the soup, where the challot? Where, oh where, is the potato kugel?" Esti spoke to the kitchen gently. She said, I will show you a new way.

The freezer had grown blooms of ice, stretching pawlike across its walls and ceiling. She turned it off at the plug and smiled to hear its comfortable purr judder to a halt. She opened the door and began to remove the packets and boxes of food. She placed towels around the foot of the freezer. She found she was singing, a song from long ago, when she had been a schoolgirl.

At seven a.m., the telephone began to ring. There were, Esti knew, a very limited number of reasons that she might be telephoned at seven a.m. Mrs. Mannheim, the headmistress of the school, might, for example, have something important to say to her about certain things that might have been seen in the school playground the previous day. Esti walked into the hallway and stared at the telephone, sending her unwelcoming thoughts down the wires. It stopped ringing. A few minutes later it began again. She picked up the handset, walked into the kitchen, and put the telephone in the fridge. It continued to ring, cold and muffled. Esti was satisfied.

At eight o'clock she found herself deeply hungry. She made a stack of thick pancakes, anointed with lemon and sugar. She ate, rolling each crisp, warm mouthful across her tongue, chewing with delight. She could not remember the last time she had cooked like this only for herself. Was her food always this good? It had never been quite this delicious, surely? The telephone rang again, shivering in the fridge. She could just hear it if she placed her ear to the refrigerator door. She listened courteously until it was done. Shortly afterward, she heard the sound of stirring upstairs. Ronit? No, not loud enough, no banging. Just gentle, methodical movement. She walked upstairs.

Dovid was sitting on the side of the bed. He looked tired and sad. His hair was rumpled, his skin hadn't quite lost the previous day's grayness. She touched his forehead, brushing his fringe to one side. She rested one fingertip between his eyes, at the place where his frown had creased a deep line.

"How is it in here?"

"It's all right. A bit fuzzy still."

"Does it hurt?"

"No, not really. Only as much as it always does. Esti?"

Dovid's hands were folded in front of him, but she could see the words forming in his head. She felt resentful. This was not how they were. This was not how they had lived, all these years. This, at least, they were never supposed to have: questions and recriminations, interrogations and assaults. Where they were together, they were together. Where they were separate, nothing further should be attempted. Even now, with the idea of a notion of a beginning of life within her, there should be no questions.

Dovid said, "Can we go out? For a walk?"

Esti looked at him for a long time, taking him in: his hair, fine and brown, thinning on top, the constant rosy blush at the sides of his cheeks, the little rounded belly peering over his trousers. Downstairs, in the fridge, the telephone began to ring again.

"Yes. Let's do that."

There are parks in Hendon. There are parks and trees, with wild grass growing and open-faced hills sweeping down to the Brent Cross Flyover and the A41. Once upon a time, long ago, there were farms here and farm people. Traces remain: stone-built houses and ancient roads with crooked names, though London has silted up this place that once was farmland. In the center of the city, the land has quite forgotten that it was ever tilled and sown, though once it was. But Hendon, lacking age and wealth, remembers the seed and the soil.

We who live in Hendon now like to imagine ourselves elsewhere. We carry our homeland on our backs, unpacking it where we find ourselves, never too thoroughly nor too well, for we will have to pack it up again one day. Hendon does not exist; it is only where we are, which is the least of all ways to describe us. Nonetheless there is a kind of beauty here, in the scratched-open places and the remains of agriculture. All beauty touches the human heart, be it only so small as an ant or a spider. Our ancestors, we can be sure, felt a sense of it in Poland or in Russia, in Spain and Portugal and Egypt and Syria and Babylon and Rome. Why should we regret that we find a sort of kindness in the tamed land of Hendon? It is not our place, and we are not its people, but we have found affection here. And, as King David told us, God is in all places, high and low, distant and near at hand. As surely as He is anywhere, God is in Hendon.

Esti and Dovid sat on the remains of a fallen tree and looked down the hillside toward the curve of the North Circular Road.

"Well," said Dovid.

"Well," said Esti.

They sat for a moment in silence. The morning was warm, the sun beginning to burn the dew from the grass.

"So," said Dovid, "did you do anything interesting yesterday?"

Esti looked up at him. He was smiling a nervous half-smile.

She remembered this, from a long time ago. She wrinkled her nose.

"Let me think. No . . . I can't think of . . . oh, wait, I finished all the washing-up."

Dovid nodded. "Right."

"How about you?"

Dovid glanced up at the tree bending its branches over them, and at the sky beyond that: an uncertain blue, turning to white.

"Apart from the shul board? No, not much. Boring day really. I had a bit of a headache."

Esti nodded. Without analysis, she rested her head on his shoulder. He put his arm around her waist. It was solid and warm. They looked out over the hillside, down toward the children's playground, the tennis courts, and the rushing tides of the North Circular.

He said, "Did you ever lie on your back on a hill like this—a place with a big sky? When you were a child?"

She said, "I think so. I can't remember."

He squeezed her waist. "Let's do it now. Let's lie on our backs and look at the clouds."

Yes, she said in her heart, yes.

"Someone might see."

He smiled at that.

"They already know. I think we can safely say they've worked it out."

It was better, side by side, looking upward together. She did not have to look at him and remember his face. She was not confused by the things she felt sorry for and the things she did not. She was simplified by the many-colored clouds, the sky, the birds. A glinting airplane left a white trail. They decided what shapes the clouds were: a teacup, a rhinoceros, the letter W, a man in a boat.

She thought to herself, we could remain here forever, like this. Nothing need ever be said. Perhaps this is what is meant by love.

She gathered her courage. She thought, this is not about love. Love is not the answer to anything. But speech, at least, can defeat silence.

She said, "What you saw, yesterday. Me and Ronit, what you saw . . ."

She stopped there. Love urged her to remain silent. Love is a secret thing, a hidden thing. It feeds in dark places. She said to her heart, I am *tired* of you. Her heart said, if you say this you will never be able to go back. She agreed that this was the case.

She said, "What you saw. It wasn't the first time. It began long ago."

The clouds moved silently through the sky, carrying shapes with them that would become other shapes and further shapes. Nothing remaining the same, not even for an instant. That was the truth of it.

She said, "It began when we were schoolgirls. Before I ever knew you. And it has . . ." She stopped again. Where were the moon and the stars when she needed them? Where was the gentle comfort of the night?

She said, "It has always been this way with me. No other way. I think I will never be any different than this."

Behind the sky, the stars and the moon continued to turn. In front of the sky, the clouds continued to be swept up by the winds and carried around the globe. It occurred to Esti that the world is very large and that Hendon is very small.

Dovid raised himself up on his elbows. He looked out toward the trees and the motorway beyond. Esti could see his face. He was smiling.

He said, "Have you thought all this time that I didn't know?"

See? said Esti's heart. Now look what you've done. Nothing will ever be the same. Even the past isn't the same anymore. Every element of your life must be reevaluated. Time to stop now. Say nothing. Be nothing.

She said, "Since when?"

He said, "Since before we were married, I think. In a way. Not completely."

She said, "Then why?"

He said, "I just. I didn't want you to shrink like this. I thought I could keep you safe. I was wrong. I'm sorry."

He leaned back and looked at the sky.

"If you want to go, I won't try to stop you."

"If I want to go with Ronit?"

"Yes. Or not. If you want to go. Away."

"Do you want me to go?"

Dovid thought, this is only pain. All that this can possibly be is pain. It cannot do anything significant.

He said, "I don't want you to stay if you want to go."

She thought of how that might work. She would go away, carrying the baby inside her like a present to be unwrapped elsewhere. She would live in some other, contrary fashion. She would be free to do as she pleased. She might become another sort of person entirely: make friends with a one-legged ex-fireman, set up her own pie-making business, cut off her hair and take up her skirts, draw and paint and learn the bassoon, take a lover to whom she might feed ripe strawberries and climb to the top of a tree in midwinter to gaze at the moon. She saw her life, in that moment, as a sort of fabric laid out before her, to be cut and shaped to her desire. She might choose something else. She might write her own story, for this, too, is a life that exists.

She laced her fingers into his. She said:

"Have you been happy, Dovid? Have I made you a bit happy?"

There was a long pause. She watched the clouds drift by, white, yellow, pink, gray. At last, he said, "Yes."

Her heart said, silence, silence is best. Say nothing now. Consider. Reflect.

She said, "I'm pregnant. We. We are pregnant."

They walked together back through Hendon toward the house. Hendon was busying itself for Friday. In the butcher's shop, the baker's, the greengrocer's, the delicatessen, people noticed them walking.

Esti thought, let them notice. That is for them to decide, not me. The thought made her smile. It was a new thought. Not Dovid's, not Ronit's. It did not belong to the silence that is appropriate to women. She held it tenderly in her mind. She felt there would be many more such thoughts to follow. A new way of thinking, not dominated by silence.

At home, Ronit was waiting for them, all awkwardness. Before they had entered the hallway, before they had removed their coats or shoes, she was already talking, describing plans she had made, how she needed to be on her way, would move her ticket to enable her to do so swiftly. She would leave on Sunday, they would not have to put up with her any longer, she wouldn't be attending the hesped, so at least they wouldn't have *that* to worry about. Maybe she could even move the ticket to Saturday, except that Hartog probably wouldn't like it and anyway it didn't seem respectful somehow, did they know what she meant?

Esti found the new place in her thoughts, the place that had opened up in the park. She saw that Ronit was afraid, that she was running away. Ronit thought she was running away from God, but in fact she was fleeing from silence. She would need to be shown that it did not need to be feared. That ceasing to flee from it did not mean that it had to be embraced.

Ronit said, "Umm . . . Esti, where's the telephone?"

I wanted to go. When I woke up that morning, all I wanted was to leave as soon as I could. It was quite clear to me that I'd been here too long, that everything would be much better for all concerned if I left. I packed in a hurry, gathering as many items of clothing as I could find, not worrying too much about the rest. It was ten o'clock, probably enough time to rearrange my flight for tonight, to call Hartog to set up our little assignation, to go. But no, bollocks, today was Friday. No driving for Hartog tonight. Well, maybe I could persuade him to let me go anyway, without an escort.

Except, a little snag. Phone nowhere to be found. Once or twice I thought I heard a faint ringing somewhere in the house, but wasn't able to trace it before the sound disappeared again. I asked God if He was deliberately concealing it from me for the purposes of teaching me a valuable moral lesson of some sort, but He remained resolutely silent on the subject.

In a kind of sadness, I pulled my cell phone out of a pocket in my bag and turned it on. It beeped mournfully, searching for a signal, then one long tone when it realized it couldn't find one. It was too far from home. I knew exactly how it felt.

I waited for Esti and Dovid. They took too long to come back. The sun was already low in the sky and I couldn't believe I was noticing this sort of thing and worrying about Friday by the time they reappeared. I thought maybe they'd been arguing, then I decided that one of them had probably killed the other, like Cain and Abel in a field somewhere.

I tried to argue with my father so many times. He was a difficult man to argue with. He believed in silence. It doesn't make for rip-roaring, gut-busting, passionate debate, trying to argue with someone who believes in silence. I could shout my lungs hollow at him and he wouldn't respond. He'd listen, with all appearance of attention, and when I was finished, he'd wait for a few moments and then turn back to his books. Dr. Feingold reminds me of him, just a little. In the velvety softness of her silence, in the pause after I finish speaking.

When he did speak, it was in allegory and metaphor.

When I was sixteen, the year before I left home forever, he found out that I'd been eating in a bakery that he didn't approve of. It wasn't a *nonkosher* bakery, God forbid, there was no ham or bacon, no cheese mixed with chicken or beef with butter. It had a certificate on its wall to prove that a Rabbi had been in there to watch the food being prepared. But it wasn't one of *our* bakeries, not supervised by Rabbis *we* trusted. For a small people, we do seem to enjoy subdividing. In any case, the news found its way to my father's ears that I had bought an egg sandwich from this bakery, and when I got home from school he beckoned me into his study. He said, "They tell me you have eaten from Streit's Bakery?" A hollow sensation in my stomach, a sudden dip and swoop. "Don't you know that we don't eat from there?" Yes, I knew. He looked at me, just looked. He said, "I'm disappointed in you. You know better than this." And there was a throbbing in my head, a kind of pressure from the inside, and I found that I was shouting. I can't remember everything I said. I know it wasn't all about egg sandwiches. I remember that I said, "It's no wonder that I hate you so much, because you never listen!" I remember that I said, "I wish I were dead like my mother!"

He said nothing. He listened, and when I'd finished shouting he turned back to his work.

My mother gave me my name: Ronit. It's not a usual name for where I come from, not typical. I should have been called Raisel, or Rivka, or Raeli. But my mother liked the name. Ronit. The joyful song of angels. I think about that sometimes; I could have changed my name when I moved to New York and changed everything else, but I didn't. Ronit: a song of joy, a voice raised in delight. The name my mother gave me.

They told me, those who would tell me, that my father and mother used to laugh together, before she died. That they could make each other laugh in a roomful of strangers with nothing more than a look. I have no way to tell. I can't remember her and I never heard him say three words together on the subject. She was the aching, absent heart at the middle of our lives and the words could never be spoken.

The next day, he told me the story of Cain and Abel, the sons of Adam and Eve. They argued in a field, and Cain killed Abel. But that verse, the place where the Torah tells us what they argued *about*, is unfinished. The line says, "And Cain said to his brother Abel." It doesn't say, "And Cain spoke to his brother" or "And Cain talked to his brother." It uses the word *vayomer*: he said. Something should come afterward. But it doesn't. It stops. The next sentence is: "And it happened when they were in the field that Cain rose up against Abel his brother and killed him."

My father said, over this, we pass in silence. Even the Torah does not enter into arguments between close family. Even the Torah uses silence here. That also made me shout at him. I can't stand revisiting those memories now. Shouting at this old, silent man. And the truth is, I understood what he meant.

Once Esti and Dovid returned, and Esti had passed me the phone, cold and covered in condensation, I called Hartog.

As he picked up the telephone, he was sniggering as though he'd just heard a wonderful joke.

"Hartog?" I said.

"Miss Krushka? Do forgive me; my wife and I were just laughing over . . ."

Plague? Pestilence? Flood? The death of innocents? I almost said.

" . . . well, it doesn't matter. What can I do for you, Miss Krushka?"

For all the world like we were friends. Reasonable people. Hartog, Hartog, I wanted to say, boychick, why can't we be honest with each other? Neither of us is a reasonable person.

"I was calling to say . . . that you won, Hartog. I know you wanted me to go before the hesped. Fine. I'm going, sooner than you asked. I'll go tomorrow night, or Sunday. A whole week early."

You weasel, you hound, you lowlife pond scum.

There was an intake of breath on the other end of the line. I could almost imagine the man smirking, mouthing to his wife, something. Perhaps I'm paranoid. Doesn't mean, of course, that they're not out to get me.

"Now, now, Miss Krushka, remember our little talk. Delighted as I am to hear that you're so eager to return home, I must insist that you stay until the day before the hesped, as we had agreed. I wouldn't . . ." He chuckled, a wheezy asthmatic sound. "I wouldn't want you having second thoughts and deciding to come *back*."

"Surely you don't—"

"No, no, Miss Krushka. We will keep to the original plan. The hesped is next Monday. You will fly out next Sunday evening. As you board the plane you will have your effects, and not before. And as you board the plane, you will receive your check." I could almost hear him smirking on the other end of the line. "I'm sure we understand each other."

I put down the phone and listened to the hum of the house or, possibly, the ringing in my ears. In the kitchen, Esti and Dovid were preparing the food for Shabbat. Together. They were talking in low voices.

I thought, I can't stay here. But I can't leave. Not if I want Hartog's money, my father's things.

In the kitchen, Esti said something that made Dovid laugh. I hadn't remembered what a deep laugh he has, a rich vibrato thrum. I didn't understand how this was possible: Esti and Dovid laughing in the kitchen. I picked up the telephone and listened to the purr of the dial tone until it turned angry.

I thought, I don't need his fucking money and I don't need his bagful of trinkets. The one thing that I wanted was those candlesticks, and I never found them. So I thought, New York. My real life. The life I want. I can leave and never come back, I can leave tomorrow, go back to work, my job, which I enjoy, which I'm good at, which rewards me for the effort I put in and is always fully explicable under all circumstances. I could call Scott, tell him I'm coming back to the office next week, probably if I work it right manage to take the rest of my "compassionate leave" somewhere warm and sunny later in the year.

I dialed the number and, a quarter of the way across the world, I made a British number appear on a black telephone on a blond-wood desk. It rang. And rang. And rang. And clicked over to voice mail. I checked the time. Eleven in New York. I couldn't imagine Scott wouldn't be at his desk or that his secretary wouldn't pick up in his absence. I dialed again.

This time, Scott answered the phone after two rings, his voice a little ragged and out of breath, as if he'd had to sprint for the phone.

"Hi," I said, "it's me."

"I know," he said. And paused.

And in that pause, I think I knew everything, before he said a word. I knew and didn't know, as one does in these situations. I knew but did not want to acknowledge.

I said, "How are things?" Which was to say, what's wrong? Without having to say it.

He said, "Listen, Ronnie, I can only talk for a minute, okay?"

I remained silent.

"Ronnie?"

He never calls me Ronnie, not unless he's drunk.

"Yeah, I'm still here. That's okay, I only have a minute, too."

"Listen, Ronnie," he said, as if I were doing something other than listening. "It has to be over, you and me."

I kept my voice bright and cheerful. "It is over, Scott. Or don't you remember dumping me?"

"No, I mean really over. Look, it's"—he paused, gasping—"it's Cheryl. That night, when I came to see you, she followed me. To see where I went. She followed me in the car, in her robe."

I imagined Cheryl, whom I have never met, who exists for me only as a perfectly presented photograph on a desk, driving in slippers and a dressing gown. Wild.

"She sent the kids away this week, so she could tell me. If it doesn't stop now, she says she wants a divorce and I can't . . . Ronnie, I'm sorry. I had to tell her it was you, she wouldn't let it drop. We can't work together anymore. I'm sorry. I won't, I mean, I'll make sure that you don't . . . you know?"

I didn't know. I didn't say anything. This situation, which had been so easy, so blissfully simple and free from complication, had suddenly become tangled and confused.

"Yes," I said. "I understand. Don't worry. I won't be coming back to the office. I resign."

And while Scott was muttering and worrying and telling me I didn't have to do that, and while I was assuring him that I could because, of course, I'd had a sudden windfall, I found that I was thinking only: yes. This is what happens. If you buy chickens, you should expect that one day, they're going to come home to roost. See? This is what you get.

I'm an oddity. I know it. Even in New York, where everyone's just a little bit Jewish, I don't make that much sense. The Orthodox world is tight; you don't tend to meet that many "lapsed Orthodox Jews." People from my background just *don't* leap the tracks, go and bat for the other team. Except when they do.

There are a few of us out there; I've met them from time to time at dinner parties and movie outings. People will say, "Ronit! You *must* talk to *Trent*. He grew up in *Monsey*!" And there will be Trent, looking perfectly normal, not as if he could recite the Ten Commandments in Hebrew or anything. I tend to avoid these people. Sometimes, they're mad. The ones who went too fast, who ran away from Orthodoxy because they thought it was the root of all their problems and then don't know what to do when they find they still have some. And sometimes, they're not mad but have some truly tragic story: abuse, neglect, violence, oh yes, these things happen in our community, too.

Something that made them, understandably, turn their faces away from anything like the place that had hurt them. And all these people, if I get close to them, if I start talking about *religion*, will inevitably share their story of escape and then ask to hear mine. How did I get out? That's easy. Why? Not so easy.

People who meet me tend to assume that because my father was a Rabbi, there must have been some explosive last scene. People who know me better think that there was some quibbling over my slightly amorphous sexuality. And, let me acknowledge it brutally now, no one has ever got close enough to me to earn the full story. So I suppose I have something in common with my father after all.

What happened was this: nothing. Nothing and everything. A series of arguments about this and that, from egg sandwiches to the teenage magazines I started to buy and bring home, to the length of my skirt. I don't think he ever knew, ever even suspected about me and Esti; his mind didn't work that way. But for all that, Esti changed my relationship with my father. With her, I began to question something. And questioning something, I questioned everything. And his answers no longer satisfied me as they had when I was a child.

We did not go out of each other's lives in a blaze of anger. We simply fell out of the habit of speaking. We lost our common language and so lost everything. There was nothing for us to say.

And now he's dead, and that's all there'll ever be. Silence. No last message for me. No final thoughts. Nothing left to interpret. Only silence.

I found I was still holding the phone in my hand, as if waiting for Scott to come back on the line and tell me it had all been a mistake and that the bricks of my life hadn't suddenly tumbled over in a disintegrated heap, revealing that there had never been any cement holding them together at all. I put down the phone, and Esti lit her candles, and it was the Sabbath.

That evening, I sat down with Esti and Dovid and we *talked the matter through*. Simple as that. Or, not really, but somewhere close to simple, somewhere in the *vicinity* of simple. It went like this. I explained my situation. In order to leave, I'd have to stay. To get away from Scott, to have months and months of money to pay my bills while I found another job and didn't have to face him and the unspecified domestic unhappiness I'd been a part of, I'd have to take Hartog's check and do what he asked. They nodded and tutted and told me that of course I was welcome as long as I needed to stay.

Then there was a long pause, of me staring at the floor and them looking at me. Kindly, I think. They were looking at me with compassion.

I said, "Esti, you should come back to New York with me. Leave, at least, but I can help you if you like."

I didn't say it quite like that. I pussyfooted a bit. I hedged around the subject. It wasn't like me at all. I got there in the end.

"Sometimes," she said, "I have thought of little else." She looked up at me. "I used to dream of coming to find you, you know. Of arriving on your doorstep one morning, with my bags in my hands and saying 'Here I am.' I used to dream that a lot." I drew breath to speak, but she continued: "It's funny, though. I never used to dream of you coming back here. Somehow, when I imagined it, I always came to find you. Isn't that strange?"

I didn't think it was strange at all.

She said, "I'm considering it." And Dovid nodded as if he, too, were considering leaving.

I said, "You can't stay here. Not like this, not now that all this has happened. Those whispers don't go away, Esti. You might think you'll be able to ignore them, but you can't. They'll grind you down a little bit day by day. You need to go somewhere there are no whispers."

She said, "Perhaps."

She said, "Maybe there's another way. I haven't quite worked it out yet. Dovid and I need to discuss it. You should stay for the week. Take Hartog's money. The shul made its money from your father anyway; it's owed to you."

I noted the way she said "Dovid and I." I couldn't work out what that meant. Any way I looked at it, the phrase seemed absurd.

I said, "Do you know what gets me?"

She said, "What's that?"

"The candlesticks. They were the only thing I really wanted here, and I never found them. My mother's candlesticks. The ones she used to light every Shabbat when I was little. They're the only thing I remember really clearly. She used to light the candles and I'd stand on a chair next to her and say the bracha with her. They were huge things, about as long as her forearm and very shiny silver; we used to polish them every Sunday."

"Silver candlesticks?"

I nodded.

"Did they have leaves and buds on them, with two bulbs along their length?"

I nodded again. "You remember them. The ones that always stood on a tray in the front hall after she died."

"They were in the house. Before your father passed away. I'm so sorry. I should have . . . I forgot. They were in the house."

She stood up and left the room. Two or three minutes later she returned, holding a bulky parcel, about a foot and a half long, wrapped up in brown paper, tied with garden string. She thrust it toward me awkwardly. I knew what it was by the weight, by the manner of wrapping, before my fingers were able to pry the knots apart. It was always my father's way. He saved wrapping paper and string, reused them over and over again. He must have tied them up himself. Esti said:

"Your father gave them to me, long ago. He said they should stay in the family but that if ever you should ask for them, they were yours."

I pulled off the string and unrolled the parcel. The brown paper crackled as I pulled off two, then three, then four layers until at last I found them, nestling among all that secondhand paper. Blackened with tarnish but still recognizable. Far more hideous than they had been in my memory, clunky rather than sinuous, spiky, ungainly, and awkward, but nonetheless. My mother's silver candlesticks, which my father had given to Esti in case I should want them.

Chapter Twelve

Jacob was left alone, and a man wrestled with him until the rising of dawn . . .
And the man said: "Let me go, for dawn has broken," and Jacob said: "I will not let you go unless you bless me."
And he said to him: "What is your name?" and he replied: "Jacob."
And he said: "You will no longer be called Jacob, but Israel, because you have wrestled with God and with men . . ."

Genesis 32:25–29

The story of Jacob's battle with the angel is obscure indeed. We are not told *why* the angel fought with him, nor how Jacob was able to defeat a powerful messenger of the Lord. All we know is this: Jacob was given a new name and that name is our purpose. We are bound to struggle not only with other men but also with God until the rising of the new dawn and the end of the earth.

Jacob's battle with that angel was neither the first nor the last of these struggles. Does not Abraham argue with God when He wishes to destroy Sodom and Gomorrah? Does not Moses challenge the judgment of God when He has decided to destroy the Children of Israel? Not for nothing did the Lord call us a stiff-necked people—a stubborn, willful, disobedient race.

This is our territory. We stand at the border, engaged in constant battle. We are nothing if we do not recognize that truth. Let us not deny that God asks; let us not doubt for a moment that He requires certain actions of us, and certain refrainings from action. He requires that we do not eat certain foods, that we honor the Sabbath day to keep it holy, that we bathe ourselves if we have become impure—these are simple things. They may be difficult to undertake or understand, but they are within our capabilities: neither revolting to mind or spirit nor harmful to the body.

But let us not deny that of the many things He asks, some few may perhaps seem to us not only difficult but also unjust, unfair. Wrong. And, in these moments, let us never doubt that we, too, have a voice within us to speak, that we, too, like Abraham and Moses, may argue with the Lord. It is our right. The simple fact of our existence has bought us the space to stand before Him and make our case.

By three p.m., the ground floor of the synagogue was filled. Names and faces whom one had only previously encountered in the pages of the *Chronicle* or, according to one's custom, the *Tribune,* mingled freely. That freedom was, of course, rather more theoretical than actual, for, although all the chairs had been removed from the floor, the room was still packed far beyond its capacity. In fact, had it not been for the mechitzah, separating the sexes so that the men took the left-hand side of the room and the women the right, the level of crowding, with its concomitant rubbing, squashing, pushing, and—let us not hesitate to say it—elbowing, would have been positively indecent.

The synagogue had become a landscape of food. Along the center of the room ran a long table, topped by another to form a T shape. There were stacks of gleaming white plates, each separated from its neighbor by a napkin and surrounded by fanned forks. There were salads: potato, coleslaw, cucumber, carrot. There was Waldorf salad and three-bean salad, barley salad and tabbouleh salad, Moroccan salad, Italian salad, and the ubiquitous tomato-cucumber-pepper salad. There was fish: a whole poached salmon, fried fish balls, boiled fish balls—both sweet and salty—herring, cold fried plaice, cod and haddock and an abstract sunset in smoked salmon, mackerel, and trout.

Many of the women lingered by the fish, and though their attention was fixed upon the food, once their plates had been filled some found a moment to speak with one another, upon matters synagogal and communal. Bending to reach for a gefilte fish ball, Mrs. Berditcher remarked to Mrs. Stone that Dovid, she had heard, would speak later in the service, and Mrs. Stone responded with a brilliant white smile.

The men, meanwhile, congregated nearer to the meat. And what meat there was! There were fried chicken wings and barbecued chicken wings, roast chicken legs, a huge dish of chicken schnitzels. There were slices of turkey, duck, and goose. There was salt beef and roast beef, pickled beef and boiled beef, smoked beef and barbecued beef. There was liver, a dish of hearts, and a calf's-foot jelly, trembling on a long, thin serving dish, a row of coy boiled eggs nestling within. There were meat pasties and meat pies, cut so that their solid, dark pink filling was displayed; there was bratwurst and liverwurst, salami and bologna. Starches accompanied these meats: saffron and coriander rice, almond and raisin rice, chickpea and lentil rice. There was kasha varnishkes and mushroom barley; there were fine squares of egg lokshen mingled with fried onion.

Among these wonders, Mench spoke to Horovitz and Abramson to Rigler. Was it true? Would Dovid speak? Why, yes. They had heard it from his own lips, or from the lips of those who *had* heard it. And his wife? Ah, she would prefer to leave, they had heard. A shame, of course, a dreadful shame, but after all, if she'd be happier elsewhere the community surely could not stand in her way.

At the top of the table was a display of desserts. It is here that the art of the kosher caterer reaches its very apex. Naturally, no dairy food may be served at a meal containing meat. Yet the best, the finest desserts are those concoctions of cream and sugar so beloved of small children. It is a mark of the great gifts of the caterers of Hendon that, to eye and to tongue, the desserts they offered were indistinguishable from the more usual dairy recipes. There was jelly cake and chocolate fudge cake, strawberry gâteau and Black Forest gâteau, orange sponge and lemon sponge. There was a great tureen of chocolate mousse topped with whipped cream (soy cream, of course), surrounded by biscuits: *langues-de-chat* and coconut macaroons, crisp chocolate chip cookies and melting Viennese fingers. There were tiny cream cakes, each one no bigger than a finger, in almost infinite variety. There was a large basket filled with Belgian chocolates: creams and truffles, nougats and pralines, liqueur-filled and marzipan-topped. The basket itself, naturally, was made of chocolate.

And by this table, shining with sugar, magnificent in its intricate glory, stood Dr. Hartog and his wife. They greeted guests. They smiled and, as appropriate, inclined their heads to indicate their quiet acceptance of the words of condolence offered to them. They, like the desserts made without dairy, were indistinguishable from the genuine and the sincere.

Dovid was in the ladies' gallery, watching. He was sitting in the front row and had pulled back the curtain—just enough to allow him to look down. Beneath him, the guests at the hesped ebbed and flowed in the main hall below. The room was already thick with people, particularly around the central table. So far, there had been one or two accidents—a smashed glass, an elbow nudged, causing a plate of food to be deposited across an elderly man's jacket. But still the people came. He picked out faces he recognized, and observed many that meant nothing to him, trying to match them to names on the guest list. He saw Hartog, of course, striding from one side of the room to the other, the crowd miraculously parting to allow him passage. Fruma was deep in discussion with one of the caterers, although Dovid could not imagine what more there might be to arrange now. Occasionally, a few words, a greeting or a name, would float upward from the crowd below. Hartog's voice was louder than usual as he boomed, "Dayan Schachter, Rebbetzin Schachter, welcome!" or "Sir Leon, Lady Birberry, may I offer you a seat?"

And he saw Ronit. She was dressed in a manner that could not cause offense to even the most religious of the many religious men and women here today. Her skirt was long, down to her ankles. Her blouse was buttoned up to the neck and down to the wrists. Over it she had thrown a loose, shapeless cardigan. On her head, though she was unmarried, she wore a long blond sheitel, with a deep fringe. The wig was so full, in fact, that her face was largely concealed. Dovid smiled. No one who was not looking for her would possibly know she was there.

They have this show on TV in the States—*The World's Greatest Magical Secrets Revealed*. Or something. It might be called *How Do They Saw That Lady in Half?* or *When Good Magicians Go Wild*. I can't really remember. The point is—it's a show that explains how they do all those magic tricks you see on TV. I love those shows, the ones that take you behind the scenes and show you how stuff works. I guess I just like to know what's really going on. And what always amazes me about *Magicians: How Do They Do Those Tricks?* is how simple the solutions turn out to be. I mean, you could have worked it out, it's just that you never really imagine anyone would go to that much *trouble*. Or, to put it another way, when they tell you it's impossible for a woman to fit in that tiny space where the two boxes overlap, you just sort of believe them, rather than working out for yourself whether a *really small* woman, who was prepared to be pretty uncomfortable for fifteen minutes, could fit there. That's the thing. If someone tells you something's impossible, mostly you just believe them.

The point of which is—it is technically possible to check in to, say, a transatlantic flight, check your bags, go *through* passport control, wave goodbye to your loved ones (or loathed ones, whichever is more applicable in your particular circumstances), and yet nonetheless somehow *not* leave when the plane does. You just have to be really motivated. And not be afraid to throw a shameless "Help I've just discovered I'm terrified of flying, of enclosed spaces, of food served in a plastic tray, and of the very words 'overhead bins'" fit in front of three hundred complete strangers. It's pretty easy, actually. So it is possible to convince, say, a slightly loathsome synagogue functionary that you're cruising at an altitude of thirty-five thousand feet when, in fact, you're back in Hendon, none the worse for the experience except for a slight hoarseness caused by all the screaming. Like I say, it's all a question of motivation.

The room fell silent. Hartog looked around, a slight, puzzled expression on his face. Dovid smiled a little: Hartog was probably looking for him. He pulled back a little from the rail of the ladies' gallery, watching the man's slight confusion. He would go down in a moment, of course. In a few moments. He waited. Hartog summoned Kirschbaum and Levitsky from the crowd with a quick motion of his hand. There was a whispered conversation. The three men looked around the room, bewildered. There was a further, brief conversation, resolved with a shrug and a sigh.

Hartog stepped toward the microphone at the front of the stage.

"Ladies and gentlemen," he said, "honored guests. Thank you for coming here today, to celebrate the life of Rav Krushka, may his memory be blessed."

One by one, the great Rabbis of the country, mostly elderly men themselves, took the few steps up onto the stage and spoke. One or two spoke in Yiddish, but most in English—a few still had the accented speech of those who had spent their boyhoods in Eastern Europe. They spoke words of comfort to the congregation. They spoke the words the people needed to hear, expected to hear. They spoke of the greatness of the man, of his tireless work on behalf of his congregation, of the passing of a light from our world.

Dovid, listening, found himself thinking of those last six months of the Rav's life. He thought of the mornings when he would wake to hear the Rav wheezing or coughing and coughing without respite. He would knock quietly on the old man's door and, as he entered, the Rav would raise a hand in greeting while he choked and retched, as though the cough was merely an interruption, an unexpected visitor who would soon be gone. Dovid remembered how he used to hold one of the plastic bowls—once white, but now yellowed with the constant scalding cleanings—in front of the Rav. He would place his hand on the old man's back and would rub softly, coaxing out the phlegm and blood, feeling each vertebra sharp beneath his palm. And when the sticky mess had been deposited in the bowl—more and more as each day passed—he would clean the Rav, wipe his face with a damp rag, sit holding his knotted hand as he regained his strength. It was not respect that made him do so, not the qualities that were being discussed today, not faith nor greatness in learning. It was none of these things, although these things had certainly been part of the man.

Dovid had a small headache, a thin blue fog, an ice crystal or two floating past his face. In his pocket, though, was a packet of pills Ronit had arranged for him. She had taken him, like a child, to a doctor. The doctor had given him pills. It was simple. He had not taken a pill yet but he tapped the box in his pocket from time to time, just to remind his headache that it was there. It seemed to be working. The headache was behaving well.

It was time. The words had been spoken, as had other words, following words, and fine ones. It was time for him to speak now. Dovid had rehearsed this moment with Hartog several times. Hartog had talked him through it. Dovid would go up to the stage and would read a carefully prepared speech about the life and work of the Rav, touching on his family, his great contribution to the community. He and Hartog had written the speech together. It was a good speech. It contained beautiful, moving thoughts on the strength of the community's spirit and the importance of continuity. When it was done, Dovid knew that all present would agree that the Rav had found a worthy heir. The thing would be done.

Hartog was becoming increasingly agitated. It occurred to

Dovid that Hartog did not think to look upward—it did not even cross his mind to look there, in the ladies' gallery. For some reason, this thought amused him.

I listened as man after man walked up the stairs to the stage and spoke about my father. I had met most of these Rabbis at one time or another; they might have recognized me if I hadn't kept my head down, behaved like a demure Jewish woman. I listened as they described a man I'd never known.

"The Rav was brilliant," they said. "His thoughts were quick and lucid."

"The Rav was a giant among men," they said. "We were awed by him."

"The Rav had astonishing kindness," they said. "His heart was filled with the love of the Jewish people."

Well. Maybe it's true. I have no way of knowing.

I was four years old when my mother died. It's young enough that I might never think of her. Old enough that the knowledge would always be with me. And I don't. And it is.

There's nothing to think of, of course. What do I remember? A sensation of warmth, a brown skirt and a pair of legs, a laugh as she talked to someone on the telephone, a time when I was ill in bed—a fever, perhaps spots—and she brought me soup and fed it to me with a spoon. A pair of candlesticks. A pickle bowl. The cream-colored shoes she wore on Shabbat.

I remember the aftermath more clearly. Mourning, sitting on a low stool, the women of Hendon showing me kindness, brushing my hair, dressing me, giving me food, and they were kind indeed but they weren't my mother and so nothing could help. It wasn't my father who did these things, who made the food or laid out my clothes; he had his studies. It was a succession of women, first the women of the community and then housekeepers, one after another, as interchangeable as grains of sand or the stars of the sky.

And there was never a hesped for my mother. There were no great men lined up to speak words of praise for her, no banquet to memorialize her. For a woman cannot be a Rabbi, and only a Rabbi can be a scholar of such note, and only a scholar of note will be honored with a hesped.

These are subtle things. We don't condone wife beating here, or genital mutilation, or honor killings. We don't demand head-to-toe coverings, or cast-down eyes, or that a woman must not go out in public unaccompanied. We are modern. We live modern lives. All we demand is that women keep to their allotted areas; a woman is private, while a man is public. The correct mode for a man is speech, while the correct mode for a woman is silence.

I've spent a long time proving that this isn't so. I've spent a long time insisting that no one else can tell me when to speak and when to remain silent. So much so that it's hard for me to tell when I want to be quiet.

In another life, another me would have been at the hesped because I had a plan, some sort of grand caper to make Hartog suffer or to make myself more noticeable. But it wasn't that. I was there because they wanted me there. They had asked me. They had something planned.

So I stood in silence and I listened. It's this concept I've been working on.

"Ladies and gentlemen, we had been hoping, that is, er, we had been expecting that Rabbi Dovid Krushka, the Rav's nephew, would join us today, to speak a few words. Unfortunately, as you know, Rabbi Krushka has been far from well recently . . ."

It's now, thought Dovid. If I am to do it, it's now.

He pulled back the curtain. He drew a breath. The crowd was silent. He would not have to be loud, but loud enough.

He said, "I am here."

Heads twisted and necks craned. Women nudged their neighbors. There was a sort of laughing gasp as the people saw that Dovid was standing in the *ladies' gallery*. Some of the congregation wondered privately if it might not be forbidden for him to be there. The thing seemed a terrible, forbidden mingling.

Hartog looked at Dovid, motioning wildly, beckoning him down to the stage.

Dovid acquiesced. He dropped the curtain in front of his face, stepped back, and walked down the stairs to the main hall to take his place on the stage. Somewhere between the ladies' gallery and the stage, though, he found a companion. For, as Dovid walked onto the stage, he was accompanied by his wife. They were holding hands, Dovid's right hand in Esti's left. In the instant it took every eye to swivel, those linked hands were the only important feature in the room. With Esti, Dovid stood before the microphone.

"My wife," he said, "would like to say a few words."

He took a pace to the side. Esti took a pace forward. Their hands remained interlinked. This was important. Had Dovid let go, had he stepped away from her, had he retreated to the back of the stage, there would have been remonstrances and mutterings. The people would have asked, "What is this?" and "Why?" They would have whispered against her. As it was, they stood together and Esti spoke. Perhaps the simplest thing of all.

"Speech," she said. "One month ago, the Rav gave us his thoughts on the matter of speech. On its importance, on the holiness of each word that proceeds from our mouths. He told us that, with speech, we imitate God. As God created this world with speech, so, too, we create worlds with our words. What world," said Esti, "have we created with our words in this past month?"

The hall was utterly silent.

"The way to honor a man, surely, is to hearken to his words? To reflect on them, to contemplate them, to discuss and debate them. Did not our sages demonstrate their respect for one another by argument, by constantly toiling in each other's words, by point and counterpoint? This is what I would do today, to consider the words of the Rav."

Esti looked down at her hand, at the place where it was interlinked with Dovid's, then back up at the people. She took a breath and began again.

"A long time ago, I had a conversation with the Rav. I was fifteen and I told him . . ." She paused, seeming unsure how to proceed. "I told him that I had experienced improper desires." A buzz in the hall, a sharp noise like the humming of insects. "I told him that my friend, my dear school friend and I . . ." Again, she broke off. Whatever this deed was, these desires, there appeared to be no words to describe them. "You must understand," she said, "that I wanted to behave properly, to follow the Torah, to keep the mitzvot. I sought the Rav's advice. I told him . . ." She gulped, took another breath, and spat out the words. "I told him that I had desired another woman. That she had desired me."

Buzzing again. A whispering, metallic sound as three hundred people put down their wineglasses and napkins, ceased to chew their mouthfuls of excellent food.

Esti held up her hand and the crowd fell silent again. She continued to speak, softly, in a measured tone.

"The Rav listened with compassion. He told me that this matter did not surprise him, that it did not shock him. He was kind and he was sympathetic. He listened to me with seriousness; he understood these were not simply childish fantasies. He explained that to act on such desires is forbidden. I had already understood this. He explained further that the desire itself is not forbidden. I had understood this, also. He told me that, if I felt able, I should marry— a quiet man, a man who would not make demands upon me. Someone, he said, who hears the voice of Hashem in the world. Someone capable of silence. In this, the Rav was right. May his memory be blessed."

Around the hall, there was a low murmured "May his memory be blessed" as three hundred people found, with relief, a sentence to which they knew how to respond.

"The Rav also told me that I should remain silent regarding my desires. That no good would be served if I were to communicate them to my husband, to the others in the community. He explained that certain things must remain secret, that it is better not to speak of them, that the *community* would do better if they were never spoken of. Some topics, he told me, are best discussed only in private—they should not be aired. The Rav was a wise man, a good man, learned in Torah. In so many matters, his understanding was deep. But in this matter he was wrong. May his memory be blessed."

Again, a ripple of agreement in the congregation, perhaps a little more uncertain this time.

"Speech," she said. "It is the gift of creation. For God created the world from speech and so our speech, too, is the power to create. Let us examine, for a moment, God's creation. He spoke, and the world came into being. If God had valued silence above all, He would never have spoken to create the world. If He had prized only the silence of his creations, He would never have given a part of it the gift of speech. Our words are powerful. Our words are real. This does not mean, however, that we should remain silent forever. Rather, we must measure our words. We must be sure that we use them, like the Almighty, to create and not to destroy.

"There have been those"—she paused, smiling a little—"there have been those who have wished me gone. There have been those who have found my mere presence an abomination, who have lived in fear of what might be said about me, what one might say to another. We should not be afraid of words, or of speaking the truth openly. That is why I am speaking today. I am not afraid to speak the truth.

"I have desired that which is forbidden to me. I continue to desire it. And yet, I am here. I obey the commandments. It is possible"—Esti smiled—"as long as I do not have to do so in silence."

Here is the difference between New York and London. In New York, that would have been the showstopper. When Esti finished talking, walked off the stage with Dovid, when they left the hall, that would have been the end of the event. There would have been riotous applause, or perhaps angry shouting, something loud and dramatic, anyway.

But, because this is Britain, that's not what happened. There was a pause, a minute or two. A great quantity of whispered conversation, some pursed lips, some eye rolling, and then the event simply continued, speaker after speaker. There's something both admirable and hateful about this. The stolid refusal to become dramatic is also the inability to respond to serious things seriously, with depth. That next half hour was proof, if proof was needed, that what we say about ourselves is not true. There is a myth—many of us believe it—that we are wanderers, unaffected by the place in which we live, hearkening only to the commandments of the Lord. It's a lie. These British Jews were British—they shuffled awkwardly, looked at their feet, and drank tea.

Having said that, there were a couple of gratifying responses. Hinda Rochel Berditcher and Fruma Hartog looked at each other over the peach and apricot pavlova. I was watching them from across the hall, from behind this ridiculous wig. Hinda Rochel was evidently attempting to be calm, consoling, speaking oiled words. Fruma was white, even more so than normal. Hinda Rochel offered to cut her a piece of cake. Fruma refused, lips tightly shut like a baby refusing a spoonful of mashed liver. Hinda Rochel put out a hand and touched Fruma's arm. Fruma shook her off and said, and I could read her lips quite well even from across the hall, "Don't touch me."

It wasn't much, but it made me smile.

And then there was Hartog. I have to confess, I had almost intended to speak to him, to show myself. My outfit represented something, as clothing always does. It showed that I wasn't there for myself, I was there for Esti and Dovid because they'd asked me to be there. Because this was their way of making their peace with my father and with me, with our pasts. Esti had rustled up the clothes from the various appropriate shops in Golders Green. But, I'd sort of thought, I'd contemplated the possibility that at the end of the hesped, as everyone was filing out, I'd walk up to Hartog, to show myself to him, to say . . . "Well, I came anyway, you tosser. Now what are you going to do?" I didn't want him to have even that victory, even thinking he'd managed to get rid of me even to that extent.

So, as the crowd was streaming out of the hesped I made my way toward him. The food had been eaten, the speeches had been made. The people were ambling home, muttering among themselves about Esti, sure, but also, I noticed, about the excellent food, the excellent speeches, the *properness* of such a celebration of the Rav's life. Yes, we don't do things in a hurry. Not Orthodox Jews, not the people of Britain. I spotted Hartog in the lobby and headed in his general direction. I still thought I might speak to him, but as I came closer, I found the desire ebbing away. It was enough. Something had changed here. As much as could ever change. I found, and was surprised to find, that I didn't *want* to confront him.

I passed right by him in the lobby. He was wearing a fixed smile, staring at the crowd leaving the hall without focusing on any one person, even those who shook him by the hand. Admittedly, I wasn't wearing my usual clothes. But still, he looked right through me as I passed, didn't register my presence. Except, as I walked by him, I turned my head a little and looked back. He reached his hand up quickly to his face: I thought he'd seen me and was going to call me back, or was stifling a gasp. No. He pinched his nose in the palm of his hand, drew his hand away, and looked at it. The tips of his fingers were red. He shoved his hand into his pocket and drew out a crumpled hand-kerchief, trying to stem the thin trickle of blood dribbling from his nose, just as if someone had punched him in the face.

Chapter Thirteen

It is not for you to complete the task, but neither are you free to refrain from it.

Pirkei Avot 2:20

There is a story told in the Talmud. We know that every word in the Talmud is the true word of God, so it follows that this story, too, is true.

A story is told of several Rabbis, arguing over an abstruse point of law. One of them, Rabbi Eliezer, vehemently disagreed with the other sages. After long debate, he at last said, "If the law is as I say, may this carob tree prove it!" And the carob tree uprooted itself from its place. But the sages said, "No proof can be brought from a carob tree."

And Rabbi Eliezer said, "If the law is as I say, may this stream of water prove it!" And the stream began to flow backward. But the sages said, "No proof can be brought from a stream."

And Rabbi Eliezer said, "If the law is as I say, may the walls of the study house prove it!" And the walls of the study house began to bend inward. But Rabbi Joshua rebuked them, saying, "When the sages debate, what right have you to interfere?" So, out of respect for Rabbi Joshua, the walls did not fall, but out of respect for

Rabbi Eliezer, they did not return to their place; hence they are still bent to this day.

And Rabbi Eliezer said, "If the law is as I say, may Heaven prove it!" And a voice came from Heaven, saying, "Why do you disagree with Rabbi Eliezer, seeing the law is always as he says?" And Rabbi Joshua stood up and said, "It is not in Heaven! It is not for a divine voice to decide the law, for in the Torah it is written that the majority opinion shall prevail." And the sages followed the majority opinion in their ruling, and not the opinion of Rabbi Eliezer.

And from this we learn that we are not to look to Heaven to solve the difficulties of our lives, that we are not to interpret signs and wonders to live our lives by them. We learn that there is value in making our own choices, even if God Himself communicates clearly that the choices we make are wrong. We learn that we may argue with God, that we may disobey His direct commandments and yet delight Him with our actions. We learn of God's compassion for us—in the end, broader than we can understand.

For the story does not end there. We read that, later, Rabbi Nathan met the prophet Elijah in a dream. And he said to the prophet, "What did the Almighty do, when Rabbi Joshua said 'It is not in Heaven!'?" And Elijah replied, "At that moment, God laughed with joy, saying, 'My children have defeated Me, My children have defeated Me.'"

God has given the world to us, for a spell. He has given us His Torah. And, like a good parent, like a loving father, He has joyfully set us free. It is not in Heaven.

In the cemetery, a small crowd—forty or fifty people, far fewer than attended the hesped—has gathered by the side of a grave. It is a year since the Rav died, and time, in the way of things, to place the headstone by the site where his body rests. The ceremony is simple; it will not take long.

Ronit has returned to Hendon for her father's stone setting. She looks up at the pale blue morning sky, streaked with white and gray, and thinks of how only the day before, she had been there, on a plane. She had been in the morning. She had a strange dream as the plane was passing through the night across the Atlantic, but she doesn't think she's going to tell anyone about it. It's just between her and the morning.

She's holding the baby, just a few days shy of three months. They've named him Moshe, after her father, and she's not sure how she feels about the Freudian significance of holding a child named after her dad, but she's not worrying too much about that either.

Esti and Dovid stand together loosely, both looking forward rather than at each other, as though at any moment they might realize they were standing too close to a complete stranger and walk away from each other. But they don't. They remain together, and when Esti moves forward, Dovid goes with her. Watching them, Ronit thinks about people who stay married even if one partner changes sex, or loses several key appendages or their mind. She knows that's kind of patronizing, but she's just trying to get her head around it.

Esti is watching Ronit, too. She's thinking that Ronit seems less, now, than she did before. It's not that she is less, Esti knows that, but that she used to seem too much. There was a time when Esti thought that Ronit's face contained the world, but now, well, it's just a face. She's grateful for that, grateful for the change, because it's not good to see the world in a face that doesn't belong to you, that's always turning away from you.

She doesn't see the world in Dovid's face either, but she can see it's a better face than she thought. He is kind and he has a surprisingly good sense of humor. These things aren't everything, but for now, they're enough to make the journey not unappealing to her. She thinks if she had the choice to make again, the original choice from all those years ago, she'd still choose the same. It seems quite clear to her. Esti finds that, these days, she's quite clear about a lot of things, as though a sort of fog had lifted from her brain. It's as if she herself had been brought into focus, like a telescope drawing down the moon. She surprises herself, quite often, by thinking: it's fine. Everything is just fine.

A year, of course, makes all things seem easy. In a year, a mere stirring in the belly becomes a child—tiny and unknowable, his eyes clear blue and his hands grasping. In a year, the grass grows over a grave, softening its edges. In a year, the depths of grief become less raw, what was shocking becomes commonplace, what was talked of constantly becomes old and stale.

All things, when measured in spans of years, seem simple. But human lives do not occur in years but slowly, day by day. A year may be easy, but its days are hard indeed.

So. It has been a year. The grass has grown over the Rav's grave and Esti and Dovid's tiny son blinks in the autumn sunlight. But it has not been easy. There have been those, not a few, who have left the Rav's synagogue: some with great noise and commotion and others more quietly, slipping out between one Sabbath and the next. There has been whispering and there has been shouting. Esti and Dovid have found themselves, perhaps, with fewer Shabbat invitations than they had previously enjoyed. Some people—though not as many as they feared—make their excuses to avoid speaking with them. They are still muttered of in Hendon, though not as often as was once the case.

And yet, with all this, things are fine. Certain things are possible. This, and this, but not this. Certain things will forever remain impossible. But within what is possible, there is room to live. Those people who remain at the synagogue have come to value Esti and Dovid's continued presence. Esti speaks to the congregation at the stone-setting ceremony, as she has done from time to time over the year. A few simple words over the Rav's grave and they are done. The people in attendance smile and thank her for her thoughts.

Esti and Dovid have bought a telescope. Through it, they examine the face of the moon, identifying the mountains and craters.

Disobedience

After dark, once the baby is asleep, they place the telescope at the open window of the spare bedroom, taking turns to squint through the eyepiece. They sweep the telescope's eye across the sky, focusing on far-distant stars. They name them to each other, marveling at the distance. Even among other people, they often mention one of these names, perhaps Arcturus or Rigel, as a secret signal to each other. The signal means: I'm still here.

Last night I dreamed that I flew over Hendon. The wind was around me, above and below, and filling my lungs. And beneath me, Hendon was spread out. At first, I saw its dried streets, the identical mock-Tudor houses. I saw the fitted wardrobes, the two-car families, the jobs for life in accountancy or law. I saw the kitchens that were more kosher than anyone else's kitchens, skirts that were longer, tights that were thicker, sheitels that were attached more firmly than anyone else's. I saw the study of Torah and the practice of good deeds and kindness, and I saw the gossip and the slander and the public humiliation.

And I said, "Lord, can there be passion in Hendon? Can there be desire or despair, can there be grief or joy, can there be wonder or mystery? Lord," I said, "can this place live?"

And the Lord said to me, My child, if I will it, it will live.

And behold, I saw the Lord lift the roof from each house, as if with a mighty hand and outstretched arm. And the Lord spoke in turn to each person in each house, filling their hearts with His light. And I watched. And behold, when He was finished, nothing much changed.

And I said, "Lord, what does this mean?"

And the Lord said, My child, my joy, things here are slow to change, for this is a stiff-necked and disobedient people, but at least they are still willing to listen.

Ronit remains for five days in London. She asks after Hartog, who had not been present at the stone setting, and learns that he has joined another synagogue. There will, of course, always be somewhere for Hartog to go. Dovid is the Rabbi now, although he does not enjoy the title. "Call me Dovid," he says to the people who visit his house. There are those who find this informality disturbing, who seek again the order and rigidity they knew in their youths. They call him Rabbi and he does not protest. They continue to come to the house, however. They come, sometimes, to see his wife rather than him. She is known as a good listener; no problem is too great for her ears, no trouble too shocking.

Ronit returns to New York. On the plane, she reads her father's book, and although in places it irritates her beyond measure, she is pleased to have done so. She has discussed her father with Dr. Feingold, who suggests that perhaps she could learn to remember what good there was in their relationship, to appreciate it, and to understand that no parent can give his child everything she needs. Ronit wonders if this amounts to the same as honoring him as recommended in the Ten Commandments and decides that it probably doesn't, but she doesn't much care. She'll do what she can and rely on the rest to be unimportant.

She's come to recognize that there is a tiny, tenuous area where good sense intersects with fundamentalist religion. She's trying out how it feels to live in that area, at least some of the time. So she took some time off, using Hartog's money to good effect, and found a new job where she doesn't have to share office space with a married man she used to sleep with. Good sense and religion agreed on that one. And sometimes, she does the stuff. Only if she wants to. She has Friday night dinner at her place, lighting the candles in those huge silver candlesticks, roasting a chicken. Sometimes, she even prays. Although she calls it "having words with God" and it's not clear that her soul is humbled by it.

She takes a vacation in the south of the United States and is amazed by the quantity of sky there at her disposal every time she chooses to tip her face upward. She thinks about that: looking up, looking down, about how the sky is always there, wherever you go. You can choose to look at it, or not, but whichever you do it'll still be there, a thing of beauty and light. She finds this strangely comforting.

Disobedience

* * *

I've been thinking about two states of being—being gay, being Jewish. They have a lot in common. You don't choose it, that's the first thing. If you are, you are. There's nothing you can do to change it. Some people might deny this, but even if you're only "a little bit gay" or "a little bit Jewish," that's enough for you to identify yourself if you want.

The second thing is that both those states—gayness, Jewishness—are invisible. Which makes it interesting. Because while you don't have a choice about what you *are*, you have a choice about what you show. You always have a choice about whether you "out" yourself. Every time you meet someone new, it's a decision. You always have a choice about whether you *practice*.

Practice, of course, means a lot of different things. Probably something different to everyone. You can practice every day, or just once in a while. But if you don't ever practice, you'll never know what it could have meant to you. You'll never know who you might have been. If you don't practice, you'll probably even feel awkward claiming that identity: if it has no function in your life, what's the point of saying it? It's still there, of course. It'll never go away. But if you don't practice, it can never change your life.

Honestly, with the world the way it is, it's probably easier not to practice. You'll fit in better. If that's what you want. Me, though, I've never been that interested in fitting in.

So, I've come to a conclusion. I can't be an Orthodox Jew. I don't have it in me and I never did. But I can't not be one either. There's something fierce and old and tender about that life that keeps on calling me back, and I suppose it always will. I guess that doesn't sound like much of a conclusion, but it's the only one I've got. Dr. Feingold calls it "learning to forgive myself." I call it learning that you don't always have to answer every request. Sometimes it's enough to note it and say: maybe I'll get to this, and maybe I won't.

I had another dream a few nights ago. I was in some kind of outdoor restaurant, with trees and bushes growing all around. I was having lunch with this older guy—he kind of reminded me of my dad. We were just laughing, chatting, shooting the breeze when the waiter slid over with the wine list. I glanced through it and I said:

"Y'know what? I'll have a Calvados."

And the guy I was having lunch with leaned over and shook his head a little bit. He said, "You know you're not supposed to have that."

I winked at him and said, "I've got to make my own choices. It'll be fine. You just wait and see."

He said, "Hey, you can't know that for certain."

And I raised my glass to him, looking at the way the light refracted through the amber liquid. I downed it in one. It was warm and delicious, like all forbidden things. I put my glass on the table and raised an eyebrow. I said:

"It'll be fine. I have faith."

And he threw back his head and laughed.

Acknowledgments

For boundless enthusiasm and belief, thanks to Veronique Baxter and Kate Barker, as well as Elena Lappin, Paul Magrs, and Patricia Duncker. For financial encouragement, thanks to the Asham Literary Trust and to the David Higham Agency.

Thanks to Ann Fine and Kristen Nelson of the Casa Libre and to Frances Sjoberg and the staff at the University of Arizona Poetry Center for providing a quiet summer in the desert. Thanks to Tash Aw, Philip Craggs, Siobhán Herron, Yannick Hill, Jen Kabat, Lesley Levene, and Helena Pickup. Special thanks to Diana Evans for the title and other wonders.

Thanks to my family, especially my grandmother Lily Alderman and my brother Eliot Alderman. Thanks to Vivien Burgoyne, Deborah Cooper, Dr. Benjamin Ellis, Jack Ferro, Yoz and Bob Grahame, Rabbi Sammy, and Liat Jackman and Andrea Phillips. Thanks to Esther Donoff, Russell, Daniella and Benjy. Thanks to Dena Grabinar and Perry Wald for support, faith, and the provision of safe harbor.

About the Author

Naomi Alderman is a graduate of Oxford University and the University of East Anglia's Creative Writing MA and has published award-winning short fiction in a number of anthologies. She has worked as an editor and game designer, and spent several years living in New York. She grew up in the Orthodox Jewish community in Hendon, where she now lives.

Disobedience

1. *Disobedience* gives the reader insight into life in a tight-knit, religious community. Do you think Hendon is different from Jewish communities in the United States? How so?

2. Ronit's married lover, Scott, once told her that "you belong in three places: the place you grew up, the place where you went to college, and the place where the person you love is." Do you agree? Ronit left Hendon but she notes that "while I can give up being Orthodox, I can't give up being a Jew." How much does your heritage contribute to the person you become?

3. In addition to examining the concept of whether or not one can go home again, what are the novel's other themes? Why do you think the author chose the title *Disobedience*?

4. The narration of the novel shifts between first person and third person. How does this affect the storytelling? Why do you think each chapter starts with an excerpt from a Jewish prayer?

5. When first studying under Rav Krushka, Dovid begins to experience blinding migraines accompanied by flashes of vivid color. Do you think, as the Rav did, that Dovid was receiving visions from God or was he just suffering from stress-induced headaches? Discuss the importance of color during these episodes.

6. Within their community, it is widely assumed that "the correct mode for a man is speech, while the correct mode for a woman is silence." What are the different expectations for men and women in Hendon? How does Esti fit in? How does she change from the beginning of the novel to her speech at the Rav's memorial service?

7. When Ronit and Esti rekindle their old feelings for each other, Esti muses, "Loving Ronit seemed, already, to demand some denial of herself. Or perhaps, she reflected later, all love demands that." Do you agree?

8. The only possession Ronit wants from her father's house is a set of silver candlesticks she remembered from Shabbat dinners of her

youth. What do these candlesticks represent and why are they so important to her?

9. What do you think was Ronit's true intention when standing behind Esti in the kitchen, giving her the gift of hydrangeas, just as she did when they were younger? Why do you think Ronit told the Hartogs and the Goldfarbs that she was a lesbian with a girlfriend back in New York?

10. The novel eloquently ruminates over the concepts of time, love, and family, as in this passage: "Often it may seem that time has taken us very far from our origin. But if we only take a few more steps, we will round the corner and see a familiar place. . . . But although the view may be similar, it will never be identical; we should remember that there is no return." How does this apply to Ronit's journey?

11. What is the significance of the Bible story of David, Jonathan, and King Saul? What does it mean to Esti?

12. Why do you think Ronit ignored Hartog's warning, disguised herself, and attended the memorial service? Why doesn't she confront Hartog afterward?

13. Esti and Dovid decide to stay together and have their baby. Do you think their marriage will be a happy one? Can you think of other examples of successful marriages that relied more on partnership than love? Will Dovid make a good rabbi? And what of Ronit at the end of the novel? Is she happy?

14. What new insight did you gain from reading *Disobedience*? Did you learn something about yourself, someone you know, or communities like Hendon?

Q&A WITH NAOMI ALDERMAN

You came from a world quite similar to Ronit's. Your father is a columnist for the *Jewish Chronicle* and members of your family are strict Orthodox Jews. How much of your personal experience did you draw upon for *Disobedience*?

Certainly the Orthodox world is portrayed entirely from my own experience—apart from a few points of Jewish law, absolutely no research was necessary to present a picture of the community I grew up in! And I have lived in Manhattan, like Ronit. And I have debilitating migraines, like Dovid. More deeply, like most adults, I know what it is to love, to desire, to have my heart broken, to want someone who doesn't want me and to be desired by someone whom I do not desire. I have been confused and angry, resentful and cowardly, I've done things I wasn't proud of as well as things that have filled me with pride in myself. These are universal experiences, I think, and happen in the world of the Orthodox Jews no less than they happen anywhere else.

In an interview with *The Guardian*, when referring to your faith and ideals, you commented, "It was like holding two glass vessels in my hand—Here is feminism and equal rights and here is Judaism, and it took me a long time to kind of bash them together." How did you reconcile the two?

Hah! I don't think it's possible to reconcile the two! All it's possible to do is continue to live being both Orthodox and feminist and see how that works out. I think there's a dishonesty in denying that parts of Judaism are misogynist. You can erase those bits if you like, but then why can't you just erase anything that doesn't please you? And once you've done that, what's left? And if everyone makes a version that pleases them, where is the powerful communal patterned life? I prefer the grainy-textured, gamey, too-rich-for-some Orthodoxy to the homogenized, pasteurized version. Having said that, parts of Orthodoxy continue to make me so angry I could scream. And I think that saying that is part of the point. If there turns out to be a world to come, and if one has an interview with one's maker there, I shall have some angry points to make which I anticipate will be met with the sort of good humor and patience I think my creator possesses.

What do you think are the biggest differences between British Jews and American Jews? How do you think the book will be received in America?

That's a big question. I wouldn't like to say that Jews in Britain are different from Jews in America in a national-determinism kind of way. But the communities operate in different ways. Certainly the U.S. Jewish community is more confident than the community in the UK. And the U.S. Jewish community is more accepted as a foundational part of the United States than is the position with British Jews. Now, which of those came first? Are British Jews less confident because Britain has an established church and public schools here put on Nativity plays at Christmas (but not Exodus plays at Passover)? Or are British Jews less accepted as part of the wallpaper of British life because we don't speak up for ourselves? Or is there some vicious circle going on? Not that I have any answers for this . . . And I don't really know how the book will be received in America—well, I hope! And I hope American readers will forgive me for going to lengths to explain bits of Jewish tradition and custom with which they may already be familiar.

You won the Orange Award for New Writers for *Disobedience*—quite a coup for your first novel. Were you surprised at the reaction to the book, both from critics and relatives?

Yes. In that, while I was writing the book, I was fairly frequently convinced that it was the worst book ever written, and that I'd be lucky if my agent didn't phone me up and tell me so when I sent her the manuscript. So perhaps I'm not the best judge of my own work, who knows? I've been pleasantly surprised that the book's been so well received in England, that most of the reviews have been good, and that my family have been incredibly supportive. The worst reviews I've received have come without exception from Orthodox Jews, which surprised me on one level—I hoped the Jewish press here might be happy for my success—but on another level wasn't surprising at all. No community likes to see itself written about, especially one which has concentrated as hard on remaining invisible as the Orthodox community in Britain.

To use a biblical term, what was the genesis of *Disobedience*? What would you like readers to take away from the novel?

I can actually pinpoint the precise genesis of the novel—it was when, living in New York City, I went to see the movie *Trembling before G-d*, a documentary about Orthodox Jewish homosexual men and women. The film was so deeply moving and drew my attention to an aspect of my religion I hadn't properly considered until then. I came to realize how, simply by being an Orthodox Jew and not contemplating this issue, I had been complicit in the suffering of people in my community. Over the next few weeks, walking around Manhattan, I found myself thinking about it over and over again, until a story began to form in my mind. It started off as a short story, which eventually grew into the novel.

Readers might assume, given your background, that Ronit Krushka is you. How much of yourself, if any, is in your characters?

I hope, I *hope* that I am not quite so royally mucked up as Ronit. Perhaps she's the person I fear I am. Or the person who, while writing the novel, I feared I might become if I wasn't careful. I think there's a person I can project who's quite similar to her: mouthy, fearless, apt to shoot herself in the foot just to prove she can. But there's a reason Ronit and Esti have such a strong bond. Beneath everything, Ronit is just as scared by life as Esti, which is why Esti annoys her so much. So both these women come from me—they are part of my internal dance of confidence and fear, of quiet calm and raucous anger, of inward insight and outward denial. All of us contain worlds, don't we? As for Dovid, he has my headaches, the headaches I've suffered from since I was at least eighteen months old (they are my very earliest memory). Pain like that changes who you are as a child, even if no one tells you it's a gift from God. All of my characters contain parts of me. Ultimately, though, I think they've all grown beyond that and assumed their own identities, which is very satisfying.

Your next novel is about a group of friends at your alma mater, Oxford University. What issues will you be examining in this novel?

I don't really like to talk about the next book, lest I jinx it out of existence, but since you ask . . . it's a book about the nature of friendship and the limits of love, I think. About whether selfless love really exists, and if it does what the point is. It's also, I find, about how puzzling Christianity appears if you happen to be Jewish.

If you were to visit Ronit, Dovid, and Esti in ten years, what might they be up to?

Hmmm. You know, while writing the novel I assiduously avoided asking myself this question. I wanted the readers to be able to make up their own minds, or at least to be able to wonder. All I can imagine is one or two possible futures, which are probably less valid than whatever the readers come up with by themselves. I think they will all be fundamentally okay. Ronit might be a bit more able to receive the advice of Dr. Feingold, Esti might leave the community eventually or she might not, and if she does she might take Dovid with her. Or maybe not. The truth is, if I ever came back to write about them, I'd probably be as surprised as anyone else. And if God thinks it's so important not to be prescriptive about our futures, I can't do anything less for my characters!